3/13

Praise for Kelly Jamieson

D0809236

"*Rule of Three* is a b   ...ern love story... I was drawn to the three main characters; they are strong, loving, independent, and utterly comfortable in who they are and what they want."

~ *Fresh Fiction*

"Dag and Chris are both lovable, funny, smoking hot characters so it's easy to see why Kassidy jumps at the first opportunity to have both men in her bed. This author has a gift of writing characters that people can relate to which helps lock the reader in for the whole book."

~ *Guilty Pleasures Book Reviews*

"*Rule of Three* absolutely blew me away. I wasn't expecting the emotionally complex story that I got. *Rule of Three* is a novel filled with love, passion, and more layers than most novels with twisted, complicated plots."

~ *Sizzling Hot Book Reviews*

Look for these titles by *Kelly Jamieson*

Now Available:

Love Me

Friends with Benefits

Love Me More

2 Hot 2 Handle

Lost and Found

One Wicked Night

Sweet Deal

Hot Ride

Print Anthology

Love 2 Love U

Rule of Three

Kelly Jamieson

Fic
413-9948

Samhain Publishing, Ltd.
11821 Mason Montgomery Road, 4B
Cincinnati, OH 45249
www.samhainpublishing.com

Rule of Three
Copyright © 2013 by Kelly Jamieson
Print ISBN: 978-1-60928-893-8
Digital ISBN: 978-1-60928-696-5

Editing by Sue Ellen Gower
Cover by Scott Carpenter

First Samhain Publishing, Ltd. electronic publication: February 2012
First Samhain Publishing, Ltd. print publication: January 2013

Chapter One

"In the shower?" Kassidy looped her arms around Chris's neck and gave him a sexy look up through her eyelashes. "That's where you want to have sex for the first time in our new home?"

Chris pressed her up against the kitchen counter with his hips and rubbed his jaw against hers. "Well, if you'd rather do it here, I'm good with that too."

Kassidy glanced around the messy kitchen, still piled with boxes from the move, and laughed, a bubbly joy rising inside her. "You're a sex maniac."

"You knew that," he murmured, and she melted against him, against his big, hard body. She peered up at his face, his strong, square chin, dark green eyes and short nose. So handsome, so big, so knee-weakeningly male. "And you moved in with me anyway."

She nuzzled the side of his neck, inhaling the warm, sexy male smell of him, let her fingers climb his chest to his shoulders. "Yeah. I must be crazy."

"Hmmm. I think—" he pulled her hair aside so he could kiss the side of her neck, "—you're a bit of a sex maniac too. Admit it. You love it."

Heat flared between Kassidy's thighs and she pressed closer. Chris's mouth on her neck, nibbling down to where it met her shoulder, sent hot shivers sliding over her.

She did love it. She loved him. She was a sex maniac for *him*. They'd been together for a year now, and she was still as hot for him as the day they'd met.

"I'm just trying to be efficient," Chris continued, his lips on her collarbone in the open V of her T-shirt. Her head fell back and she tried to focus her distracted thoughts.

"Efficient..."

Then she remembered. Chris's old friend Dag was in town and they were meeting him for dinner. "God, Chris!" She managed to get her wrist into her field of vision so she could see her watch. "We have to get ready!"

"I know. That's what I'm saying. In the shower."

She laughed as she let him drag her into the bathroom— *their* bathroom, the one off *their* bedroom, theirs!

And they did indeed have sex for the first time in their new home together in the shower.

It was quick but hot, bodies slicked up with water and soapy suds, a cloud of scented steam surrounding them. He lifted her against the wall of the shower, pinned her there with his body while his mouth devoured hers and his cock impaled her. The feel of him inside her, big, hot, hard, filling her, fucking her, sent tingles radiating over her body from where they joined.

She tilted her pelvis to the right angle so her clit bumped his pelvic bone with every hard thrust. Pressure built, burned, pleasure filling her to the point of overload then bursting out of her.

"Jesus." Chris gasped, his cheek against her wet hair. His hands tightened on her thighs and he came too, pulsing inside her. "Jesus Christ. I love you, Kass."

"Mmm." She wrapped her arms around his neck tightly. "Love you too. So much."

After, he toweled her off with gentle hands and left her to blow-dry her hair while he dressed. He appeared in the doorway of the bathroom moments later, dressed in black pants and a gray sweater layered over a white T-shirt. Yum.

"You need another hour?" he asked, and she swatted him with the hair brush and laughed.

"I won't take that long. And it's your fault, dragging me into the shower like that."

He grinned and stood beside her at the counter while he ran a brush through his short hair, a lighter golden brown than her mink brown. She turned off the blow dryer and reached a hand out to tousle the top of his hair. He always wanted it neat and perfect, but it looked good messed up just a bit. He shook his head but smiled and left the hair alone.

She'd laid out her clothes earlier as she'd been unpacking and putting things away, so her white jeans and silky pink blouse lay on the chair.

"You must be happy to see Dag after all these years," she said as she dressed. Chris watched her and the heated look in his eyes almost made her want to strip everything off again and roll into bed with him. But they could do that later.

"Yeah." His eyes lit up. "Man, I've missed that guy."

She smiled. She'd never met Dag, but she'd heard a lot about Chris's friend from college. They'd been best buds until Dag had moved away for business, first to Los Angeles then San Francisco. Strangely, he'd never come back to Chicago, not even to visit. Until now.

She moved to the dresser against the wall and quickly darkened her eyes with shadow, brushed some rosiness over her cheeks, though they were still flushed from the hot shower and hot sex.

"So why's he back after all this time?"

"I'm not sure. I mean, I know he sold his business, so he's basically unemployed."

"Can you call someone who's a multi-millionaire unemployed?" she asked with a smile.

"He doesn't have a job. Ergo, he's unemployed. He says he's here to look at business opportunities. Something to invest in."

"Mmm." She took one last look at herself in the mirror. She wanted to look nice when she met Chris's best friend. She knew how much Chris had missed him, how much it had bugged him that Dag had never come back for even a visit. She tipped her head to one side.

"You look gorgeous," Chris said, coming up behind her and laying his hands on her shoulders. He met her eyes in the mirror and smiled. "As always."

She smiled back at him. "Thank you." She glanced around. "Just need my shoes… Oh there they are." She stepped into the strappy high-heeled sandals. The jeans made her legs look longer and the pink top fluttered over her bare arms. Yeah, she looked okay.

"Ready."

"Let's go. Don't wanna keep Dag waiting." He grinned and the excitement and anticipation of seeing his friend gleamed in his eyes.

Dag sat in the restaurant at the table set for three, waiting for Chris and his girlfriend to arrive. Kassidy. He hadn't met her. She'd been nowhere in the picture when he'd moved from Chicago to Los Angeles six years ago. He wasn't surprised to know there was a woman in Chris's life. He sighed as he tapped his fingers on the table.

The sleek, modern steakhouse occupied part of the main floor of the trendy boutique hotel he was staying at in downtown Chicago. He watched the sexy blonde hostess seat another couple, leading them through dark wood tables and chocolate-brown leather chairs. This was the first time he'd been back and it felt weird. He'd been a college student for most of the time he'd lived in Chicago, then had started his first job at Ensign Technology. It had only been a year after that that he'd decided he had to get away.

And now he was going to see Chris again after all these years. Yeah, they'd talked on the phone, although less often lately, and they'd emailed, but...

There he was. Dag forced a smile and stood so they'd see him. Chris spotted him and a genuinely happy grin spread across his face. He started toward Dag, holding the hand of a slender, dark-haired woman.

"Dagster! Man! I can't believe you're here!"

Chris released the girl and reached for Dag's hand to shake it, but with his other hand grabbed Dag's shoulder and pulled him in for a masculine hug. Dag's stomach tightened and he closed his eyes briefly at the contact.

Chris's smile was so sincere and warm when they drew apart it made Dag's chest hurt. "Good to see you, buddy."

"You too," Dag said. He turned his gaze to the woman standing just behind Chris. "This must be Kassidy."

"This is." Chris reached for her and drew her forward. She extended a hand, all fine bones and soft skin, and Dag shook it.

Their eyes connected. Silky dark hair brushed her shoulders. Her smooth cheeks grew a little pinker as they looked at each other. Her unusual mouth—wide and full

11

lipped—curved into a smile, and brown eyes sparkled with gold flecks. What eyes! Now that's what you'd call bedroom eyes—big and long lashed and sexy as fucking hell. She was gorgeous.

Shit.

"Hi, Kassidy. Good to meet you."

"Dag. I've heard so much about you."

"Oh now, that makes me nervous." He sent her a smile and she blinked at him and grew even pinker. "Let's have a seat."

He held Kassidy's chair for her so she was seated between him and Chris, Dag facing his old friend across the square table.

The waitress approached to take drink orders. Dag requested Scotch, Chris went with his usual beer and Kassidy ordered a glass of Pinot Grigio.

"So." Chris shot him a grin and shook his head. "I can't believe you're back in town. What the hell, man? You were too busy making money to even come back and visit once in a while?"

Dag laughed. "I guess so. I didn't plan it that way. It has been a long time, huh?"

"Too long." Chris's smile faded. "I would've visited you, but it seemed like every time I suggested it you were too busy traveling or having meetings or something."

Dag's chest tightened but he gave his friend a rueful smile. "I know. It never seemed to work out."

"Are you here to stay?"

"I don't know. I've got a few business meetings lined up next week. I'll have to see what develops." He smiled at Kassidy. "Chris didn't tell me how gorgeous you are. Wow." He put a hand over his chest and turned back to Chris. "How the hell did you hook up with someone this good looking?"

Chris's smile broadened and he glanced at Kassidy. "Yeah, she's pretty sweet."

She rolled her eyes. "You're talking about me like I'm not even here."

Chris reached over and covered her hand on the white tablecloth. "I know you're here, sweetheart." Their eyes met in a shared exchange that had Dag's stomach rolling over.

"This looks serious," he drawled, watching them eye each other. His gaze moved between them. "Chris. What's up, man?"

Chris looked at him. "We just bought a condo and moved in together," he said. Pride and obvious love shone on his face. "As of today."

"Wow." Dag nodded, heart descending slowly in his chest. "That's great. Where's the new place?"

The waitress arrived with their drinks as they described the condo to him, and the same warmth and affection sparkled in Kassidy's eyes as they talked. She was as happy as if she'd just won a multi-million-dollar lottery, shacked up with Chris. Dag's chest tightened.

"How'd you two meet?" he asked, picking up his Scotch and taking a big, burning mouthful.

"At work. We both work at RBM."

Dag lifted a brow at Kassidy. "And what do you do there, Kassidy?"

She smiled. "I'm in Human Resources. Training and Development."

"Cool."

She glanced at Chris. "Just over a year ago I was assigned a training project for Chris's department. That's how we met." Her eyes moved over Chris warmly. "We started going out after the project was done."

"That's okay?" Dag asked. "I mean, RBM doesn't have any policies against that kind of thing?"

"No." She shook her head, her silky hair sliding. "You have to use some judgment of course. But since that project, we haven't worked directly together again, and the company is so huge, we often don't even see each other during the day. Right now I'm working on a project for our marketing division."

"I see. That's great."

"Yeah. I really love it. This time I'll have to travel a bit, as I'll be delivering training in Minneapolis and Detroit later this year."

Chris frowned at that. "Yeah."

Chris was going to miss her. How touching.

Then Chris looked at him. "What about you, man? No wife, no girlfriend?"

Dag laughed. "No. I'm not ready to settle down."

"Will you ever be?" Chris shook his head, smiling.

"Who knows?" Dag had had all kinds of relationships, but the idea of spending the rest of his life with one person scared the crap out of him. He changed the subject. "What about you, buddy? How's work? Vice President of Product Development. Impressive."

Chris grinned. "Hell yeah. Didn't I tell you I'd be VP by the time I'm thirty?"

"Just under the wire, huh?" Dag returned the smile. "Turning thirty next month, aren't you?"

"That's right. And you the month after that."

"Yeah."

"You've done all right too."

"Yup." Dag swallowed more Scotch. "And I've been having a

blast."

"Making a living off fun," Chris said with a grin.

"You bet." He wasn't going to apologize. The online games and fantasy sports he'd developed had become hugely popular. And what was wrong with fun? Much as he admired Chris and his business sense, he couldn't do what Chris did—slaving in a corporate box developing data storage solutions. Thankfully it took all kinds.

The waitress returned to take their order but they hadn't even looked at their menus yet, so they spent the next few moments studying the selections. Finally, Dag closed his.

"Let me guess," Chris said with a grin. "Steak."

"Prime rib."

"Close enough. I knew you'd order a big hunk of beef."

"Probably because you want the same thing," Kassidy said dryly. She, too, closed her menu.

"I'm betting you're a chicken or fish kind of girl," Dag said, watching her. "Or maybe salad."

She reached for her glass of wine with a graceful motion of her hand and flashed him a look. A faintly hostile look. "Chicken or fish kind of girl?"

He tipped his head to one side. "Don't tell me you want beef too?"

She gave him a slow smile that sent heat sliding right through him. "I believe I will have a steak tonight," she said softly.

"Attagirl," he replied, holding her gaze. Another flash of heat jolted him.

Huh. Something flowed between them, something warm and magnetic, something that felt a lot like...attraction. He could not be feeling that for his best buddy's girlfriend, for

15

Chrissake. He tossed back the rest of his Scotch.

And yet, better he flirt with her than... *Hell.* Luckily Chris knew what he was like. Chris would know it didn't mean anything. Dag flirted with every female he met—that was just him.

Her smile went a little crooked, her eyes grew wary and she broke the connection to look down at her wine.

"Well, if we're all having beef, let's order a nice bottle of red wine," Dag said. They looked over the wine list, and when the waitress returned, he ordered a bottle of Shiraz he knew was excellent.

He saw Kassidy and Chris exchange a glance.

"What?"

"That wine..." Kassidy began.

Chris just shook his head and laughed. "Quit showing off, asshole. We know you're loaded."

Ah. Hell. The money he'd made still blew his fucking mind. Him, a kid who'd grown up with nothing, less than nothing in fact. But he must be getting used to the good life because he hadn't even thought twice about ordering an expensive wine. He just ordered it because it he liked it. He forced an answering grin. "Didn't need to do that, huh?"

Kassidy's pretty lips pressed tightly together. Had he pissed her off? He leaned toward her, close enough that he caught a whiff of her scent—vanilla and amber, warm and sexy, sweet and provocative.

"Sorry," he said, laying his hand on her bare forearm. He curled his fingers around her and gave a gentle squeeze. "I didn't even think. I'm buying dinner and I like that wine. So let's just enjoy it."

Her big eyes met his, mouth still pinched. He held her gaze, ignoring the sparks ricocheting inside his body, trying to disregard the softness of her skin, the hitch of her breath. Then her lips softened.

"Thank you," she said politely. "That's very nice of you."

He *had* pissed her off. What? *What?*

Suddenly his entire focus became trying to get back to that place where they'd been locked in an eye clinch, warm and sensual. Because this was his friend's girlfriend. It was important they get along.

And it was important Chris not know how he was really feeling.

Chapter Two

Chris watched the exchange between Dag and Kassidy. Damn, he wanted Dag to like Kassidy. Because she was so important to him. They hadn't talked marriage, but that's probably where they were headed. It was...right.

But he also wanted Kassidy to like Dag. First, he wanted her to *know* Dag. The guy had showed him what hard work was. Motivated him. Kicked his ass when he tried to slack off. He knew he'd been lucky in life and Dag had definitely not, and he'd learned from Dag that rewards were so much sweeter when you'd worked for them. When you'd earned them. Chris had always wished Kassidy could meet him, could know how big a part Dag had played in shaping who he was. And finally he was here.

Typical Dag, even though he'd come across as mocking and sardonic, he was looking at Kassidy as if she were dessert and he'd missed his last three meals. But he always did that. The guy was a chick magnet, no question, yet he'd never been serious about anyone, basically a man-whore who'd slept his way around campus and continued it in the business world when they'd graduated. Was Chris jealous? Nah. There might be a tiny element of jealousy there, but Chris had to admit to a tinge of admiration for the ease with which the guy attracted girls, and truthfully, he'd reaped the benefits of that magnetism himself, with some of the things they'd done.

But Kassidy...didn't seem impressed. Chris's stomach tightened as he sipped his wine, watching them eye each other, Dag with heated interest, Kassidy with wariness.

"This wine is very nice," Kassidy said. She set the glass of ruby Shiraz down. She was being all polite and he could tell Dag had pissed her off when he'd ordered the wine. She hated pretention and she hated people who showed off their money.

"Thanks," Dag replied, sitting back so the waitress could place his dinner in front of him. Chris smiled at the girl as she served him his, and picked up his knife and fork. The charbroiled smell of the meat rose to his nose. Damn, it smelled good and he was starved.

"How's your steak, sweetheart?" he asked Kassidy.

"Delicious." She smiled at him.

The weird thing was, Dag wasn't the type to show off his money. Chris had made the joke about it, but really, it *had* been a joke. Because he knew Dag, and that wasn't him. Or at least it never had been before. Because Dag had never had money. Had making it big changed him?

"So, you're out of a job," Chris said, trying to get things back on track.

Dag laughed. "Yeah. It feels weird."

"I heard you made a killing when you sold to Momentum Media."

"I did okay." Dag made a face.

Now that was more like it—more like Dag to downplay his success. The seven-figure deal had been in the news a month or so ago.

"What are you going to do with all that money?" Chris asked.

"That money is my freedom to do whatever I want." Dag grinned. "You know I don't like being tied down to stuff." He shrugged and cut a piece of meat. "Like I said, I have a few meetings lined up. I need something new to sink my teeth into."

"You always need something new." They shared a smile. "What kinds of ideas do you have?"

They talked business for the next while as they ate, and Chris watched Kassidy listen to them. She was relaxing, he could tell, thank god.

The conversation fell to reminiscing about college days, which also left Kassidy out, but she laughed at their stories and asked questions, and seemed to warm up to Dag a bit.

"How did you two end up friends?" she asked.

Chris grinned and shot Dag a glance. "Mostly because we were in all the same classes. And we were the two best-looking dudes on campus."

Kassidy laughed. "Well, yeah, I can see that."

One corner of Dag's mouth lifted. "We had other things in common too." He slanted a glance at Chris. Oh yeah. Chris didn't exactly want to go there, not with Kassidy, not now. But yeah, he and Dag had shared some good times.

"I should set something up for all the old gang," Chris said. "You remember Jeff and Sarah? And Cole." He named a few others. "How about next Friday we all go out somewhere? You should see everyone while you're here."

"Sounds good." Dag leaned back in his chair, his dinner finished. "More wine, Kassidy?" He lifted the bottle.

"Sure. Thanks."

He filled her glass then Chris's, and drained the small amount left in the bottle into his own glass. "Should we order another? Or do you want to go somewhere for a drink?"

"Let's just go in the bar here," Chris suggested.

"We'd invite you back to our place, but it's a bit of a mess," Kassidy said. "We just finished moving in today and there's still unpacking to do."

"That's okay. Although I don't mind a mess, believe me."

"Um...maybe tomorrow..." Kassidy flashed a look at Chris.

"Yeah. Come for dinner tomorrow." The place wasn't that bad.

"Actually...I have tickets for the Cubs game. I was going to see if you wanted to come."

Chris leaned forward. "Cubs game! Yeah, that'd be great." And he'd get to see more of Dag while he was here.

"I just have two tickets," Dag said apologetically to Kassidy. "I don't know if you like baseball..."

"I don't mind it," she said with a smile. "But that's okay. You two should go. Catch up. I'll get things straightened up at home and you can come back for dinner after."

"Great."

There. Perfect. Things were looking up. Kassidy didn't mind him going out with Dag and they'd all have dinner together after. It was all gonna be good.

"You guys have two of everything." Hailey held up the toaster. "What are you going to do with this?"

"I don't know." Kassidy sighed. "There are so many things we don't need. Keep that toaster, it's better than mine."

Her sister had come over to help with some of the unpacking while Chris and Dag were at the baseball game, although she hadn't actually been that much help.

21

Hailey set the toaster on the counter in the kitchen and began unpacking dishes. "So what's Chris's friend like?"

Kassidy's stomach clenched. "He's um...interesting."

Hailey paused and looked at her. "Interesting? What the hell does that mean? Was he a jerk?"

"Not exactly. He's..." How could she describe Dag to Hailey without her sister getting all the wrong ideas? Dag was...unexpected. She, too, had expected Chris's best friend to be someone more like him. But Dag was clearly different. A rebel, where Chris always followed the rules. A bad boy compared to Chris's golden goodness. Intense dark eyes that looked right inside you. Shaggy dark hair falling over his eyes in a sexy swoop, dark sideburns that dipped into stubble shadowing a square jaw, and the wickedest smile she'd ever seen. A smile that made her think bad thoughts. About her boyfriend's best friend.

She gave herself a mental slap on the back of the hand.

"Kass? Hello? Anybody home?"

Kassidy's gaze flew to Hailey's face. "Oh...um...he's okay. He's kind of annoying, actually."

"Really. How so?"

Kassidy set some kitchen towels into a drawer. "Apparently he's filthy rich."

"Oh. One of those. Talking about money all the time, huh?"

"Well...no."

Hailey heaved a sigh. "Jeez, Kass, did you like him or not?"

"I guess I did. You know." She shrugged. "I hardly know him. He's coming for dinner later." She looked around the kitchen. "What was I thinking when I invited him? This place is a disaster."

"Order pizza."

"Yeah, that'll impress him."

Hailey lifted a brow. "You want to impress him?"

"No!" Kassidy sighed. She felt as confused as she knew she sounded. The evening had been a strange combination of comfortable friendship and sexual sparks that had made her pussy clench. Dag just oozed sex. Everything about him said lickable, kissable, fuckable. She'd been squirming in her seat all evening.

Maybe she'd just been all worked up from the quickie in the shower with Chris just before they'd left. And they'd certainly burned up the sheets when they'd gotten home last night.

When Dag looked at her, she'd sensed a sort of predatory attraction, which was ridiculous, layered over animosity. As if he liked her, but he didn't want to like her. Maybe he thought she wasn't good enough for his friend. But then, she got the feeling he *did* think she was good enough for *him.*

That was just so wrong.

"Okay," she said, closing up the cardboard box she'd just emptied. "Pretty much done in here, which is good. I can cook dinner, anyway. Now I just have to finish putting some clothes away."

Hailey glanced at her watch. "I should get going."

"Oh. I was going to see if you wanted to stay for dinner too. You could meet Dag."

"Much as I'd love to meet a boring friend of Chris's, I have other plans." Hailey's contempt for Chris and Kassidy's corporate careers and conventional life annoyed Kassidy, but she let it slide off her like she always did. "Got a hot date."

"Oh. Really."

Two years younger than Kassidy, Hailey'd always been the

wild child of the family, causing their parents no end of anxiety. When Hailey had started smoking at age fourteen, Kassidy had been horrified. When Hailey'd started doing drugs, she'd been shocked. The drinking and partying had in truth made her a little envious...and the boys...well, Kassidy couldn't even imagine that. She'd had three steady boyfriends in her entire life, including Chris. She much preferred that to a string of meaningless sexual encounters with guys she didn't even know.

And Hailey showed no signs of settling down. She'd dropped out of college to work as a bartender, and still did. Kassidy had no idea how Hailey lived the lifestyle she did off the kind of money she made bartending—maybe she didn't want to know. Hailey's licentious lifestyle had always made her a little uncomfortable.

"Well, have fun," she told her sister. "Thanks for helping."

"No prob."

"Hey, Mom and Dad's thirtieth anniversary is coming up. I was thinking we should plan something for them."

Hailey frowned. "We just did something for their twenty-fifth."

"That was five years ago!"

"But twenty-five is the big one. We don't need to do something for their thirtieth."

Kassidy blew out a breath. "Sure. Never mind. Chris and I will do something."

Jesus, Hailey could be annoying, especially when it came to their parents.

Hailey took off with a wave and Kassidy wandered into the bedroom, her irritation with her sister scraping away some of the pleasure she felt from living with Chris. She opened a drawer and saw Chris's socks and underwear shoved inside in a jumble. Shaking her head, she removed everything and carefully replaced it, neat and organized. He'd be so happy when he saw that.

She sat on the bed and looked around the room, now nice and neat, the mix of their belongings a happy symbol of their two lives now linked together in cohabitation. She let the happiness swell inside her again. She loved Chris so much, and seeing her moisturizer sitting beside his aftershave sent a wave of contentment through her.

She glanced at her watch. Better get dinner started. In her new kitchen, she laid the cookbook open on the shiny granite counter and looked back and forth from it as she prepared the Greek chicken casserole, adding chicken to tomatoes and black olives. She crumbled feta cheese on top and popped it into the oven to bake. The guys would be back any minute.

She set out salad ingredients, and then, because they weren't home yet, used the extra time to fix herself up, changing from rolled-up sweatpants and a T-shirt into a pair of knee-length shorts and a loose camisole top.

She was ready. The casserole was ready. Chris and Dag still weren't back. They must have gone out somewhere after the game. With another glance at her watch, she sighed. The casserole sat on the stove. It would keep.

Then she heard the key in the lock and hurried toward the door. Chris and Dag walked in, bringing the smell of fresh air and sunshine with them. Their eyes sparkled, their faces were tanned from sitting in the sun all afternoon at Wrigley Field and they looked like they'd been laughing.

"Hey, sweetheart, sorry we're late," Chris said, hugging her and kissing her mouth. He smelled like beer. Not obnoxiously, like he was drunk, just as if he'd had a few.

"It's my fault," Dag said from behind him, and she met his

sexy dark eyes. Once again that little current of electricity jolted her as their eyes met and held. "These are for you."

He held out a cellophane cone full of pale pink and fuchsia gerbera daisies, all bright and cheery. She'd been ready to be annoyed, but the sweet gesture softened her up, even though she totally recognized it as sucking up.

"Thank you." She moved to take them from him. He opened his arms for a hug. She hesitated. For some reason she did not want to touch him. But she moved toward him anyway and gave him one of those superficial, barely touching hugs you give a near-stranger or an uncle you haven't seen for years.

But that wasn't good enough for him, and he pulled her in and gave her a quick squeeze that pressed her breasts into his chest and sent fire licking over her. It was over in a second but she had to swallow and clasp her hands tightly around the flowers. She focused on them instead of Dag.

"They're beautiful," she said. "I love them."

Dag smiled, his dark eyes crinkling and warm. Both he and Chris were bright-eyed and suntanned and happy, and her heart swelled at seeing Chris so relaxed and cheerful. A surge of gratitude toward Dag rose inside her, gratitude for coming back to see his old friend, for bringing such a smile to his face and a sparkle to his eyes. Not that Chris had been miserable. She just knew this meant a lot to him. So she sent a warm smile Dag's way, and once again their gazes hooked together and hung there, suspended, as if she couldn't look away.

"Come on in," Chris said, leading the way into the living room. Dag looked around and Kassidy moved to the kitchen to find a vase for the flowers, hands unsteady, stomach quivering.

She could not remember where she'd put the vases. Likely Hailey had unpacked them. She searched through cupboards, flustered—*Where are the vases, dammit?*—and listened to the guys talking about the condo.

"Nice," Dag said. "Really nice."

"Three bedrooms," Chris said. "One's going to be my home office eventually. Still have some work to do."

She found a vase and arranged the flowers then carried them to the living room and set them on a side table. "Dinner'll be ready in a few minutes," she said. "I just have to cook the pasta and toss the salad."

"How about another beer?" Chris offered Dag. They followed her into the kitchen. It seemed very confined in that small space with those two big guys moving around.

"Who won the game?" she asked, filling a pot with water.

"Phillies won, three to two."

"Cubs kinda sucked," Dag added.

"It's early in the season," Chris said. "Thanks for the game, man." And he looped an arm around Dag's neck and pulled him in for a brief squeeze.

She watched the hug then turned away to run water into the big pot for the pasta, the image of that brief embrace lingering in her head. Stuck there. Making her feel...she didn't know what. And she didn't know why. Maybe it was because she'd never seen Chris do that with any of his other friends. As she set the pot on the stove to boil, she kept thinking about it, even as they moved out of the kitchen with their drinks.

She liked seeing Chris do that. Once again, she wasn't sure why. Maybe it was because of what had happened when Chris met her friend Steve. Steve had been one of her best friends in high school, part of the crowd she hung around with, and he was gay. He'd never "come out"—he just always was out. As far back as she could remember, everyone knew it and accepted it. He was a great guy. He had boyfriends, and so did she.

Then in the summer after graduation, he'd been attacked by some kind of sick homophobes after coming out of a gay bar downtown. He'd been close to dying, in the hospital for weeks with serious injuries. She and all her friends had spent hours at the hospital visiting him, sick with grief and rage over what had happened to him. He'd recovered, but after that he'd moved away. They still kept in touch, and when he'd come back for a visit last year, she'd been anxious for Chris to meet him and his new partner. It didn't bother her at all, but Chris was cool, almost awkward around Steve and Ryan, and that troubled her a little.

She'd tried to talk to Chris about it after. He really didn't even want to talk about it. Like many guys, she guessed, the idea of two guys together was—what was the word—distasteful? Repellent? She wasn't sure. She remembered having those kinds of conversations with male friends over drinks in college, trying to get insight into the male perspective of why the idea of two girls together was a turn-on for them but not two guys. She'd even broached *that* idea to Chris, in an attempt to understand where he was coming from, but he had *not* wanted to talk about. Even the two-girls scenario.

Anyway. She didn't think Chris was homophobic, but seeing him physically showing casual affection for a male friend made her feel good. She liked it.

After dinner, she didn't have anything for dessert and Chris said, "I've got the perfect thing." And he pulled the bottle of Limoncello out of the freezer.

So they poured icy-cold lemony shots of the liqueur and drank them, talking and laughing about all kinds of things, until about ten o'clock when Dag said, "Man. I can't drive back to the hotel like this. What is that stuff? I'm plastered."

Chris laughed and showed him the alcohol content. "You'd

better crash here, buddy."

"I can take a taxi, I guess. Come back tomorrow for my car." It was the Memorial Day long weekend, so neither Chris nor Kassidy had to work in the morning.

"Nah. Just stay here. We have room."

Chris looked at Kassidy. She had this vague idea that it might not be a good idea but was a little buzzed too from all the drinks, so she said, "Sure. I'll just make the bed."

"I'll help," Dag insisted, following her down the hall.

"This sofa bed is from my apartment," she told him. "I just had a little studio apartment so this was all I had room for."

"So this was your bed," Dag murmured, and the sexy suggestive tone in his voice made her pulse leap.

"Um. Yeah."

He helped her pull the bed out and she found sheets and pillowcases and pillows. They both laughed as they bumped into each other trying to stretch the fitted sheet over the mattress, but she was a tad tipsy and almost fell over. Dag caught her and pulled her against him to steady her.

Their eyes met.

"Thanks for letting me stay here," Dag said, his voice a velvet stroke over her senses. "And thanks for letting me monopolize your boyfriend today. I know you two just moved in here and you probably wanted him home."

"That's okay," she said, a little breathless. Her heart had picked up speed. The warmth of Dag's body heated her. His sexy mouth curved into a smile, not far from her own, close enough for her to see the whiskers shadowing his square jaw. "He's glad you're here. Of course you should spend time together."

He nodded, eyes searching hers. She felt something, like

Dag's thoughts floating beneath the surface, but didn't know what they were. And then they moved apart and she picked up a pillow and began shaking it into a pillowcase. Dag did the same.

"There ya go," she said, and moved to the door. "Help yourself to anything you need in the bathroom."

"Yeah. Thanks, Kassidy."

She caught his eye as she walked out the door, and for some reason she thought the look in his eyes was...loneliness.

Chapter Three

Where the hell was he?

Dag blinked at the strip of brightness around the edge of the blind on the window and peered around the dim room. Jesus. Chicago. Oh yeah, he was in Chris and Kassidy's new place.

His head fell back on the pillow and he closed his eyes. Chris and Kassidy.

Why the hell had he come back here? Some kind of misguided idea that after all these years he could come back to Chicago, which he'd missed like hell, and see Chris again, who he'd also missed like hell, and it would all be okay.

He groaned and rolled over in the bed. They'd had such a great time yesterday at the Cubs game, almost like old times. They'd fallen back into easy conversation, laughing and joking like they always had.

Then they'd come home to Kassidy.

Sweet and sexy Kassidy, who was just as easy to talk to as Chris. They'd sat around drinking and talking, and hours had zipped by before he even realized it, along with the better part of a bottle of Limoncello.

Which accounted for the way his mouth felt dry as sand and his head ached faintly.

He rolled out of bed and reached for his watch on the small dresser. Nearly nine o'clock. Were Chris and Kassidy awake yet? Guess he'd find out. He dragged on his jeans before leaving the small bedroom to use the bathroom. The faint sound of a TV drifted down the short hall. Someone was up. Probably Chris. He'd never been one to sleep in or lie around in bed.

Of course, with a woman like Kassidy in bed with him, that could be a whole different story.

Dag found a toothbrush still in a cellophane package sitting on the vanity in the bathroom. Huh. That had to be from Kassidy. He ripped it open gratefully and brushed the sand out of his mouth then washed up.

He wandered out to the living room and found Chris sprawled on the couch watching TV, a cup of coffee clasped in both hands resting on his flat belly. Morning summer sunlight flooded in the arched window, glowing on the polished hardwood floors and turning Chris's light brown hair gold. He glanced up. "Hey, you're up."

"Yeah. Morning."

"Want some coffee?"

Dag made a face. Chris laughed. "Oh yeah, I forgot you hate the stuff."

"Got any Coke?"

"Yeah, I think there might be a couple of cans in the fridge. Help yourself."

"Chris." Kassidy's voice came from behind him, and Dag turned to face her. Hell, she looked just as good first thing in the morning, her face bare and pink-cheeked, hair loose around her shoulders. She shook her head at Chris. "He doesn't know where anything is. You could get up off the couch and look after your guest."

The two men just laughed, and Kassidy led Dag to the kitchen still shaking her head. She slanted him a glance as she opened the fridge door. "Coke? For breakfast?"

Dag grinned. "Yeah. Why not?" He watched her open the fridge, her movements graceful and smooth.

She glanced up at him through her eyelashes as she shrugged and reached inside for a can. "Seems weird."

"It's got sugar and caffeine. Same as a cup of coffee. Why not?

She handed him the can then a glass, her gaze skittering over his body. He hadn't put a shirt on, in fact he literally wore nothing but his jeans and they weren't even buttoned. He hadn't thought before wandering out of the bedroom half naked. And Kassidy was clearly aware of his bare chest.

Like he was aware of her bare legs below the hem of the khaki shorts she wore, her feet small and pretty with rosy-pink polished toenails. He dragged his gaze up and away from her legs.

"Are you hungry?" she asked. "We just had toast..."

Dag shook his head. "Nah. I never eat much in the morning. Coke's good, and then I'll head back to the hotel."

She nodded and picked up her mug of coffee then padded over to the couch where Chris sat. She curled up beside him and he absentmindedly slid his arm around her and pulled her closer, his hand going into her hair and playing with the silky dark strands.

Dag watched Chris's long, tanned fingers caressing Kassidy's hair, slowly rubbing a strand then dragging his fingers down the length of it. Something clenched inside him and he felt like he couldn't take his eyes off the mesmerizing motion.

He lifted the glass and took a big swallow of nose-stinging fizzy Coke. He had to get out of there. Now.

He walked across the living room to the arched window overlooking the tree-lined street. Nice neighborhood. The sun lit up the fresh green leaves of the maple trees, the sky above a perfect clear blue. He turned back to the couple snuggled up on the couch together, Chris absorbed in the news show he was watching, Kassidy watching...Dag. Heat suffused him.

He guzzled down the rest of his Coke. "I'll uh...get dressed," he said. "And get out of your way. I'm sure you have a lot to do."

"No rush, man," Chris said. "What are you doing today, anyway?"

Dag paused in the hall. "I have some business stuff to go over. To get ready for my meetings later this week."

"Oh. Okay."

Dag returned to the bedroom where he'd slept, found the rest of his clothes and quickly dressed. He pulled the sheets and blankets off the bed, folded the mattress back up into the sofa frame and replaced the cushions. Then he gathered up the bedding in his arms and took it out to Kassidy.

"What should I do with this?" he asked her.

"Oh, thank you, Dag." She rose from the couch and accepted the bundle of laundry with a smile. "You didn't need to do that. I'll just toss it in the washer right now." And she disappeared into a small room off the kitchen.

"So I'll call you later this week," Chris said, standing too. He followed Dag to the door. "We'll get things set up for Friday night. But hey, we can do lunch or something one day. If you have time."

"Yeah, sure."

Kassidy came to the door too, and Chris pulled her in front

ot him, slid his arms around her waist and rested his chin on her head. His forearms sat just below her breasts, plumping them up a bit, which made Dag notice they were braless beneath the soft cotton tank top she wore, her nipples hard little points. Another demonstration of the warm and sexy chemistry between the two of them.

Out. Of. There.

"Thanks for dinner, Kassidy. You're a great cook."

She grinned. "Thank you. Any time. It's been great getting to know you."

And he got the hell out.

On the leafy street, he sucked in big breaths full of fresh morning air as he walked to his car parked at the curb halfway down the block. Oh man. All the emotional crap twisting and turning inside him was completely unexpected. There was no fucking way he could move back to Chicago.

He rubbed his face as he unlocked his car door then slid into the vehicle. His best plan would be to get through these business meetings he had lined up, and then get the hell back to San Francisco.

Kassidy had the day off Friday and planned to do some shopping. They needed towels for the main bathroom—Chris's mismatched, well-worn towels didn't fit in with their new condo. And they needed curtains for both the extra bedrooms. When Dag had slept over, it made her want to do up the rooms nicely. Not that she anticipated having guests very often.

Dag.

She got all warm inside when she thought about seeing him that morning. Jesus, the man was walking sex. Those worn jeans sat so low on his hips she could see the twin indentations at the base of his spine when she looked at him from the back, and facing him...well she couldn't even look, afraid of what she might see. The lowest she'd let her eyes go was his six-pack abs and even that was dangerous. His silky dark hair had flopped over his forehead and those eyes had looked at her with such heat, she'd almost felt like she were burning up.

She'd felt so guilty for admiring his half-naked body she'd practically jumped onto Chris's lap to force her attention where it should be—on her handsome boyfriend. Who was equally as sexy. There was just something about Dag that kept pulling at her.

And tonight they were going to see him again. He and Chris had had lunch yesterday but hadn't invited her along. Not that she'd wanted to go. She'd had lunch with friends from work, as she usually did.

The doorbell rang just as she was checking her purse for cell phone, keys and shopping list, and when she peeked out she saw...Dag.

She didn't know why her heart started thudding in her chest, heavy and slow, taking her breath away. She unlocked the door and opened it with shaky fingers, forcing a smile.

"Hey," she said. "This is a surprise."

He smiled back at her, that wicked sexy smile that crinkled his eyes and creased his lean cheeks. "I tried to call you at work but you weren't there."

Puzzled, she tipped her head to one side. "Yeah. I mean, no. I took the day off to do some errands."

"That's what Chris told me. I called him to find out where you are. I was hoping to pick your brain."

"Me? Why?"

His eyes sparkled. "I've got this idea...met with a guy yesterday, and it got me thinking. And you're the perfect one to help me."

"Idea for what?" Thoughts buzzed around in her head. *Why me? What guy?* What was he talking about?

"Let me take you out for lunch," he said, not answering any of her questions. "And I'll explain everything."

"Uh...okay. I guess." She glanced at her watch. It wasn't even eleven yet. "Kind of early for lunch, though."

He shrugged and gave a crooked smile that sent a shaft of heat right through her. "I'm hungry."

"Let me guess. No breakfast."

"Yeah." His smile deepened. "Okay, I'll take you for a late breakfast then. No, you have lunch, I'll have breakfast."

"Whatever." Amusement glimmered inside her. "Fine. Let me get my purse." She grabbed it from the kitchen table where she'd been checking it then flicked off the lights. "I was just heading out. A few more minutes I'd have been gone."

"Lucky me," he said, and the husky timbre of his voice brushed over her. She licked her lips as she locked the door of the condo behind her.

His rental car was parked at the curb beneath the rustling green canopy of the big old maple trees in front of their building. He opened the passenger door for her and she climbed in.

"Where should we go?" he asked, fastening his seat belt.

She had no idea. There were so many places they could go, but since it was a gorgeous warm day, she tried to think of somewhere outside. "There's a little place not far from here. In fact..." She made a face. "We could probably have walked."

He slanted her a grin as he shifted gears. Something she'd

always found very sexy was a man driving a standard transmission, shifting gears smoothly like he could feel the motor revving. When she saw his hand on the gear shift, she had to swallow hard.

"Turn left at the next light," she directed him. "It's called Lombardo's."

"Sounds fancy."

"It's not. It's just a little place, but it has a nice patio."

"Sounds good."

He found the place easily, and with some kind of wicked luck he found a parking spot on the street and eased the car into it in a smooth feat of parallel parking. He did everything so easily—he seemed to Kassidy to be the kind of guy who had it all, who never had to work that hard, someone for whom things just fell into his lap.

They sat at a small table on the patio under a red-and-white-striped awning, surrounded by pots of scarlet geraniums and blue lobelia. Jazzy music played in the background for them alone, as they were the only ones there at that in-between-breakfast-and-lunch hour. Kassidy ordered coffee and Dag requested a Coke, making her smile, and the waiter left to get those while they looked at the menu.

She wasn't hungry. She was burning with curiosity. She wanted to know what Dag wanted to talk to her about. All kinds of wild thoughts ran through her imagination, none of them appropriate. At all. But then, Dag had called Chris about where to find her, so it wasn't likely that he wanted to talk to her about...inappropriate things.

He slapped his menu shut. "Steak sandwich," he ordered when the waiter returned. Kassidy requested a spinach salad.

"A steak sandwich isn't exactly breakfast," she pointed out.

He laughed. "Why not? I've never liked following rules."

That she could believe. Coke for breakfast.

He leaned back in his chair and linked his fingers behind his head. His snug black T-shirt outlined his buff torso, his arm muscles bulging from beneath the short sleeves, exposing a sexy tattoo. His teeth flashed white in his tanned face as he smiled at her. The power of that smile to captivate, to make her feel like she was the center of his attention, of his world at that moment, astonished her.

She looked away from him, down at the white mug full of black coffee. "So," she croaked. "What did you want to talk to me about?"

He leaned forward, forearms on the table, hands clasping his glass of Coke. "You work in training and development, right?"

"Yeah." She eyed him.

"And RBM is a big company, right? With more than one location?"

"Yes. We have offices in Detroit, Minneapolis and Seattle."

He started asking question about traveling to design and deliver training programs. She'd been doing a lot more traveling over the last year and really didn't enjoy it. She didn't like being away from Chris, and there always seemed to be so much time wasted sitting in airports, traveling to and from the airport, sitting in the hotel, even with her BlackBerry.

"What about informal learning?" he asked. "Social learning?"

She eyed him. His knowledge surprised her. "What about it?"

"How do people in different locations learn from each other?"

"They don't."

"Tell me what you know about social learning."

"What is this, a job interview?"

He grinned. "No. Just checking some things out."

"Well, supposedly eighty percent of what people learn comes from social learning, on the job, just talking with coworkers."

"That's a lot."

"Yes."

"What about networking?"

She frowned. "Once again, I say, what about it?"

"The role of networking in developing staff."

She could see how his mind was bounding ahead of their conversation and he had to slow himself down so he'd make sense to her. His intelligence was almost scary.

"Oh. Well, that's huge too, of course. It's not just what you know, but who you know. Knowing who to ask."

"Are there a lot of younger employees at RBM?"

She nodded. "Sure. We're a tech company. We're always recruiting."

"But being a tech company, I'm sure your older staff is comfortable with technology too."

"Yes. I suppose. What's this about?"

His grin was infectious and teased an answering smile out of her even though she had no idea where this was going. "I was talking to this guy yesterday. We got this idea for social networking."

She rolled her eyes. "Not another social networking site."

"You're not into the FriendSpace thing?"

She hitched a shoulder. "I am. A little. It keeps me in touch with friends who've moved away. Obviously I'm not into it to meet people."

"Okay, good, so you know how it all works." He leaned closer across the table. "Picture something like that in the workplace."

"We've banned our staff from accessing those kinds of sites," she replied automatically, her forehead creasing a little.

"No. I mean your *own* social networking site."

She stared at him, still not getting it.

"Designed for training and development. Information sharing. Networking."

She gazed back at him, processing what he was saying. She had a hard time grasping exactly what he was telling her, but he continued to talk, enthusiasm coloring his voice, making his eyes gleam. Obviously he'd been thinking about this and the ideas came pouring out of him. "Think about the organizational knowledge you could capture," he said. "Picture user profiles describing everyone's experience, training, education…how easy it would be for someone new to the company to know who to contact with a problem or a question. Whether that person sits in the cubicle next to them or across the country."

And her mind opened up to an incredible world of possibilities as she started envisioning it. "The relationships they could build, even long distance," she said slowly. Their lunches arrived and they ate as they continued talking, asking each other questions and throwing out suggestions, and the interest and excitement built inside her as if she'd caught it from him like a virus. A good virus.

"So, that's what you want to spend your money on?" she finally asked.

He smiled. "Well. I haven't decided for sure. I didn't plan to start off right on the ground floor with something, I was kind of looking for something already established that I could invest in. But man, I'm pumped about this."

"It's a lot of work."

"Yeah. But I think I have enough connections that I can find the people I need." He lifted a brow. "Wanna come work for me, Kassidy?"

Her mouth fell open and she stared across the table at him.

Chapter Four

"Are you serious?" she asked, blinking rapidly at him.

He laughed. "Yes and no. I'd love to have you, but I'm nowhere near ready."

"You don't even know me," she protested. "How do you know I'm any good at my job?"

"I know you're good." He winked at her and watched her cheeks bloom with color. Christ, she was gorgeous, all animated during their discussion. Once she'd gotten what he was talking about, her quick mind had thrown out things he hadn't even thought of—good ideas, but also barriers he hadn't anticipated. Problem solving with her was a rush.

"What made you go into training and development as a career?" he asked.

"Well, I actually thought of becoming a teacher. All through high school, that's what I intended to do."

"You like kids?"

She blinked at him, but smiled. "Yeah. I love kids."

"Me too. Not that I'll likely ever have any," he added. "Anyway, go on."

"I started working at my first part-time job in this office that had really horrible management, and I had all these ideas how they could improve the place. I got interested in how businesses work and making things better. So then I wanted to go into business, but since I like the aspect of teaching, I decided to specialize in training and development."

"Cool." He had a sense from those words "make things better" that she also liked to make people better. Maybe sometimes whether they wanted it or not. Which was admirable but could also be annoying. He smiled at her, liking her sense of purpose. "Anyway. You're probably happy where you are. But you never know, one day if things work out...keep it in mind. Maybe in the meantime, though, you can be a sounding board for me. Hey, I know—I could pay you a consulting fee."

She opened her mouth then closed it. Then opened it again. "Great," she said, glancing at her watch. "You owe me...two hundred dollars for the last hour."

Laughter burst from his lips and he shook his head. "Nice try."

"You're loaded," she said. "Why not?"

He studied her, hearing the slight edge in her voice. "That bugs you, doesn't it?"

"No, of course not."

"Bullshit." He rubbed his forehead. "That night at Vincent's, I wasn't showing off when I ordered that wine."

Her mouth twisted. "Yeah," she finally said. "I know."

"You and Chris aren't hurting," he said. "I know what VPs at RBM make."

"A lot more than I do," she said ruefully. She laughed. "I'm sorry. I judged you and I shouldn't have."

"Thank you. But I'm still not paying you for the last hour. Although I will buy your lunch."

"Thanks."

They exchanged a smile that now held shared experience, a

link between them that was more than just Chris.

"What are you up to this afternoon?" he asked as they walked back to his car.

"Shopping. Errands. Things for the condo. How about you?"

"Hmmm. Not much."

"Meetings are all done?"

"Yeah. Now I've got a different path though, have to give it some thought. Hey. I'll come shopping with you."

"You're kidding me."

"Nah." He shrugged and they paused beside his car, the bright midday sun glinting off the windshield. "I got nothing else to do."

"Gee, thanks."

He rolled his eyes but smiled. "Sorry. That didn't come out right. What I meant was, take pity on me, Kassidy, I'm all alone in town with nothing to do this afternoon."

"Oh, for—all right, come with me, but I'm going to Bed and Bath. Chris hates that store."

"Well, I'm not Chris." And he rounded the front of the car to jump in while she slid into the passenger seat.

What was he doing? Sure he was at a bit of a loose end, and yeah, he'd enjoyed the last hour talking to her about ideas and plans, in fact he was buzzing from the adrenaline of it. But spending time with Chris's girlfriend without Chris shouldn't be a problem. Really. Why would it?

Just that sexual tension underlying everything they said, every glance they shared, and never mind if he actually were to touch her. Then he wanted to, just to see if actual sparks would fly. Bad. Bad idea.

He followed Kassidy around the store. He'd lied to her. Well, actually no. It was true, he wasn't Chris, but truthfully Bed and

Bath wasn't his favorite store to shop in. He was more into electronics and cars. But he had to admire how she shopped—with a purpose and organized efficiency. She had a list, and headed straight for the towel department. She knew what she wanted. She selected some other bathroom accessories, and then led the way to the curtains, where she took a little longer to make her selection.

She pulled out fabrics and studied them, nibbled her bottom lip as she looked at different rods and checked prices. When she finally made her decision, she tried to lift a long package into the shopping cart.

"Let me," Dag said and easily shifted the carton into the cart.

"Two of those," she said, and he grinned.

"What's next?" he asked after they'd gone through the checkout.

"Well." She glanced sideways at him as he pushed the cart through the parking lot. "I was going to just browse around some of the shops on Armitage Avenue. There are some funky little places. But really. You don't have to come with me."

"Why not?" He loaded her purchases into the trunk of the rental car, slammed the lid shut and dusted his hands together. "Like I said, take pity on me. And if we finish early, I'll buy you a drink and we can talk more."

"We're going out tonight," she reminded him.

"I know."

They climbed into the car and he drove back toward the condo, the shopping district she wanted to look at not far from there. His memories of how to get around Chicago were coming back to him, despite having only lived there for the years he was in college. His mom was still in Springfield. Not that he ever saw her or ever wanted to.

They strolled the sunny sidewalks, wandering in and out of the little shops, and Kassidy bought a few things—cool things he actually liked. In one store, she stood there looking at chunky dark wood candle holders, each of them a little different in shape and size. She picked them up and set them down, until finally he said with amusement, "Tough decision?"

She smiled at him. "Yes. It is. I don't know which three to get."

"Then buy all of them."

"There are six."

"So?"

"It can't be an even number," she said patiently. "Don't you know the rule of three?"

He lifted an eyebrow. "Rule of three?"

"Yes. It's some kind of design rule. You have to have an odd number. Three is the best number for an arrangement."

"And you know this how?"

She grinned. "I like to watch a lot of home decorating shows on TV."

He laughed.

"Seriously. The rule of three applies to lots of things."

"If you say so." He reached out and picked up one candle holder, set it aside, picked another slightly shorter one, and another, grouping the three together. "There. There's your three."

She studied them and nodded. "Okay. Now I need candles."

She chose three pillar candles to sit on top of the candle holders, some funky office accessories for the room that was to become Chris's office, and a small rug for their bedroom.

"I'm done," she said, surveying the shopping bags he was

carrying for her out of the store. A warm smile curved her pretty mouth. "Thanks for helping."

"No problem. Now how about that drink?"

"Sure. I guess." She glanced at her watch. "Chris'll be finished work soon. I'll text him and tell him to meet us."

After dropping her purchases into his car, they walked to another outdoor patio nearby. Kassidy thumbed a message into her cell phone as they waited for a table. It was early on Friday afternoon, but the weekend happy-hour crowd had already begun to arrive at the small bar.

The hostess showed them to a small table under a bright umbrella, potted palms dancing in the breeze next to them. "This is nice," Dag said, looking around. "You know all the good places to go."

She laughed. "Actually I don't. Chris and I really don't go out much. Now my sister, on the other hand, knows everywhere. And everybody." Her phone buzzed and she flipped it open to read Chris's message. "He says he'll be here in an hour."

Dag grinned. "He's turned into a workaholic, hasn't he?"

She made a face. "Oh yeah."

Dag laughed.

"What's so funny about that?"

"If you'd known him when I met him, you'd get it."

A cute crease appeared between her eyebrows. "What does that mean?"

"Chris was a supreme slacker when we met," Dag said, leaning back in his chair.

Her frown deepened. "Hey..."

He shook his head. "He thought the world owed him everything. Well, maybe that's an exaggeration, but you gotta

48

admit, he grew up in a pretty uh...privileged lifestyle."

She still frowned at him. "I...I wouldn't say that."

"Well," he lifted a shoulder. "Maybe not from where you're coming. But compared to how I grew up, he did. Anyway, it's good to know some of that stayed with him. A workaholic. Who'da thought."

She lifted her chin. "There's nothing wrong with working hard."

He laughed out loud at that. "Nope. Nothing at all."

Her eyes narrowed. "You seem like someone who doesn't have to work very hard. Someone everything just comes to easily."

His jaw almost hit the small table. What the fuck? "You gotta be kidding me," he said slowly, staring at her.

She drew back a little. "No. Am I wrong?"

"You are so wrong." He shook his head, forced a smile. "I'm not making a very good impression on you, am I?"

She blinked. "No...I mean, yes..."

He laughed again, shook his head. Wow.

"From what Chris told me, you didn't like working for someone else so you started your company developing online games, things went crazy, you made a pile of money, sold the company for even more money and now you're resting easy looking for something else fun to do."

Well, it was true, on the surface, and he wasn't someone who particularly liked defending himself. He never gave a shit what people thought of him. But Kassidy's words burned a hole in his gut. He shrugged. "Yeah, that's pretty much it. Never wanted to slave in a corporate box working for someone else."

"There are benefits to working for someone else," she said, a little quietly as if he'd annoyed her.

49

"Sure there are. I didn't mean..."

"Chris loves his job."

"I wasn't insulting him, Kass." His gut tightened even more.

She rolled her lips in briefly. "No?" Her defense of Chris made something inside him go soft, drew him to her. Dammit.

"No. I admire Chris. He has the logical mind that I don't. He's focused, I'm all over the place sometimes. He's accomplished a lot."

She nodded slowly.

"And you too," Dag added. He looked up as the waitress approached, and ordered a beer. Kassidy asked for a mojito. He turned his attention back to her. "You obviously love what you do."

"I do, but I'm never going to be a millionaire, working in training and development, even for a big company like RBM."

"So you equate success with how much money you make."

Her eyes widened. "No! I don't. That's my point."

"Then why'd you say that?"

"Because...you..."

"Because I have money, you think that's how I define success."

She gave a short nod. He sighed. "Well, it's not. Don't get me wrong, I like money, but that's not what it's about for me. You like the security of working for someone else, but I like taking risks—it's a thrill for me. It's not good or bad, right or wrong. Everyone's different. And right now, I have money, but a couple of bad decisions could flush that all down the toilet. Whereas you know you'll get paid next week. And the week after that. Right?"

Her eyes were wide and moved over his face as she studied him and listened to him. "Yes," she finally said. "That's right."

The waitress returned with their drinks.

"So you like taking risks," she said, pulling her glass closer.

"Yeah." He grinned. "That's why I skydive."

She gasped. "Skydive? Jesus! You jump out of planes?"

"Yeah. It's a rush."

"You jump out of planes for fun." She shook her head. "Oh my god. That's crazy."

"The first time scared the hell out of me," he said. "My buddy in the plane almost had to push me out. I was hanging on by the tips of my fingers. Probably would've stayed there forever. But sometimes...you just have to jump. Take a chance."

"That's a pretty big chance to take."

"That's what makes it exciting." He lifted a shoulder. "I had to learn to slow down, to analyze and weigh things and make careful, rational decisions. I tend to rely on my gut too much, but you can analyze and weigh things and procrastinate to death. Sometimes you just need to go with your instincts. Even in business, sometimes you just have to...jump."

"So, that's what you like—taking risks."

"I also like creating, coming up with ideas."

"I could tell that earlier. You were all full of energy when we were talking about your idea."

"Yeah." He smiled. "I love that part of it. You're exactly right—it energizes me."

Their eyes met and a connection shimmered between them despite the fact that she him pegged wrong, all wrong.

"Tell me how you and Chris met," he said, picking up his beer, not sure if he really wanted to hear this story.

"We told you, we met at work."

"You were doing training for his department?"

"Yes." She smiled. "I guess we were both attracted to each other, but we waited until the project was done until we went out together. It made going to work every day pretty exciting for a while, though."

"What was it about him that attracted you?"

She tipped her head to one side and gave him a narrow-eyed look, as if she found his question odd. He probably should drop this. "Well, he's good looking, of course."

"He's pretty."

She frowned. "No, he's not."

Dag laughed. "Sure he is. He's a pretty boy."

"Well, he does have a sweet smile." Her own mouth curved. "But he's so big—I guess that's why I don't think of him as a pretty boy."

"Yeah. The big muscles save him from looking too cute."

She laughed. "And I love his shoulders." She gave a little shrug. "But I liked how he was so...accepting."

"Huh?" Dag sat back, watched her face. He hadn't expected to hear that word from her.

"I was junior on the project team. When I'd remind him about the human impacts of certain decisions, he listened to me. I really liked that. He could have ignored me, but he made me feel like I had something important to say." She looked down at her drink. "He was very focused on the project goals, very task oriented, very let's-get-it-done. But when there were problems, he'd sit back and not react. Other people would freak out and start rushing into crazy decisions. I liked how he listened to everyone, even me. Sometimes people get lost in the business decisions, and for me, it's all about the people. It's the people who make the company."

Dag nodded. Yeah. That was Chris. The way he'd accepted

Dag as his friend from the first time they'd met, despite their vastly different backgrounds, despite the fact that Chris was a golden boy who'd gotten all kinds of breaks in his life and had it all, whereas Dag had started with nothing and had had to fight for every damn thing. He'd treated Dag as an equal. Yeah, that was a good word—Chris was accepting. Of most things.

Listening to Chris's girlfriend praise him, watching her face light up as she talked about the man she loved, had something tightening hot and hard in Dag's chest.

Wanting to change the subject, he said, "You mentioned you have a sister."

"Yeah. Hailey. She's two years younger than me. You'll meet her tonight, actually—she works at the nightclub we're going to."

"Really?" He lifted a brow and took a swallow of beer.

"She's a bartender." Kassidy lifted one shoulder. "She's not exactly career oriented."

"Bartending can be a career."

"I suppose." Doubt shadowed her eyes. "She's a lot different from me."

"Hmmm. Interesting. Does she look like you?"

Kassidy's forehead furrowed. "No. I don't think so."

They ordered another drink, hopping easily from one topic to another as they talked, until Kassidy finally checked the time. "Jesus! It's almost seven. Where the hell is Chris?"

Dag hadn't realized how much time had passed either. He'd actually been having fun, lost in the pleasure of getting to know Kassidy who was surprisingly easy to talk to, surprisingly sweet and sexy. Okay, that part wasn't surprising. He'd already known that.

They were meeting friends at the club between nine and

ten; Chris had arranged it all with some of the people he knew who were still in Chicago. They needed to grab some food, and he needed to shower and change. Shit.

Kassidy had pulled out her cell phone and quickly sent off a text. Her phone buzzed in response only a moment later. "He's on his way," she said.

"Tell him to just go home," Dag suggested. "We should get going—"

"There he is." Kassidy lifted a hand, and Dag followed her gaze to where Chris was entering the patio. He strode toward them, tugging at the knot of his tie.

"Sorry, sweetheart," he said, bending to kiss Kassidy before grabbing a chair. "Little problem with the new WAFS project. Hey, Dag."

"That's okay. Dag and I were having so much fun we didn't even realize what time it was."

Chris looked between them, no doubt taking in Kassidy's flushed cheeks from several mojitos. "That's good," he said. "I could use a drink."

Dag stood. "You two go ahead and order if you want, I gotta get back to the hotel. Oh shit."

"What?" Kassidy gazed up at him.

"All your stuff is in the trunk of my car."

"Oh yeah."

"I'll bring it over in a while," Dag said. "We can all go to the club together."

"Gotta take a taxi anyway," Chris said. "You won't be in shape to drive later."

Trust Chris to be the responsible one. But despite his risk-taking behavior, Dag would never drink and drive. "We'll see," he said. "I'll see you back at your place in...what...an hour?"

"Sounds good."

As he turned away, Dag saw Chris lean over and kiss Kassidy again, this time a longer, lingering kiss, his fingertips resting on her jaw in a tender, intimate gesture, and something twisted inside him as he dragged his gaze away from the image and made his way out of the bar.

Chapter Five

Chris lifted a hand to attract the waitress's attention, ordered his favorite beer from a local microbrewery. "Kass...?"

"No. I'm good."

"Had enough?" He smiled at her. "What the hell were you and Dag doing, sitting drinking all afternoon?" She looked pretty, all sparkly eyed, flushed-cheeked.

"It wasn't all afternoon. He came shopping with me."

Chris sat back in his chair, hands on the armrests. "He went shopping with you? Why?"

"He had nothing else to do."

"Uh...when he called me this morning, it sounded like he had something pretty urgent to talk to you about."

"Oh yeah. He did." She told him about their lunch conversation.

"Wow." Chris made a face. "Sounds interesting."

Kassidy grinned at him, the evening breeze blowing a strand of hair across her face. "You aren't even a little bit interested in that, are you?"

"Well...it's not my thing."

"I know."

He reached over and gently tucked the errant hair behind

her ear. "I'm glad you two are getting along. I wanted you to like him."

"Why?"

"Because he's my friend. One of my best friends. And I want him to like you too."

Kassidy looked down at her fingers on the table. "Well. I do like him."

"And man, do I need this drink." Chris lifted the beer the waitress set in front of him. Tension still hummed in his body from all the crap he'd had to deal with all day at the office.

"Bad day?" She rested her elbow on the table, set her chin in her hand and studied him with those big brown eyes, all soft and warm.

"Yeah. Crappy day. Looks like they're going ahead with outsourcing all those jobs."

"Oh no." Her forehead creased. He knew how much she hated that plan, all the jobs that would be lost, the impact it was going to have on morale. "And then Wendy tells me she needs time off next month. Right when our project deadline is."

"Isn't she getting married next month?"

"Yeah. She wants to go on a honeymoon."

Kassidy laughed. "Well, you have to let her go for that."

He shook he head. "I can't. We have rules. Nobody gets time off when it's deadline time."

"Chris." She leaned forward. "You can't be serious. It's her honeymoon."

He met her eyes. "Rules are rules. And we gotta make that deadline."

"Oh, for...sometimes you have to bend the rules a little. I'd say that's an exception."

He made a face. "I can't let her have the time off."

"What do you think is going to happen if you say no? Even if she shows up—and chances are she'll call in sick—she's not going to be happy to be there. Is that the kind of atmosphere you want? You think she's going to be working hard for you? No! She's going to be pissed!"

He pursed his lips, thinking about it. "I don't think..."

"Don't be stubborn," she said, leaning back. "You know I'm right. Just think about it."

"Yeah. Fine." He sighed. "We're way over budget on the reliability solutions project. Someone screwed up on the projections and now the executive sponsors are having a shit fit."

"Damn."

"Yeah." Just talking to her about it made him feel better though. It was always that way with Kassidy. She knew just what to say—and just what not to say. She let him talk if he felt like it but didn't push him if he didn't.

"Tonight's gonna be a blast," he said, done talking about work. It was Friday night, time to set all that aside for a couple of days. "Everyone's looking forward to seeing Dag again." He listed off the names of all the friends who'd be there. "We're all meeting there between nine and ten."

"At Kiss."

"Yeah." He arched a brow. "That okay?" Hailey worked there and he knew Kassidy wasn't fond of hanging out around her sister. But it was one of the hottest places in town.

She shrugged and pursed her lips. "It's okay. I like it there."

He reached for her hand and squeezed. "Hailey will be working."

"I know." She paused. "We should go. I need to change."

"Yeah. Just let me finish this." He drained the beer, pleasantly bitter on his tongue, and set down the bottle. "We need our check..."

When the waitress brought the bill, Chris did a double take. "Jesus! How long were you guys sitting here? And what the fuck is Dag doing stiffing me with his fucking bar tab?"

"Uh...Chris..."

He glanced at her, saw the smile tugging her lips. Couldn't help his own smile. "That asshole," he said mildly, temper settling, and reached for his wallet. "He'll be buying the drinks tonight, that's for damn sure. It's not like he couldn't afford to clear his fucking tab before he ran out of here."

Kassidy shook her head, eyes dancing. "I think he might have done that on purpose. Just so we wouldn't think he was showing off by throwing money around."

"Fucking cheap bastard." But Chris grinned too as he tossed some bills onto the table. "Let's go."

Back at their condo, Kassidy pouted as they walked in. "I should have come home with the things I bought instead of sitting in a bar. I could have had the curtains hung already."

Chris kissed her forehead. "I'll help you tomorrow. Mmm. You smell good. Like sunshine."

She lifted her face to his so he could kiss her mouth. Then she wound her arms around his neck and pressed herself against him. Nice. He slid his hands down her back and cupped her butt, bringing her up against his hardening cock, and deepened the kiss. Heat swept over him and when they broke apart they were both breathing heavily. "What was that for?"

"I love you." Her eyes, a bit hazy, met his.

"Love you too, sweetheart." And he kissed her again. "Mmm. Maybe we have time..."

"No, we don't."

"Sure we do. Come on..." And he pulled her over to the couch, fell onto it with her on top of him. She giggled and he slid his hands inside her shorts and found her bare ass. The thong she wore covered nothing back there. He squeezed firm, warm flesh, let his fingers dip into the crevice between. She gasped against his mouth.

"Chris."

His fingers slid lower, found hot liquid. "Ah fuck, Kass, you're wet...already..."

She moaned and wriggled atop him.

"We can't let that go to waste."

"Or this." And she reached between them to find his hard-on. She rubbed him through his dress pants, rolled to the side so she could unfasten them.

"Or that," he agreed, eyes falling closed at her touch. Soft hands delved into his pants and underwear, pulled him out. His cock filled and lengthened, throbbed with need. "Suck me, sweetheart."

"Mmm." She shifted down his body and bent her head. Heat and suction surrounded him and his hips lifted in ecstasy. He dragged his eyelids open to take in the visual. He always loved to watch her give him head. Seeing her pretty mouth stretched wide around him, her cheeks hollow as she sucked, was such a turn-on, and when she lifted her gaze to meet his, fire streaked through him. He surged into her, reached down to cup the back of her head. His balls tightened, the base of his spine tingled...so close...so...

And the doorbell rang.

Fuck!

Kassidy drew back, eyes wide, mouth wet and shiny, lips

parted in sexy surprise. "What..."

"Christ. It's Dag."

And he rolled out from beneath her, to his feet, and hitched up his pants.

"Shit." Kassidy fell back against the couch cushions, eyes closed, breasts rising and falling.

"No kidding, shit." Heart hammering in his chest, balls throbbing, he thrust a hand through his hair then strode to the door and yanked it open.

"Hey." Dag walked in, arms full of shopping bags and the big cartons containing the curtain rods. His gaze skidded over Chris, fell on Kassidy, her clothes rumpled, mouth swollen, then came back to Chris, dipped to his unfastened pants. "Uh..."

"Never mind." Chris shut the door with a disgusted shake of his head, his cock still hard and aching.

"Sorry...I..."

Chris shook his head. "We're not ready yet. Just got home. Help yourself to a beer while we change." And he grabbed Kassidy's hands, tugged her up off the couch and practically dragged her into their bedroom. He shut the door, turned her around and pressed her against it with his body.

"Chris!" His name was a whisper. "Stop! We can't..."

"Gotta finish, sweets," he muttered, kissing her jaw, her neck. Urgent need pulsed in him and he fumbled his pants open again.

"God, Chris, Dag's right outside! He'll hear us..."

"Don't give a shit." He mumbled the words against her flesh, trying to get her shorts undone and off. The zipper rasped down and he skimmed them down her legs, let them fall to the floor. With one foot he dragged them away then lifted her thigh.

"Come on, Kass. Unh..." He took hold of his cock and pushed into her.

She wrapped her legs around his waist, head thunking back against the door. "Oh god..."

Harder and harder he thrust up into her, vaguely aware of the way the door rattled with each stroke, her wet heat taking him. He held her by her ass, pinned her to the door, fucked her hard, right there, with Dag only a few feet away. For some reason that thought spiraled his excitement higher and the orgasm he'd been so close to earlier edged closer.

"Come for me," he groaned beside her ear. "Come, Kass."

She slid a hand between them to find her clit, taking care of herself. Yeah. Oh yeah. The low sounds coming from her throat were loud in his ear, but that was because she was right there, her mouth right beside his head, and he swallowed his own cries of pleasure as he poured himself into her.

"Jesus," he gasped moments later. "Jesus."

Kassidy's hands gripped his back, holding herself up, and he released her and let her slide down till her feet touched the floor. He leaned his forehead on the door above her head, panting, her fingers digging into his flesh.

"Okay, now we can get ready," he finally rasped, and she gave a choked laugh.

"God, Chris. I can't believe we just did that."

"Sssh." He kissed her mouth. "I needed that." Nothing better than fast, hard sex to relieve a little stress.

"Oh, me too. Me too."

They moved apart, a little sweaty, semen leaking onto Kassidy's thighs.

"Now I need a shower," she complained, shoving her hair back. "And there's no time."

"Don't shower," he murmured. "You look good. And I want to smell you like this all night."

Her eyes closed briefly. "God, Chris. You're insatiable."

"Hell yeah."

"I can't go out like this. I'll have to wash up." And she disappeared into the bathroom.

He followed her, because he needed to wash up too, and because—now that they lived together—he could. They both stripped off their clothes in the spacious bathroom, their naked bodies reflected back in the mirror lining the wall above the double sinks. Like a porn movie almost, Kassidy's nude body a soft, curvy contrast to his darker-skinned, much bigger shape. He watched with interest as she ran water over a face cloth, poured some scented body soap onto it and washed herself. He did the same, cleaning his cock and balls, between his thighs, Kassidy's eyes on him too.

"You are so fucking hot," he said.

She smiled. "So are you."

He started to get hard again and quickly rinsed with cold water. "I'll get dressed."

He heard her moving around in the bathroom as he found the narrow black pants he wanted to wear, shrugged into a white button-down shirt that he left loose, with the cuffs rolled back on his forearms.

"I'll go wait with Dag," he called to her from the bedroom door.

"Okay."

He sauntered into the living room, a pretty good post-orgasmic buzz still flowing through his veins, to find Dag seated on the couch, a beer in his hands, staring out the window. Dag lifted his gaze to his and Chris blinked at the raw emotion blazing there before Dag schooled his features.

"Sorry, bud," Chris said, shoving his hands into his pockets. "Kassidy will be ready in a few minutes."

"Sure." Dag pressed his lips together and gave a jerky nod, looking away from Chris.

Christ. His chest ached, his dick was a fucking steel rod, his mind a jumble of mixed-up thoughts. He'd heard everything, every goddamn moan and pant and thrust. They might have thought they were being quiet, but you couldn't fuck up against a door without making noise.

Dag rubbed the back of his neck and drained his beer. So much for his plan not to drink much tonight so he could drive.

"So what all did she buy today?" Chris asked, moving across the room to look at all the shopping bags.

Who fucking cared? But Dag made himself smile and look up. "All kinds of shit," he said. "She dragged me to Bed and Bath."

Chris lifted a brow. "She dragged you? She said you had nothing better to do."

Heat crawled up Dag's cheeks. He tried to look casual. "Whatever."

"I hate that store," Chris said, apparently not even noticing Dag's discomfort. He peeked into a bag. "Huh. Towels. We've got a million towels. We both had towels."

Dag shrugged. "I guess you needed more."

"What are these? They look like flag poles."

"They're curtain rods, dipshit. Get with it."

Chris glanced at him and they both laughed. Some of the hot tension eased out of Dag and he rose to his feet. "Where should I put this?" He held up the empty bottle loosely by the

64

neck.

"I'll take it."

Chris disappeared into the kitchen, and Dag heard Kassidy's steps. He turned. She walked in, cheeks pink, eyes sparkling but otherwise looking all put together and sleek. Her dark hair hung in a silky curtain to her shoulders and she wore a short purple dress that draped over her slender body. Hot.

She tugged at the hem of the dress and bit her lip. "Damn, this dress is short."

"It looks great."

Her eyes met his. Her eyelashes fluttered and her cheeks got even pinker. "Thanks."

"Hey, you're ready." Chris walked back in. "You look awesome, sweets. I just called a taxi."

Dag didn't mention that he'd intended to drive. Now he'd have to somehow get back here tomorrow to get his car. Dammit.

"Did you see what I got today?" Kassidy asked Chris.

"Towels. Why'd we need towels?"

She frowned. "Yours are about a hundred years old, all frayed and thin."

"Oh." And Chris's eyes met Dag's in a masculine exchange of "whatever". They grinned.

"Let's go wait outside," Chris said. Kassidy picked up a little purse and walked ahead of them on sandals that consisted of a spiky heel and a couple of thin straps across the top of her foot. More hotness. Hell.

Chapter Six

They walked into Kiss through a nearly invisible entrance at the end of a narrow alleyway just off Oak Street. A long staircase descended into a room lit with low red lighting from pot lights, antique light fixtures dripping with gilt and crystal, and candles everywhere, filling the air with a warm beeswax fragrance that mingled with expensive perfumes. People crowded the dance floor, moving to the drum beat of the DJ's mix of bhangra and hip-hop.

"Looks like we're the first ones here," Chris said. "Let's find a spot." He led the way through the bar to several black leather and faux-leopard-skin sofas arranged in a small group around a low table.

Dag took in the eclectic surroundings, liking the cosmopolitan vibe of the place. Yeah, dammit, there were things about Chicago he missed. He sat on one of the black leather sofas, and Kassidy and Chris took a seat across from him.

"There's Hailey," Kassidy said. Dag shifted his gaze across the room to the artfully lit bar, with rows and rows of bottles stacked against the wall behind it glowing in the red lights. He searched for which bartender might be Kassidy's sister, finally picking out a slender dark-haired woman in a constant whirl of movement, pouring, spinning, reaching for glasses. Her short dark hair was a spiky cap on her head, but even from here he could see the resemblance to Kassidy in her build, her graceful movements and the shape of her face.

A waitress clad in a short skintight black dress approached to take their drink order and Dag smiled up at her. She returned the smile with a wink as they ordered. Dag handed over a credit card so they could run a tab.

"Oh yeah, that reminds me," Chris said. "You left without paying your bar bill this afternoon. You owe me fifty bucks."

Dag looked at Chris, saw the glint in his eye and laughed. "I figured you wouldn't mind picking up the tab."

"For you and my girlfriend sitting and drinking all afternoon without me? Not fucking likely, buddy."

Then they both laughed and shook their heads.

"There's Jeff and Sara," Kassidy said, waving a hand. Their friends began to arrive. Dag stood to greet the people he hadn't seen for so long, with handshakes and hugs and smiles and questions. Everyone was finding a seat and milling around the area when Kassidy's sister approached them.

"Hey, Kass," she said. Her gaze narrowed in on Dag and he arched a brow and returned her smile. Again, he could see a family resemblance in the shape of her mouth and eyes, but Hailey's face was thinner, her chin a little sharper, her eyes harder. Her smile held a hint of tartness instead of Kassidy's sweetness. A silver stud pierced her left eyebrow and a diamond glittered on the side of her nose. "You must be Dag."

Kassidy moved to stand beside Hailey. "Yes, this is Dag. Dag Spencer, my sister Hailey Langdon."

Hailey fastened her eyes on him and extended a hand, which he took. Interest heated her gaze. "Pleasure to meet you," she said. "You're not what I expected."

"What did you expect?"

"Mmm. Someone more like Chris, I guess." Her smile deepened.

"What makes you think I'm not like Chris?"

She moved closer to him, into his personal space. "Just an impression I get."

He laughed. "I'm guessing you're not like Kassidy either."

Her smile turned sly. "And what makes you think that?" She turned his words back to him.

"Just an impression I get." He arched a brow.

Now she laughed with appreciation. "Yeah, Kassidy's a good girl. Boring, but good."

Boring? Whoa. That wasn't a word he ever would have used to describe her, albeit he'd only known her a week. He flashed a glance Kassidy's way and saw her mouth tighten. "And you're not good?" he asked Hailey.

"I'm good at some things." She set her hand on his forearm and leaned even closer into his personal space, so close he could smell the spicy scent of patchouli. Strangely, patchouli had always given him a headache and he felt the faint throb begin deep in his head. But he smiled at her because she was Kassidy's sister. She slid her hand higher on his arm. "Very good. But...sometimes I'm a bad girl." Her voice went throaty.

Jesus. Subtlety wasn't part of her makeup.

"So, how long are you in Chicago, Dag?"

"I'm not sure." Earlier in the week his plan had been to get the hell back to San Francisco, but now he had this great idea he wanted to explore and Kassidy was the perfect one to help him with some of it. Then he'd had to listen to them fucking on the other side of their bedroom door and once again his resolve had changed to getting away from them. Christ, he didn't know what the hell he wanted, what he was doing. "Depends on business, I guess."

"I could show you around town," she said. "If you're interested."

"I might be."

Then he caught sight of Kassidy's face as she watched them flirting—and the crease in her brow and the tightness of her pretty mouth.

She should have known Hailey and Dag would hit it off. They seemed to be two of a kind—a bad boy and a self-professed bad girl, both of whom seemed to effortlessly attract attention from the opposite sex. Yeah, they would have a lot in common. Why that sent a shaft of pain slicing through her, she had no clue.

Kassidy tipped her mango martini to her lips and took a big gulp. Sweet coolness washed down her throat. She forced a smile. "Are you on a break, Hailey?"

Hailey didn't even look at her, no surprise with a gorgeous guy standing right in front of her. "Yeah. So, Dag..."

Kassidy moved away to let them talk, for a moment alone in the crowd, her stomach tight. She searched for her anchor—Chris. There he was, over talking to Cole and Tyra. She made her way over to him.

He glanced down at her as he talked, smiled, slid an arm around her to rest his hand on her hip. A feeling of security eased the stiffness inside her a little. A feeling of knowing she was loved and wanted. She had that with Chris, always.

Why did it bother her that Hailey liked Dag? Or did it bother her that Dag liked Hailey? Her eyes fell on them across the room, still talking, laughing, and that tension returned, gripping her body.

But Hailey's break couldn't last forever and a few minutes later she returned to her place behind the bar. Dag's attention turned to their friends. As the evening went on, she overheard him talking, "business meetings" and "San Francisco's great" and "nice to be back", as he moved from group to group. And it wasn't just their friends—a crowd of women formed around him, beautiful women. All the while he looked so damn gorgeous and sexy, hair falling into his eyes, his black T-shirt—not just an ordinary T-shirt but some kind of silky expensive fabric—stretched across his taut body, tucked into just the front of his black pants, a gleaming belt buckle riding low. He looked dark and dangerous and exotic.

"I need to sit down," she told Chris awhile later, her feet starting to hurt in the strappy heels she wore. She lowered herself to the soft leopard fabric of a couch. Chris sat too, and she was glad. She snuggled up to him, winding her arm through his, and sipped her drink.

"Having fun, Kass?" he asked, leaning closer.

"Mmm. Yeah."

He kissed the top of her head. "Good. Looks like Dag is too."

"Yeah." She wanted to ask if he'd seen Dag and Hailey together, but couldn't get her voice to form the words. Dag's familiar laugh carried over the music, now an African-funk blend, primal and rhythmic, as he flirted with the girls surrounding him. She felt the music inside her, like another heartbeat. Her body pulsed against Chris's.

When Dag lifted his head and his eyes met hers across the room, she turned her face to Chris and kissed the side of his neck, his skin warm and fragrant. Chris made a low noise in his throat, rested one hand on her bare thigh where her dress had ridden up. Her pussy ached. She wanted him to slide his hand higher.

They were in a nightclub surrounded by people. What the hell was she thinking? She swallowed. "I think I need another drink," she said in Chris's ear.

He drew back and smiled at her, his hand still warm on her leg. "Want me to get you one?"

"Sure."

He got up and moved toward the bar, and she could still feel the weight of Dag's gaze on her without even looking at him. When she did turn her head slightly, their eyes once again met and held. And held. And...held.

He lifted his drink to his mouth and slowly sipped, never taking his eyes off her as some girl chattered beside him.

Oh Jesus. What was happening? She was filled with all kinds of rampant, reckless feelings that she couldn't even identify, except she knew the dominant one was lust. Analyzing that just made her skin tighten up, though. She took a deep breath and crossed her legs, not bothering to pull her skirt down, wanting Dag's attention on *her*, not some nameless pretty stranger.

She turned her attention to watching other people in the bar, and it was a good place for people watching. Couples danced in sexy abandon on the dance floor, including one female couple, both of them young and pretty and dressed in short skirts and skimpy tops. Kassidy watched as they touched each other, danced closer, mesmerized by the sensuality of it.

When Chris returned with her drink, she guzzled down half of it then said, "Let's dance."

He took her hand as they walked onto the dance floor and they shifted into the rhythm of the music, moving together. He set his hands on her hips and they watched each other's faces as they danced. Then Chris's gaze drifted off to the side and she

71

followed it. He was looking at those two girls, still dancing together, bodies now pressed together, back to front, the girl in back sliding her hands over the hips and stomach of the girl in front.

She glanced at Chris's face, went onto her tiptoes to speak into his ear. "I thought two girls didn't excite you."

He smiled. "It'd be hotter if one of them was you."

Her eyes flew open wide. "What!"

He grinned and pulled her closer.

"You want to watch me and another girl?" she asked incredulously.

His breath tickled her ear. "Watching you with anybody would be a turn-on."

Holy crap. How did she not know this about him? Kassidy pulled back to look into his eyes. "Really?"

The corners of his eyes crinkled but he held her gaze steadily. "Really."

Heat suffused her body. She didn't know what to say. Chris was so...straight. Did he expect her to make that kinky fantasy come true? Or was it just that—a fantasy?

The music changed and without saying a word, they left the dance floor and returned to their couch. She picked up her drink and downed the rest of it in three big heat-quenching gulps. Oh god.

"I'll get you another one," Chris said with a knowing smile.

She sat there in a bit of a daze until the sofa dipped beside her. She turned quickly, thinking it was Chris back already with her drink, but it was Dag. His dark intent eyes fastened on her face. "How're you doing?"

"Good!" She gave him a bright smile. "You? Having fun?"

He shrugged, sipped his drink again—Scotch? Probably.

Chris returned with drinks. He couldn't sit beside Kassidy because Dag was there now, but she didn't want him to sit far away on another couch. Then Dag shifted away from her, pulling her with him so there was room for Chris on her other side. She took her drink from Chris, shoulder-to-shoulder with big, warm maleness on both sides of her.

Other friends came and sat too, and they all talked and laughed while Kassidy tried to ignore the achy fullness in her pelvis.

After a while, Dag said, "Come dance with me, Kassidy." He set down his drink and rose to his feet. He held out a hand, and she looked at Chris, who smiled and nodded. She took Dag's hand and followed him back to the dance floor, feeling a little like she were being led down a dark downtown alley at midnight, nerves fluttering in her tummy and her pulse leaping.

They moved to the music, a throbbing Latin drumbeat. Dag was a good dancer—of course—nothing flamboyant, but he knew how to move his body with an athletic grace. She let herself absorb the music, let it move her body, never taking her eyes off his face. When the rhythm slowed and merged into a slower song, he slid his hands over her waist, hips, around almost onto her ass. His heat enveloped her, the scent of his sultry aftershave filled her head as she slid her arms over his shoulders. Their hips moved together to the beat of the music.

Sex.

It felt like sex. Liquid heat slid through her body and pooled between her legs.

She bit her lip and looked over to where Chris sat. He'd crossed one ankle over the other knee, one arm stretched out along the back of the couch, looking so big and handsome and watching them.

Watching you with anyone would be a turn-on.

73

He lifted his chin in acknowledgement of Kassidy's glance. She was almost afraid to tear her gaze away from him and return it to the dangerous man she was dancing with.

"Chris is watching," Dag said.

"Yes."

"He likes to watch."

Dag knew that about him?

Their gazes locked. His hands slid lower on her hips, to just below the curve of her ass and his fingers moved. Dear god, he was pulling up her skirt. And it was short enough to begin with. Her pussy pulsed.

The silky fabric slid higher, bunching a little beneath Dag's fingers. "What are you doing?" she asked him through tight lips.

"Giving your boyfriend a show," he said with a wicked glint in his eye.

"And everyone else in the bar."

But she didn't stop him.

"Nobody else is paying any attention to us," he said. "They're all watching those girls."

The female couple was now dancing even dirtier, grinding their bodies together. They were so beautiful and sexy it was hard to take her eyes off them.

"Hot," Dag said. They watched. The girls turned to face each other again, and then they kissed. A long, lingering kiss on the mouth, hands buried in each other's long hair.

Dag and Kassidy looked at each other. The air sizzled around them. They were both aroused and maybe that was why she let him continue to ease the skirt of her dress up, his hands on her hips sliding the fabric higher. She looked back at Chris, now with both feet on the floor, leaning forward with elbows on his knees, still watching them, his gaze scorching her with erotic intensity.

And maybe that's why she still didn't stop Dag. She was pretty sure the cheeks of her butt were showing now—she was wearing a pair of cheeky panties, but they didn't cover much.

Then Chris was striding toward them, joining them on the dance floor. He pressed against her back, his erection hard against her, and nuzzled her neck. The three of them danced together, hard bodies pressed against her front and back.

Chris pulled her hair aside to mutter in her ear. "That was so fucking sexy." She pressed her ass back against him, tightened her fingers on Dag's shoulders.

"Your girlfriend is hot, Chris," Dag said.

"I know."

The music picked up pace again and they continued dancing, still close, just changing the tempo. Heat sizzled up and down Kassidy's spine and she felt hypnotized by the beat of the music, the hot desire of two men, lost in the utter sensuality of it. She lifted one arm above her head and hooked it around Chris's neck, four hands on her body. Her breasts swelled and her nipples tingled. She ached to be touched there.

By the time they decided to leave the dance floor, every nerve ending in her body was on fire, sizzling and snapping with sexual tension.

The three of them sat on the couch side by side again, damp with perspiration and a little breathless. Some of their friends had already left, others had disappeared, perhaps into the crowd on the dance floor, and they were alone. Chris set his hand on her bare thigh and picked up his drink with his other hand.

"I should get going," Dag said. "I'll come by for my car tomorrow."

"Why don't you just stay at our place again?" Chris said. "Saves you a trip tomorrow."

Kassidy's blood surged in her veins, hot and scary, as she waited for Dag's response. A response that seemed...significant. Weighty. A response that took forever.

"Okay," Dag finally said.

Her chest tightened.

"I'm ready to go too," Chris added. "Kassidy?"

"Sure." She licked her lips.

A couple of yellow cabs waited on Oak Street when they emerged from the alley where the club was and Dag lifted a hand. One pulled up and all three of them climbed into the back. The night air had cooled her heated skin, but now inside the taxi the air was heavy, pulsing with thick arousal. There was enough sexual energy in that vehicle to power the small hybrid car for many miles. Her heart pounded all the way home, and she stared at her bare knees, once again in the middle of the two men. It was only a short ride back to their place, and when she unlocked the door and let them into the condo, her heart sped up even more. She could hardly breathe, the sense of anticipation tightening her lungs.

They walked into the condo, Chris leading the way and flicking on a lamp. He turned and the three of them stood there, snared in a net of erotic tension.

Chris held out a hand to Kassidy and she drifted across the living room to take it without a word. He slid his hand into her hair, cupped the back of her head and kissed her. She melted into him, already a semi-liquid puddle of arousal.

"Watching you dance with Dag was fucking hot," he whispered against the corner of her mouth.

Questions backed up in her brain but none of them came

out of her mouth. Then Chris did the same thing Dag had done, started sliding up the skirt of her dress, baring the back of her thighs to Dag.

This was a dangerous game they were playing. She was so turned on, so fevered with hunger, it made her afraid of what she might do. They were just fooling around, making each other—all three of them—hot and bothered. How far would they go?

"What panties are you wearing?" Chris murmured.

Her throat was so tight she could barely speak.

"Show us," he urged.

She couldn't move, her body locked into place, her heart racing.

"She's not going to show us her panties," Dag said. "Kassidy's a good girl. Isn't that what your sister said?"

His words mocked her, the words her sister had used, her sister who always made fun of her and made her feel like a straight-laced prude, even though she wasn't. She was different from Hailey, sure, but it wasn't like she was totally naïve.

She didn't want to be a good girl. And she wanted Dag to know that. The sexual tension that had been building inside her for the last week, so much that fast, hard sex with Chris in the shower and even up against the bedroom door had still not quite satisfied her, was leading her into doing naughty things. A heavy ache pulsed in her pelvis.

She took a step back, lifting up her dress. She glanced at Dag, who stood there watching them with scorching intensity, his mouth a tight line of self-control.

"Nice," Chris said. "Don't you think, Dag?"

"Very nice."

Her panties were a band of pink lace around her hips. She

bit her bottom lip, knowing how wet they were. Dag smiled at her. Her fingers trembled, clutching the fabric of her dress.

"You haven't told her, have you?" Dag looked at Chris.

Chris's eyes met Dag's. Kassidy's gaze darted back and forth between them.

"Told me what?"

"No," Chris said.

"Are you afraid Kassidy will be shocked?" Dag continued. "Because she is a good girl."

"Told me what?"

Chris's eyes narrowed and his body tensed next to her. Dag's eyes gleamed and his wicked smile made her body pulse again.

"Told you..." Dag's gaze moved over her face. "About the threesomes we used to have."

Her mouth did drop open a little. Okay, she wasn't naïve, but the idea that Chris and Dag had done that...gave her a jolt. She turned to Chris.

He gave her a sheepish little smile. "It was a long time ago."

Wow.

She wasn't jealous. She knew Chris had had girlfriends before her. She even knew some of them. They were all done and gone before she came along.

"Does that disgust you, Kassidy?" Dag asked.

"No." She had to close her eyes against the wave of heated arousal that shimmered through her body, a sharp, forbidden thrill.

"Or does it turn you on?"

How could she admit that to Dag...to Chris!

She met Chris's gaze. "It turns me on."

"Oh sweetie." Chris's voice was a groan.

They were just talking about it. It wasn't like they were going to do it.

"Who did you do it with?" The words slid out of her mouth.

They exchanged a glance then Chris said, "It doesn't matter who, sweetheart. Like I said, it was a long time ago. Before you."

Curiosity scorched her. She wanted to know what happened—who did what to whom. The idea of two men making love to her at the same time seemed incredibly hot. Her skin tingled and tightened with electric pulses of heat and longing.

Their eyes met once again, exchanging some kind of wordless communication. She wanted to know what they were thinking. What if they wanted to do it? What if they wanted to share her, like they apparently had shared girls before?

A moan leaked out of her. Her breasts swelled and ached, her nipples tingled and her pussy clenched hard at the idea of being with two men.

Chris was such a conservative guy, she could hardly believe what they were telling her. His earlier revelation that he wanted to watch her with someone else had been a prelude to this shocker. But then he looked into her eyes and sparkles shot through her body at the question she saw on his face.

It wasn't because of her sister. She had nothing to prove to Hailey. Kassidy was her own person and comfortable with how she lived her life. But at that moment, she wanted to be the bad girl. She wanted excitement. She wanted that adrenaline rush that Dag got from taking risks, making dangerous business deals, jumping out of airplanes. And she wanted Dag.

She licked her lips and turned her attention to Dag. He watched her with hot, predatory eyes, his beautifully shaped mouth smiling slightly, and she knew he wanted her too. She'd known it all along.

She would never cheat on Chris. Never. She'd never been tempted, not even once. If he wanted this, it wouldn't be cheating. But it was the baddest thing she'd ever contemplated doing in her entire, careful life.

Once again she met her boyfriend's eyes. "Do you want to?" he finally asked out loud.

She couldn't do it. She wanted to. How could she do something like that? Arousal swelled and burned inside her, and she countered, "Do *you* want to?"

Chapter Seven

It was clear they both wanted to, but were each afraid to say it. Afraid of what the other would think. What it would mean.

"Jump," Dag said.

Kassidy knew exactly what he meant after their conversation about skydiving. How you could analyze and debate the pros and cons, consider everything before making a decision. Sometimes you just had to do it. And deal with the consequences after.

"Yes," she breathed.

"Fuck," Dag muttered.

This could be the biggest mistake she'd ever made.

I don't think I can do this. The words seemed loud in her head, but she hadn't spoken them out loud. Determination to be bad, to show Dag, the rebel, she could be bad too, mingled with a desire to equally prove to Chris that she wasn't shocked by the revelation about his past, and she was just as up for naughty fun as he was.

But uncertainty weakened her knees, made her hands tremble. She had no idea what to do. The arousal that had heated her earlier had been crowded out by nerves. They stood there in the living room, in the dark, the lamp in the corner the only illumination.

"Why?" she asked.

They looked back at her. "Why what?" Dag said.

"Why did you do it?"

Another shared look that reminded her of their long—and apparently intimate—history. "I don't know," Dag said. "I guess there were girls we both liked and we wanted to share."

A gazillion questions bounced around in her brain. Were there serious feeling involved? How did that work? Wasn't there jealousy? Or were those girls just slutty whores who slept with two guys for the fun of it?

Oh stop. She couldn't think of those girls as slutty whores because she was about to become one of them. There was nothing wrong about enjoying the pleasure of sex with two gorgeous men, especially when one was the man she loved and the other was someone he cared about and trusted.

"I never thought a lot about why," Chris said. "It just seemed like the thing to do."

Dag had turned to look at Chris when he spoke. His eyes moved as he studied his friend, his eyebrows drawn, his mouth tense, his hands in loose fists, and Kassidy sensed emotions inside him, inside Dag, expanding. His chest lifted and his Adam's apple moved as he swallowed.

Something inside her caught, twisted. And she realized she wasn't just doing this for herself. She was doing it for them.

Dag couldn't believe they were doing this. What the fuck had happened tonight?

He studied Chris, wanting to know what was going on in his friend's head. Yeah, they'd shared girls before, but never someone one of them had actually had a real relationship with.

And much as he wanted to do it, for so very many reasons, he didn't want Chris and Kassidy to jeopardize their relationship for...this.

But Kassidy's eyes were hazy and full of lust, her body practically quivering with need. Her mouth tempted him, Christ, he had to have it, taste it.

And he'd get to be with Chris while he was doing it.

Complex emotions rose and fell in him, fragments of thoughts spun away even as he tried to marshal them together into coherency. But his balls were on fire, his dick so hard it hurt, and all those hormones pounding through him were destroying his ability to resist temptation.

He moved toward Kassidy, standing next to Chris, and Chris moved too so they stood like they had on the dance floor, him behind her, the sweet curve of her ass pressing into him, Chris in front of her. Dag started at her shoulders, dragged his hands over slender bones down the soft skin of her arms, onto her hips. His fingers dug into the warm resilience of her flesh beneath the silky dress. She'd let the hem drop so her ass was covered once again, but he'd seen the sweetness that was under there and wanted to touch it.

She let out a moan as the two men pressed her between them, and he smelled her hair, a soft scent that was sweet and sexy, a mix of vanilla and amber.

"So hot," he whispered. "Aren't you, Kassidy?"

Another whimper escaped her mouth. He nudged her hair aside to find the warm side of her neck, inhaled her scent again and opened his mouth on her skin. He sucked lightly, dragged his tongue over her. Sweet.

"Ah, sweetheart." Chris drew her arms up and over his shoulders. "I love you for this. So much. Come on. Let's go in the bedroom."

He kissed her mouth and then stepped back. The three of them moved together down the short hall and into the bedroom where Chris had nailed her up against the door earlier. Jesus. Dag's cock twitched. And now here he was in there with them.

Chris flicked on a lamp beside the bed and started unbuttoning his shirt. Dag watched as his bare chest appeared, took in the ripped pecs and abs, the flex of biceps as Chris tossed the shirt aside. Dag moved to Kassidy.

"Let me," he murmured, and once again he drew up the hem of her dress inch by silky inch. She moved her hips as the dress rose higher and he met her eyes as he pulled it up over her waist and then...her breasts. The dress was loose and she lifted her arms for him to tug it over her head, the full mounds of her breasts right there in front of him, swelling over the edge of a pink lace bra that matched the little strip of lace around her hips.

She had a beautiful body—smooth curves, golden skin, the surprise of a diamond glinting in her belly button. He flicked it with a finger. "That's nice."

"Thank you."

Dag glanced at Chris, who had lowered himself to the side of the bed, wearing just his black pants, watching them with hot eyes.

Dag wanted to kiss her. God, he wanted to. His lips parted and he studied her mouth, the pouty bottom lip, the sweet bow of her top lip, the way her teeth gleamed whitely through the slight opening. He heard her indrawn breath as she realized he was looking at her mouth and her lips parted more.

He slid a hand beneath her hair to the back of her neck then glanced once more at Chris, as if to make sure the guy was still okay with this, because, Jesus Christ, he was going to kiss her, kiss her with everything he fucking had.

Chris gave him a slow up-and-down motion of his head as he reached for the fastener of his pants and released it. He rubbed his hard-on beneath the black fabric.

And Dag turned back to Kassidy, bent his head and took her mouth. She opened for him immediately with a soft sound in her throat, her mouth sinfully soft, sweetly delicious and warm as summer. Her hands came to rest on his chest. He wanted her to rub there, but they'd get to that. He kissed her, again and again, long, deep kisses, licked her mouth, found her tongue and played with it. Her body melted against him, all warm, soft skin and pink lace. Jesus.

His other arm slid around her, palm on her back, pressing her against him, her breasts soft, her pussy hot. Damp heat poured off her, in fact, he could smell it, tantalizing feminine arousal. He got lost in it, in everything, the feel of her body in his arms, the taste of her mouth, the vanilla and warm amber and girl scent of her, so much that he forgot about Chris watching them and drifted off on a cloud of erotic pleasure.

This woman...dammit, she affected him. Like no other. What was it about her?

He lifted his head and they gazed at each other, panting, wet-mouthed, blazing eyes.

"Dag."

Her breathy voice saying his name like that undid him all over again, and he groaned. "This is insane."

"Yeah."

And then they both turned to Chris, who had taken his cock out and was stroking it. Kassidy made a little noise as if a gasp had stuck in her throat. "Oh god," she said.

Dag watched Chris's hand pull up the thick length of his cock then back down. He'd seen it before. They'd done this before. But still his blood raced fast and hot through his veins at the sight.

He set Kassidy in front of him, settled his hands on her hips. She glanced over her shoulder at him, wide-eyed at the sight of Chris jerking off.

"C'mere, Kass." Chris lifted his chin. "Come and suck me."

Dag helped her move forward, nudging her with his hands on her hips, and with another glance at him, she went to her knees beside the bed, between Chris's legs. When her mouth closed over the head of his cock, more flames threatened to explode in Dag's balls. Now it was his turn to press against his throbbing erection. He wasn't sure if he could even walk, he was so hard. But he managed to move up behind Kassidy and gather her hair back to hold it for her at the nape of her neck.

"Oh yeah, Kass. So good." Chris threw his head back, eyes closed, hands on the bed on either side of him. "Oh...yeah."

Dag peered over her shoulders to watch her slide up and down on Chris's shaft, dark and ridged with veins, her mouth stretched wide. She rested her hands on his thighs and her head bobbed. When she let the gleaming crown slide out of her mouth and sat back a bit to catch her breath, Dag lifted her beneath her arms to stand.

"Now suck Dag," Chris said, his eyes dark, face flushed.

A string of curses ran through Dag's mind, and he yanked his T-shirt out from his pants and rapidly unbuckled his belt. Yeah, he wanted to feel her mouth on him too, and he knew Chris liked to watch that, but hell, he wanted to make this good for Kassidy.

He stripped out of his clothes, but as she went to drop to her knees once again, he held her up. "No."

She blinked at him, and he lifted her into his arms and carried her over to the bed. He laid her down, nudging Chris aside, who stood and stepped out of his pants. The two men stood side by side, looking down at beautiful Kassidy stretched out on the bed, wearing pink lace and a blush. She bent one knee, licked her lips.

"Ladies first," Dag said, a smile tugging his lips. "Wanna make this good for you, babe."

Her mouth curved sweetly as he climbed onto the bed, shifted her over a little more to make room for Chris. The mattress dipped with Chris's weight as he again sat, and then Chris found the clasp of her bra and Dag slipped his fingers into her panties and slid them down over her legs.

He let out a breath as he viewed her naked body, perfect breasts round and tipped with small brown nipples, nipples that made his mouth water and long to suck them. His gaze moved over the dip of her waist and curve of her hips, and then to the tiny triangle of dark hair just above her slit.

"Beautiful, Kassidy," he whispered, unable to resist touching her, his palms cruising over her thighs.

Chris covered her breasts with his hands and squeezed then brushed his fingertips over taut nipples. "So beautiful."

"You are, sweetheart." Chris bent his head and took a nipple in his mouth, just like Dag wanted to do. And why not? He moved up her body on the opposite side of Chris and they each suckled on her for long moments. Her nipple fit perfectly to his tongue and he closed his lips over the tip of it while his eyelids drifted shut. And sucked. Sweet. So fucking sweet.

He could smell Chris's hair now, a darker, masculine scent, his head only inches from his own as they made love to Kassidy's gorgeous breasts. Her body quivered and twitched, and Dag laid a hand flat on her belly.

"Oh god," she said, her legs sliding against the bedcovers. "God, that feels good!" And her hand forked into his hair and grabbed on. Sensation rocketed from his scalp to his cock.

"Both of you...sucking on me...at the same time. Oh my god." Her head tossed on the pillow and they kept on loving her nipples with their lips and tongues and the very edge of Dag's teeth.

His hand crept lower...lower. His fingertips brushed the curls there, dragged through them, slipped lower still. Her thighs parted for him, and his fingers found her wetness. Jesus.

"Ah Christ, Kassidy." He lifted his head from her nipple to speak then pressed a kiss against the top curve of her breast. "You're so fucking wet. Unbelievable."

"What...do you...expect?" Her words came out jerky and soft. "God, Dag." Her thighs spread even more, giving him more access, and he dragged his fingers through her folds, silky soft, completely bare below the triangle of hair and dripping wet. He probed with the tip of his middle finger, found her entrance and pushed in just a little. Wet heat sucked at him and he groaned.

"Wanna taste you," he muttered. "Now."

"Do it," Chris spoke from beside him, low and husky, and Dag needed no further urging. He kissed his way down her torso, taking that little diamond barbell in his mouth and giving it a quick tug before continuing down. He knelt between Kassidy's legs, pushed them apart with his palms on each thigh. Warm feminine spice rose to his nostrils and he had to study her for a moment before he tasted.

"That is the prettiest pussy I've ever seen," he said on a groan. "Perfect. So pink and perfect."

Her legs twitched restlessly again and Dag watched Chris continue to suck on her nipples, moving to the one where his own mouth had been a moment ago. Chris's big hand cupped the soft flesh and he rubbed the nipple over his bottom lip in a sensuous gesture. Heat flashed inside Dag.

With another groan he bent his head, inhaled deeply and

ran his tongue over her. She jerked against him, cried out softly, and once again one of her hands fisted in his hair. He licked at her sweet cream, her smooth flesh, pressed kisses there, soft kisses, suckling kisses, first one side then the other. He kissed higher, one side, the other side, then finally pressed his mouth over her clit and kissed her there. The swollen bud pulsed against his lips and she gasped and tugged harder on his hair.

He licked, swallowed her delicate taste, licked again as her body quaked beneath him. He pushed a finger inside her, her body closing around him in a hot, wet embrace, then added another finger. Her soft cries increased and he lifted his gaze to again watch Chris make love to her breasts, her other hand fisted in his hair, fingers bent tightly.

"Oh my god, I can't take any more," she panted. "Too...much."

"Not yet it isn't." He smiled against her pretty pussy. "Not yet, sweetheart." He wanted to make her come, wanted her to come in his mouth, wanted to give her so much pleasure. He licked some more, finding her clit with his tongue, the hard edge of it, tonguing it from side to side. Then he closed his lips over it and sucked.

Her hips lifted and a long, ragged cry was dragged from deep within her. He held on, sucking, drawing out her orgasm, her body tight and throbbing. Heated cream poured over his fingers. His cock throbbed insistently, his balls drew up, and for a moment he feared he'd lost the battle to keep his own orgasm at bay. Breathing through it, he managed to control the spiraling sensation, finally releasing her quivery little clit.

He rested his cheek against her thigh, catching his breath, heart racing. Holy fuck. He'd felt that orgasm almost as much as she had, which kind of freaked him out. He slid his fingers out of her, his whole hand wet. "Ah..." A small groan rumbled out of him. He lifted heavy eyelids and met Chris's eyes. Heat washed over him at the fierce arousal on Chris's face.

"She came hard," Chris murmured. "Didn't you, sweetheart?"

Her only response was a groan.

"Good job," Chris said, a smile flirting with his lips. "I just about came too, that was so hot."

Oh man. Dag had forgotten the easy way the two of them had with a girl, the total lack of jealousy or competitiveness, just a mutual desire to please and be pleased. There was no one else in the world he'd ever done this with, despite the wild and wicked experiences he'd allowed himself to try when living in San Francisco. Nothing had ever felt this right. Or so fucking terrifying.

Chapter Eight

Chris rubbed a hand across his face and sprawled onto his back beside Kassidy, his neck and shoulders tight from the posture he'd been holding. He hadn't felt it while he'd been sucking her nipples, focused on the lush sensation of her breasts in his hands, in his mouth, and the wicked hotness of watching Dag go down on her. Seeing Dag's mouth on Kassidy's pussy turned him on to the point of pain. Knowing the intensity of the pleasure she would feel with two men, one sucking her tender nipples, the other sucking her sweet clit.

And he knew from experience just what Dag was feeling too, the taste of her, the feel of her softness against his tongue, the way she tightened around him when she came. Fuck.

He wanted to be inside her, now. He turned his head on the pillow so his mouth was beside her ear. "Wanna fuck you, Kass," he whispered. "Wanna fuck you hard. Now."

Her head moved in assent, and he climbed over her. He glanced at Dag now stretched out on the bed on the other side of Kassidy, his mouth shiny with her juices, his cheekbones wearing a stain of color. His hair was a mess from Kassidy's fingers in it and he'd fisted his own cock. Christ, he looked even bigger than he'd been years ago when they'd done this. The guy was hung, no doubt about that.

"Wait," Chris said. "Turn over, sweetheart." And he helped

her roll to her stomach then pulled her hips up. She lifted her head and turned to look at him, hair falling across her face in a sexy sweep. "Dag, move over in front of her."

Chris had no problem taking charge, in the office or in the bedroom. It came naturally to him, and Dag smiled as he seemed to realize what Chris was directing, shifted over until he was right in front of Kassidy, his thick, engorged cock jutting up. Kassidy's gasp was audible.

Yeah, that was pretty much every chick's reaction when they saw Dag's package. And yet, Chris had never been envious. In a way, he almost felt...proud when girls were so impressed by his friend.

Dag stretched his legs out on either side of her, long muscled legs lightly covered with dark hair, and stuffed two pillows behind his back.

"Dag needs to come too," Chris said. The idea of Dag's cock tunneling into Kassidy's mouth almost sent him right over the edge of the orgasm cliff right then and there. Because...this was Kassidy.

Was he a sick, twisted perv? He'd never questioned the urges that had led him and Dag to do what they'd done. He'd just enjoyed it, reveled in it, took as much pleasure from it as he could get. But for the first time he wondered what drove him to do this.

Only with Dag. Never with any other guy. Never.

He shoved those thoughts away as he pushed his body into Kassidy's, her pussy dripping with cream. Her heat on his cock scalded him as he moved inside her, and he released a long, low groan. "Fuck, Kass." He shoved her thighs wider, went deeper inside her. "Fuck. So hot. So wet. Suck him. Suck Dag's cock."

He watched with avid interest as she took Dag's dick in her small hand—couldn't even close her fingers all the way around it—and gazed at it for a long moment. The smooth, round head shone with pre-come.

"Like it?" Chris asked her, hands holding her hips, throbbing inside her, unable to take his eyes off her fist around Dag's cock.

"Mmm."

"You love giving head, don't you, sweetheart."

"Mmmhmm."

Chris slanted an aren't-we-lucky glance at Dag, whose lips quirked, but then Dag's eyes fell closed. His chin lifted, his mouth a straight line, and his hands went to Kassidy's hair, holding her hair back, holding her head as she closed her mouth over him.

There was no way she could take all of Dag, nobody could, but she knew how to curl her fingers around the base and slide them up and down while she sucked the head of his cock. Chris just wished he could see more of her face.

Chris lifted a hand to rub his chest as he watched, noting Dag's hips lifting, his breathing quicken. He was going to come. Would Kassidy swallow? She always did with him, but she'd confessed once he was the first guy she'd ever done that with.

"Ah, baby," Dag groaned.

Chris reached around under her, found her clit, which jumped at his touch. He rubbed, her soft cries distant through the roaring in his ears. Her pussy rippled and convulsed around his dick and he knew she was coming again.

He stayed on his knees between her legs and fucked her, throwing his hips against her ass again and again, the tight drag and pull of her cunt on his cock sending sparks cascading over his body in heat and light, in electric tingles that grew at the base of his spine then raced outward as pleasure exploded in him and he poured it into Kassidy.

"Oh hell, I'm coming," Dag grunted. "Fuck. Oh yeah..." And with a stretched-out rough groan, he held Kassidy's head against him. She held him there, inside her, taking it all, then lifted her head. Dag reached over with his index finger, swiped something off her face, his come no doubt, and popped it into her mouth.

"Fuck," Dag muttered. "Holy shit."

Chris's orgasm wrenched at him, his skin crawling with waves of pleasure, his head spinning as Kassidy bent her head and licked over Dag's cock delicately, and then pressed the sweetest kiss right to the tip, making Dag shiver.

That was hot. Fucking hot.

"Oh man." Chris slumped forward over Kassidy, sweat beading on his brow and chest, heart thudding, lungs straining for air. His cock continued to pulse inside her, and she continued to clasp him with small, tight contractions. "Oh man, sweetheart. That was fast. Sorry."

"That's okay."

She'd gotten another orgasm out of it, so sure, it was okay. Dag shifted to the side, Chris slowly pulled out of her slick heat, and the three of them stretched out on the bed, bodies pressed together at their sides. Chris laid his hand on Kassidy's back, his fingers brushing what he realized was Dag's hand, also stroking her. He turned his face into her hair, just breathing in her scent.

"You guys," Kassidy whispered. "What you did to me..."

"Oh yeah. You deserve it, sweetheart. You're so damn hot and sweet."

"I've never... Oh god."

Chris lifted his head and smoothed her hair off her face,

smiling down at her. "Good?"

"So good." She blinked at him then she turned her head to Dag, lying there watching them, his hand still resting on the small of her back.

"C'mere," Dag said. And he moved his face toward her and kissed her. As their mouths joined, Chris stroked a hand down her sleek back, over the curve of her ass then back up. Awe and amazement swelled in him, along with a touch of disbelief that this had happened.

He'd thought that had all ended when Dag had left. And he was being completely honest when he said he hadn't missed it. The threesomes. Because there was nobody else he'd ever do it with. And now, only Kassidy. Just these two people who meant the most to him and who he now shared with each other.

Kassidy awoke in the morning to a feeling of heavy heat, surrounded by two men in the king-size bed.

Oh dear god. She was in bed with two men.

What had they done?

She squeezed her eyes closed and her body tensed as if trying to shrink away from the two male naked bodies on either side of her. Images ran through her mind, reliving highlights of last night, and she almost groaned aloud.

She searched inside herself for her feelings about all this, trying to figure them out. Because she had a lot of feelings and they were all tangled up into a mass inside her and indecipherable. She guessed that was called confusion.

There was no denying the arousal that lingered, low down in her womb, an insistent throb that couldn't possibly mean she wanted more sex. Could it? Holy crap. She'd had three orgasms last night by the time they fell asleep and that was a first. Her body tingled at the thought.

Chris. Oh god, Chris. Terror at what he might be feeling today gripped her and stole her breath. But as she went over things in her mind, she knew he'd wanted to do it too. Unless her memory was playing tricks on her, she didn't think it was a case of him being pushed to do something he didn't want. Truly, he'd made her feel strong and special and amazing for doing that. She'd seen no signs of jealousy, just...arousal.

If she'd done anything that would hurt Chris, she didn't think she could survive it. If he woke up and was upset about this, she was going to die. She couldn't shake the vague guilty feeling that she'd cheated on him with his best friend. Except he'd been right there, participating. She pressed a hand to her stomach, quivering with nerves.

And with even more guilt, she had to admit she'd enjoyed every minute of it. Which was also freaking her out a bit.

What did that say about her, the fact that she'd enjoyed it so much? The pleasure of having two men focus all their attention on her, telling her how beautiful she was, how hot, how sexy, knowing they couldn't keep their hands off her, knowing when they got inside her they came so fast and hard there was no question that she'd aroused them.

That was about the hottest thing of all.

She stretched her aching body, trying not to disturb the sleeping men, her thighs sticky and sore. Even her jaw twinged a little, from giving two blow jobs, and oh dear god, Dag had a huge cock.

Dag. What about him? How was he going to feel today? For some reason she wasn't so concerned about him, and it wasn't that she didn't care about him, it was more a feeling that he'd been the instigator, and that his wicked bad-boy image meant he'd likely done this before and thought nothing of it.

Of course, Chris had done it before too.

That boggled her mind. She turned her head on the pillow to look first at Chris then at Dag, his dark face soft in sleep, his jaw shaded with stubble, the wicked look replaced with vulnerability. She longed to reach out and brush his hair off his forehead or rub her fingers over that sexy tattoo on his arm but she restrained herself.

Who was this man? This man who walked back into their lives and had them doing depraved, sinful things. Chris and Kassidy, the poster couple for nice and normal, nothing but vanilla and commitment.

Would they do that again? Or was that just a one-time, hot-as-sin night of decadent pleasure? What did this all mean? What would happen now?

As she studied Dag, his eyelashes fluttered, long and dark against his high cheekbones, and then he opened his eyes. His mouth tipped up at the corners when he saw her.

"Kassidy." His voice was a low rasp.

She gave him a tremulous smile back, filled with uncertainty.

He reached for her, not saying another word, pulled her head down to his chest and wrapped his arms around her, so big, so strong, so hot.

"Are you okay?" he whispered to her.

"I don't know."

For a moment they were silent as he stroked her hair. The tenderness of the gesture eased some of the panic fluttering inside her. "Are you regretting what we did?" he finally asked.

"I-I'm not sure." How could she tell him that it depended on Chris's reaction? That was her biggest fear, that Chris would see her differently, or be pissed off that she'd gone along with things and actually given his best friend a blow job. Her stomach tightened unpleasantly.

"Lots of people would think this is wrong," Dag said. "Immoral. Evil."

"Um. Yeah."

"I've done things that are bad. Really bad."

"You have?" She stared at him, concern pinching her eyebrows together.

"Yeah. Things I'm not going to talk about. I just want you to know that when I did those things, I felt...bad. Degraded. Like I wanted to puke, sometimes."

"Oh Dag." Her body tightened and ached for him, her eyes searching his face. What on earth could he have done that was that bad?

"But this didn't feel like that. It's never felt like that with Chris...and now...with you. It's..." He closed his eyes against her inquiring, anxious scrutiny. "This feels...right."

Her breath squeezed out of her as she continued to stare at him. Curiosity pricked her and she wanted to know more about what he'd done, what he had to compare this to, because lord knew, she had nothing. An emotion, soft and warm, unfurled from the mass in her chest and that emotion she recognized— as caring. She cared about Dag.

He was Chris's best friend, and even though she'd only known him a week, she hoped he was now her friend too.

Then she gave a snort of laughter that had his eyes flying open.

"What's so funny?" His thick, straight eyebrows sloped together.

"I was just thinking that I hope you and I are friends now

too, but then the ludicrousness of that hit me." She choked on another little laugh and he grinned.

"Very good friends," he said with an evil lift of one eyebrow. Then his smile softened. "I mean that, Kassidy."

Chris made a noise beside them and she turned to look at him. He was awake too. His eyes met hers. "Kass, sweetie."

She rolled toward him, giving Dag her back, not trying to be rude, but that moment was between Chris and her, an important, private moment. Lying on the pillow, they stared at each other, all her questions and uncertainties no doubt visible in her eyes. Her stomach squeezed, her heart thudded as she waited for him to say something.

"I love you," he said. Relief cascaded through her, intense and weakening. "Thank you."

"I love you too," she whispered, lifting a hand to his stubbled cheek. "So much." It seemed important to tell him that right then. She wanted to pour it all out of her, how she'd woken up full of shame and guilt and worry, and she was glad he wasn't angry or hurt about what they'd done.

And how screwed up was that?

She tried to make herself think about how both of them should be feeling—ashamed, mortified, deviant even. Why weren't they feeling that way? Because they *were* deviant?

She had a hard time accepting that. She didn't feel deviant. Even though her boyfriend had shared her with another man, it felt as if he'd given her something. A gift. Something so special and rare, she hadn't even known she'd wanted it.

Four hands on her body. Two mouths on her skin. Her eyes drifted closed as Dag's hands reached for her from behind and they took her again with lips and tongues and fingers. She wasn't sure who touched her where until she dragged open her eyes and saw Dag's darker head at her breast and Chris's fingers between her legs. They petted her and stroked her and licked her. Heat flashed beneath her skin and shimmered over her whole body.

What had she done to deserve this much pleasure? She wanted to give it all back to them, and for the first time the fact that there were two of them overwhelmed her just a little. If she could have sucked on both of them at the same time, she would have. If she could have fucked them both at the same time, she would have.

And when the thought pierced her orgasmic haze that she could in fact fuck two men at the same time, her stomach cartwheeled and she pressed a hand there. God. Oh god. That was so far beyond anything she'd even fantasized about. The idea alarmed her, embarrassed her, enticed her.

But that wasn't what Chris and Dag had in mind for her just then. "You want to fuck her, don't you?" Chris said to Dag.

Dag looked at her. Then looked at Chris. But said nothing.

"Kassidy?" Chris turned to her. Her breath stuttered in her throat and her chest tightened. Like last night, the only question she had was, "Do you want me to?" but this time she didn't say it. This time she knew.

"Yes," she whispered.

Dag moved over her, his body big and muscled and hot, his face taut with control, eyes dark. He pressed her into the mattress, one hand coming up to cup her face, and he kissed her, long, deep kisses that reached far inside her. His lips sucked at hers, his tongue licked inside her mouth, found hers. She made a noise in her throat, slid her hands over his satiny shoulders, down his back and up, into his hair. She wanted to touch him everywhere. With a gasp, he lifted his mouth from hers then pressed his open mouth to her jaw, nipped her, licked a path down her throat and sucked on the pulse in the hollow of her throat. She arched against him, his erection insistent against her thigh.

She turned her head on the pillow to find Chris, again watching avidly, his cock in his fist. And while Dag kissed his way down her body, between her breasts, small pulls on each nipple, over her tummy and lower, Chris moved on his knees toward her and fed her his cock. It filled her mouth, thick and hot, and she closed her eyes and floated, mindless, lost in the sensuality of it, nothing but sensation, Chris in her mouth and throat, Dag's tongue dragging across her flesh, lips sucking at her nipples, fingers sliding inside her and rubbing over her clit, rubbing circles that started a tingling, a buzzing, a tightening.

"Inside me!" she gasped, letting Chris's cock slide from her lips, her hips moving. She was so close and she wanted the sensation of Dag inside her when she came. She waited agonizing seconds as Dag donned a condom then moved over her. Her knees bent and her hips lifted, her heels dug into the bed and she couldn't stop the cry that fell from her lips as Dag pushed inside her, so big it hurt. The pain was brief though as her body adjusted to him and grew wetter around him. He filled her exquisitely, intensifying the sparkles swirling inside her, coiling up into a sharp, hard point of pleasure and then bursting.

"Fuck, Kassidy." The words burst from Dag's lips and she opened her eyes to look at him, his face tightened into a grimace of pleasure and pain. Her gaze riveted to the compelling sight—his dark hair falling across his forehead, his beautiful mouth parted, eyes flashing. "You're so fucking tight and hot. When you came...aw, here I go..." And he came inside her in tight, hard jerks of his body, his hands tight on her legs, holding them up, his body a big, dark triangle of muscle between her thighs.

Another ripple of pleasure washed over her, not as intense,

more of a warm shimmery glow, and oh god, it was wonderful. Amazing.

Then Chris came too in hot spurts across her breasts. She reached a hand out and laid it on his hard thigh, then with her other hand she reached down and drew her fingers through his semen, rubbed it in slow, languid circles as they collapsed and fought for breath.

Wow. Just...wow.

Chapter Nine

Things got a little weird when they ate breakfast, the three of them in the kitchen, but Chris and Dag kept insulting each other and joking around until they were all laughing and Kassidy had to shake her head. They started talking about last night and the friends Dag hadn't seen for so long.

"Kevin's lost half his hair already," Dag said. "I can't believe that."

"Yeah, the poor fucker."

"Actually, your hairline looks a little higher than the last time I saw you," Dag said.

"Fuck off, it is not. At least I haven't packed on the pounds like you have."

Dag snorted. "As if. You wish you had my svelte physique."

"Svelte? Ha!"

There wasn't an ounce of fat on either guy. Chris had always been muscular and he worked out to stay that way. Dag was a couple inches taller, his muscles a little less bulky but no less impressive, his shoulders wide, his hips lean.

"Okay," Dag finally said, draining his coffee. "I'm off back to the hotel."

"What're you up to today?"

"I gotta get some work done. I've got more meetings set up

for next week."

"I thought you were done."

"Nah. After I got this great idea and talked to your most excellent and intelligent girlfriend here, I got on the phone and set up some more. Different people to talk to. I need to get some things ready."

"Okay. So we'll talk to you tomorrow maybe."

"Yeah. Sure." Dag turned to Kassidy. "If I have questions, can I call you?"

"Of course."

He was leaving.

Of course he was leaving. They couldn't have sex twenty-four-seven, and she and Chris had lots to do—new curtains to put up, pictures she wanted hung, and she had her Saturday afternoon yoga class.

When he was gone, she turned to Chris, desperate to talk about it, to reassure herself yet again that he was okay with what had happened, to ask him about what he and Dag had done in the past, and, even though in her head she thought what they'd done was absolutely depraved and kinky, to make sure Chris didn't think any less of her because of it.

But when she kept asking questions, Chris started to get annoyed. "Yes, I'm sure. I still love you. I'm not mad. I wanted to do it. Can we just drop it for now?"

"But I want to know...you and Dag...you did that before. I want to understand..."

"What's to understand?" Chris stood on a stepladder in the spare room trying to install the new curtain rod. "Hand me the drill."

"There's a lot to understand." She picked up the power tool and held it up to him. For a moment, the sound of the drill drowned out any further talk. "What we did...that's not...normal."

"Sure it is." Chris drilled again. "What's normal anyway? If we all wanted it, then it's fine. We're not hurting anyone."

She bit her lip. No. They weren't hurting anyone.

Chris clearly didn't want to talk anymore about it. Which was just like him, dammit. He'd never been one to talk about how he felt. In fact, the day he'd told her he loved her she'd damn near died. But right now, she could have exploded with all the questions inside her, the pressure that built up with wanting to know more, including...was it going to happen again?

The next afternoon, Dag met Chris and Kassidy at the beach, lazing away a sunny June Sunday on the shore of Lake Michigan, people watching, but mostly watching each other, Kassidy in a tiny bikini that exposed maximum flesh to the sun for it to turn it a deep golden hue, gleaming with the sunscreen Dag and Chris helped her apply with tantalizing strokes of both their hands.

As they ate dinner together that evening at Chris and Kassidy's, Dag sensed the tension in Kassidy, from the way she kept looking at him then Chris, then him again. He observed the uncertain flickers of her eyes, the slight tremor in her hands and he knew she was struggling.

She was wondering what was going to happen. She was afraid of what was going to happen. Even though she'd loved it. She'd been more into the threesome than any girl Dag could recall. Why that was, he couldn't say and didn't want to think too much about. He certainly didn't believe it was because she was any less committed to Chris. The bond between the two of them was almost tangible. Substantial. Enviable.

No, she definitely loved Chris. So what she had to be feeling was guilt. Something stirred inside him that he'd made Kassidy feel bad.

After dinner, Chris went to the bathroom and Dag and Kassidy wandered into the living room. Kassidy curled up on the couch and Dag stood in front of her. "Do you want me to leave?" he asked, meeting her eyes steadily.

She just gazed back at him.

"We don't have to do it again," he said, voice low and gruff. "It can be a one-time crazy thing that happened. If you want me to apologize and leave and never come back, I will."

Still she said nothing, looking at him with those big dark eyes.

"Kassidy? Is that what you want? I don't want to do anything to make you feel bad."

"You didn't make me feel bad," she whispered. The corners of her mouth lifted a tad. "I'm doing that just fine all by myself."

"Ah hell. Don't beat yourself up about it, sweetheart." His heart turned over in his chest.

"I tried to talk to Chris about it, to understand...but he didn't want to talk."

"You can talk to me."

He meant that, even though he knew this wasn't going to be the time. He sat beside her and took her hand in both his. "Seriously, Kassidy. I never wanted to hurt you."

"You didn't," she said again, turning her hand in his so their palms met, fingers curled around each other. "You can't take the blame for what happened."

"I will if you want me to. If it will make you feel better."

Her eyes went even bigger and liquidy. "Oh Dag." Her lips

quivered. "You're not such a bad boy after all."

His cheeks heated and he looked away.

And then she leaned forward and kissed his mouth.

His heart stuttered, his blood sizzled through his veins, and his chest went soft and warm. And his resolve that once would be the only time it ever happened somehow faltered in the face of her sweetness.

"You didn't answer my question," he said quietly, their hands still joined.

"No. I don't want you to go."

Chris walked back into the room as Kassidy drew back and she and Dag both looked at him. He lifted a brow.

Dag gave a small jerk of his head, indicating Chris should sit on the other side of Kassidy, and Chris gave a slow smile as he did so.

They kissed for a long while, Dag and Chris taking turns kissing Kassidy, their hands getting bolder, touching her, caressing her. She slipped an arm around each of their shoulders, turning her mouth from one to the other. Dag slid his hand beneath her T-shirt as he kissed her, found her soft breast and cupped her through her bra. She moaned into his mouth.

Heat wrapped around his cock, burned in his balls. He watched Chris kiss her, their mouths fused, so close to his own he could see the golden stubble on Chris's jaw, his gilt-tipped eyelashes, the smooth curve of Kassidy's cheek. Chris cupped her jaw, his fingers long on her face.

Dag slid both hands now up under her shirt, pushing it up over her breasts, revealing the simple pink cotton T-shirt bra, cut low to reveal enticing softness. When Chris pulled back, Dag said, "Sit forward, babe. That's it." And he lifted the shirt over her head. Then his fingers went to the button and zipper of the shorts she wore, opened them and dragged her hips forward on the couch so he could get the shorts off.

"Such a pretty body," he murmured. His gaze wandered over her body, her tanned skin from their day at the beach a contrast to her pink cotton underwear. She bit her lip.

"Yeah," Chris agreed, sweeping a hand down her arm. "So sweet, Kass. I wanna lick you all over."

"I want to see your bodies," she said, sprawled on the couch, peering at them from beneath lowered lashes. The corners of her mouth tipped up.

Dag willingly reached behind his neck to drag his own T-shirt off, and Chris did the same. Clothing littered the living room floor. Kassidy smoothed a palm up each male chest. Sensations slid through Dag at her touch, hot and sharp, straight to his groin where his dick swelled.

Chris bent his head to fulfill his wish, dragged his tongue from the tip of Kassidy's shoulder up the side of her neck, making Dag even harder. "Mmm," Chris said. "Wanna eat you up, sweetheart."

Dag slid to the floor, dragged Kassidy's ass right to the edge of the couch so she was almost lying, her head tucked up against the back cushions. While Chris nibbled and licked his way across her chest, Dag dragged her panties off and spread her legs. She was wet, so slick and hot, it made his mind hum and his ears buzz. He could hardly think for wanting to taste her, feel her. Another ragged groan tore from her throat as he gazed at her pussy. Then he leaned in to taste. Sweet. Succulent. She gasped and a small tremor went through her body. Heat slid down his spine and settled deep in his balls.

He barely noticed the bra being tossed aside as he held her thighs wide with his palms, using his thumbs to part her folds for his tongue to probe and lick, her cream like honey on his tongue, her soft cries of pleasure sweet to his ears.

"Good, Dag?" Chris murmured, his mouth against a nipple. Kassidy writhed beneath them.

"Yeah. So good. Love your pussy, Kassidy. So hot and wet."

Dag kissed and sucked and licked more. She cried out. His cock strained against his jeans, so he reached down and freed it. "Wanna fuck you, babe," he groaned. "So bad. I want inside you. Inside your tight little pussy."

She moaned again, hips lifting against his mouth. He pressed a closed-mouth kiss to her clit, then gently sucked it in, flicked his tongue over it.

"Oh yeah!" Her voice sounded thick. "That feels so good. Oh god."

Her hand had wrapped around the back of Chris's head as he moved from one nipple to the other, and Dag stood, stripped off his jeans and underwear and rolled on a condom from his pocket. He knelt again between her legs, this time lifting her ankles high, guiding them to his shoulders, and then he pushed into her. He watched himself enter her, her pussy pulling him in, accepting his girth as if she was made for him.

Fuck. He gritted his teeth. She was tight, and so fucking hot she was scalding his cock. Pleasure licked up every nerve ending like flames, a fiery wave of heat over his body. His balls tightened, pressure gathering, fast and hard. He tightened his buttocks as his hips thrust back and forth, in and out of her. Still holding her ankles, he turned his head and kissed her there, swept his tongue over the fragile bones and soft skin, then pressed her calf to his cheek.

He dragged his gaze up her body, over the flush tinting her chest, breasts rosy from Chris's attention, and her eyes opened and met his over Chris's bent head. Awareness sizzled between them, a connection, hot and bright, their gazes locked on each other.

"So good," she whispered. "It's so good."

Chris made a small noise, reached a hand down between her legs and rubbed, seeming to know exactly how she liked it. When she came, her eyes fell closed, her body tightened around him in rippling waves that almost sent him over, soft noises leaking from her mouth.

Chris laid a last kiss on her chest, between her breasts, rolled off the couch and ripped off his pants too, then knelt beside her, offering his stiff dick to her mouth. She turned her head and opened for him. Chris rubbed the head over her lips, around and around, and she turned her gaze up to him, eyes big, gaze fastened on his face as he stroked his cock over her mouth.

"Lick it," he whispered.

Her tongue came out and stroked over Chris. That was so fucking hot.

Chris pushed inside her then. "Take it all," he murmured, watching her. "Take it all, sweetheart. You know how to do it. Show Dag how you can do it."

Dag kept his gaze trained on the sight, Chris's long, thick flesh disappearing farther and farther into her mouth. She blinked, made a small noise, but held Chris's gaze as he slowly filled her mouth and throat. He released his cock, slid his hand around the back of her head, pulling her to him. Jesus! Right to the root she took him, until her nose pressed into Chris's pubes, and then he pulled out. She gave a little gasp.

"Good girl," Chris said, pushing in again, sliding in and out of her pretty mouth. Her cheeks hollowed as she sucked. Dag caught glimpses of tongue then Chris pulled out.

"Put out your tongue," he ordered her. She did and he

tapped his cock on it, one, two, three times. Then again. Chris groaned, on his knees, his muscled body taut, tanned, gleaming in the lamplight, the paler cheeks of his ass clenched tight.

Once again, Dag couldn't believe this was happening. It had been so long. Seeing Chris like that, enthralled, fucking Kassidy's mouth in a quick, hard rhythm, the rapture on his face made Dag's heart expand in his chest. His own cock surged too and now there was no holding back, his orgasm exploding in his balls, pleasure racing through his body, through every vein, out of his cock.

"Aaah," he cried out. "Ah fuck, Kassidy, baby, coming inside you..." And a long groan tore from him as he poured into her, hands tight on her ankles.

"Me too," Chris grunted, quickening the rhythm. Kassidy curled her fingers around the base of his cock, sucked him with greedy wantonness until he spurted in long streams onto her face, in her mouth. Dag watched, heart pounding, ears buzzing, still pulsing inside Kassidy's hot little body, watched her suck and lick Chris then swipe her fingers over the cream on her face and pop them in her mouth. Oh man. Oh man.

He fell forward onto her body, gasping for air, felt one of her hands come to rest on his damp back, fingers moving in small strokes.

"You are so hot, sweetheart." Chris's words penetrated the fog Dag's brain was in and he felt Chris move on the couch, realized Chris had bent to kiss Kassidy. Her fingers still caressed his back, though, up and down in small strokes.

"The hottest," he mumbled in agreement.

He heaved himself up onto the couch and collapsed beside Kassidy, laying an arm across her stomach. He pressed a kiss to her shoulder, his eyes closed. Once again, she'd destroyed him. The two of them had destroyed him, but Kassidy... He'd never been with a woman who turned him on, turned him inside out like she did.

Kassidy tried to breathe. She still tasted Chris in her mouth, her lips humming and burning from taking him so deep, her pussy still pulsing. She licked her lips, let a smile curve her lips, sank into Dag's hot body on one side of her and Chris's on the other. She'd loved sucking Chris with Dag watching, his eyes hot and intent, his big cock fucking her at the same time, both of them inside her.

What had happened to her? Kassidy, the good girl. Good girl gone wild was apparently what had happened. Once again she'd had the chance to put a stop to this. But she hadn't.

Her heart softened and expanded in her chest at remembering Dag's words, his offer to take the blame for this, to end it if that's what she wanted. God, he was nice, so much nicer than she'd thought when she'd first met him, that wicked glint in his eye, that bad-boy smile and mocking attitude giving off a whole different impression. There was a lot he kept hidden, she was sure of it, carefully hidden way down deep, and Kassidy had a feeling even Chris didn't know all of it.

The way he'd watched both of them. He'd watched her, yeah, as he'd fucked her, but his gaze had moved over Chris too, watching his cock slide in and out, watching Chris's face as she'd sucked him off.

All day long, especially when Dag and Chris had both rubbed sunscreen all over her body, she'd felt as if her senses had been electrified. As if every touch sizzled, the coconut scent of the sun lotion intense and sexy, the sun hot on her skin, the sounds of the water rolling onto the beach a sensual rhythm. She felt sexy. Desirable. Desired.

By two men.

She didn't even care what people at the beach must've thought watching two men rub lotion onto her body with such wickedly sexy strokes.

Dag and Chris started nibbling on her again, little kisses and licks over her shoulders and neck. She shivered, gave a small laugh and hunched her shoulders against the tickling.

"Whatsamatter, Kass?" Chris murmured against her skin. "Too soon?"

"Not for me," she gasped as Dag kissed his way down her chest, over the slope of her breast and then kissed her nipple. Ooooh. Gawd. Her eyes drifted closed. "But you..."

"Hmmm. Doesn't seem to be a problem." And Chris tapped her thigh with his hardening cock.

"Not for me," Dag said. He sucked her nipple in, her tender nipple, and heat zapped through her. He too rubbed his cock over her leg. He'd gotten rid of the condom in a pile of crumpled tissues on the table. Their condo was turning into a sex palace.

They were both hard again. Already. For her. How could she not be melted by that, completely, totally softened and liquefied?

"Bedroom," she whispered.

"No." Chris licked her jaw. "The couch is so..."

"Full of possibilities?" Dag suggested, looking up from her breast with gleaming dark eyes.

"Yeah." The two men exchanged heavy eye contact. Oh lord, what did they have planned for her now?

"This time it's my turn to fuck you, sweetheart," Chris said.

"Um...wow. Okay." Her insides went all heavy and achy. Again. Already. Dag's fingers slid down there and played between her thighs.

113

"She's wet. So wet."

"Good."

Chris gave her a hard kiss on the mouth then moved away. "Lie down, sweetie. On your back."

Dag moved too, hands helping her down, and then Chris lifted her ankles up onto the couch and turned her body. She felt like a doll, a little helpless, a little used, but not in a bad way. They laid her on the couch, her head on the armrest, and Dag slid off to stand beside the couch while Chris knelt between her legs.

Chris smiled down at her, his face still wearing a flush, hair tousled. His chest, wide and muscled, his golden-brown hair in the center of it tapering down in a swirl of lighter gold around his belly button, then farther down to the thick nest of brown hair around his cock. He, too, had gotten tanned today at the beach, a nice golden tan that emphasized his muscles. He lifted her knees up and back and planted one of his feet on the floor, the couch too narrow.

She blinked at him and reached a hand out to touch Dag's thigh, her head spinning a little. Then Dag slid his hands into her hair, turned her head to face him and angled her chin up. She met his eyes, dark and dangerous, and as he fed his cock into her mouth, Chris pushed inside her.

Dag held her jaw with one hand, his other hand pressed to his groin at the base of his cock, and fucked her mouth. She'd taken Chris deep, something she'd practiced and learned how to do, relaxing her throat, swallowing him, but there was no way she could do that to Dag. She raised her eyes to his face again, a little whisper of worry inside her that he might try to make her do it, but his eyes reassured her, his strokes firm but not aggressive.

"As much as you want, babe," he murmured, watching her

face with erotic hunger. "As much as you can."

She wanted to swallow him, all of him, his thick length filling her mouth, bumping the back of her throat.

"It's good," he mumbled. "So good. As much as you can, that's good, baby." His smile warmed her.

Chris plunged into her again and again, hands on her inner thighs, pushing them wide for him.

"Christ, Kass, look at you. Sucking Dag's cock like that. Oh man." The urgent drag of sensation in her pussy, in and out, in and out, started pleasure building, a faint buzz of pleasure at first, growing bigger, faster, higher. She used her own fingers between her legs to accelerate it, rubbing her clit. "Oh yeah, sweetheart, yeah, do it..." Chris's voice trailed off into a groan.

"Gonna come, Kassidy." Dag's words dragged her gaze back to him. "In your mouth...aw, fuck, yeah..." And a grimace contorted his mouth, his eyes squeezed shut almost as if he were in pain and the taste of him flowed over her tongue and down her throat as she sucked and swallowed. "Oh yeah, baby, that's so good. Sooo good."

"Yes, now..." Chris was coming too, pumping inside her in hard pounding strokes that rocked her body, jiggled her breasts, and sent her over too, flying high. Dag's cock slid out of her mouth, and he bent and kissed her as she came. She left her body, she didn't know where she went, but she floated and throbbed and soared on sensation.

Dag seemed to end up at Chris and Kassidy's place a lot over the next week. During the day he met with other investors and business people he needed to get his venture started. In the evenings he spent time with Chris and Kassidy, sometimes with Chris doing guy stuff, but often with Kassidy, picking her brain for the training and development knowledge he needed.

What would he have done without her? She was a godsend, a treasure trove of information, experience and ideas. Advice from a human resources professional with experience in training and development was invaluable.

"You've done a ton of work on this," she said slowly on Thursday night. She and Dag sat at the dining room table while Chris watched a baseball game on television not far away. Dag's creation was coming together nicely, and the research he'd done showed he had something new and different and marketable.

He shrugged. "Yeah. Well. There's a lot to do."

She sent him a funny, almost puzzled look. "Just remember, we call it talent development now. You'll want to use the latest buzzwords when you're talking to people—investors or buyers."

"Talent development," he repeated, typing on his laptop.

"Learning and development has to be aligned with corporate strategic initiatives," she continued. "For us, and probably most organizations these days, competencies are an important focus."

"How do you train on those?" he asked.

"We hire external consultants who've developed specific programs on things like client service, problem solving, teamwork."

"That must be expensive."

"Yes."

"Okay." He typed again, fingers clicking away on the keyboard. "What do you think about doing that kind of training online?"

She frowned. "Hard to say. A lot of the learning comes from the interactive classroom experience where people share their experiences and learn from each other's questions."

"But if you could do it in real time? With the ability to share information and ask questions?"

"It could work."

How could he test his product before he got too far into this? Maybe develop a prototype and get someone to try it. Once again, Kassidy.

He looked up at her, curled up cross-legged on the chair in a pair of short shorts and a tank top, her hair loose on her shoulders. "Would you try it? If I build a prototype. I need to know how well it works."

"Wouldn't you need more people?"

"Yeah. But I don't have more people. Well, there could be you and me and Chris. Chris would do it too."

"A class of three," she said with a smile. "What are we going to learn?"

"I need some content."

"Hang on."

She disappeared down the hall and returned with some books and folders. "I can't give you stuff from RBM obviously, but here are some training materials from courses I've taken. You can use this just as sample materials."

"Perfect." Excitement gripped him as always when he was working on creating something new. "Thanks, Kass. What would I do without you?"

Her pleased smile warmed him and he winked at her.

"Who's winning the game?" he called to Chris.

"Cubs. Three nothing. You guys done?"

"Just about." He had a few more questions for Kassidy. "So what about recruitment?" he asked. "Internal recruitment. I assume you often hire from within."

"I'm not the expert on that," she said. "But, yes."

And they talked for another hour. Kassidy was passionate about her work and seemed to love to talk about it. Her knowledge impressed him. She was so much more than just a pretty face, but he should have known Chris wouldn't hook up with someone who didn't have more going on than looks. And she seemed impressed with all his work too, which gave him a warm, satisfied feeling inside.

And, like almost every other night that week, he ended up staying over at their place, sleeping with Kassidy and Chris in what was becoming the sweetest, hottest, almost daily routine.

Chapter Ten

Kassidy was just coming out of a meeting Friday afternoon, laughing at a joke her boss had made, when Chris appeared in the hall. It was unusual for him to be on her floor; they usually didn't see each other during the day.

"Hi," she said with a smile, walking toward him, her steps slowing at the expression on his face. "What's wrong?" Her heart gave a jump in her chest. "Dag...?"

"No. It's your mom."

Kassidy frowned and Chris took hold of her upper arms.

"She had an accident. A car accident."

"Oh my god. Is she okay?" Her legs started to shake.

"She's in the hospital. I'm going to take you there."

"But...I have a meeting..."

"Come on. We'll tell Paul." Kassidy's boss, Paul, had just disappeared into his office.

"Chris...she's alive, isn't she?" Fear held her in a tight grip, made it hard to breathe.

"Yes." His grim mouth didn't reassure her, though, and she stumbled along after him down the carpeted hall and into Paul's office.

Chris told him what had happened.

"Go," Paul said immediately. "Call me later."

Kassidy nodded, unable to put thoughts together. "Tell Julie...the project folder's on my desk...my purse..." She turned to Chris and he took her hand, his warm and strong.

"We'll get it. Come on." He led her next to her own cubicle, found her purse and the suit jacket she'd draped over the back of her chair.

"What hospital is she at? What happened?"

"I don't know much," he replied as they rode down the elevator to the underground parking garage. "Your dad called me. He sounded...upset."

"Oh god. He's not good at stuff like this." Kassidy pressed a hand to her stomach. Please, please, her mom had to be okay. She wiped her mouth and stared into space. The elevator stopped on the eleventh floor, then the ninth floor, the fifth, the fourth... God! Didn't these people know they were in a hurry!

Her skin crawled with impatience and nerves tightened her stomach. She licked her lips and glanced at Chris.

"It'll be okay," he said, rubbing his hand up and down her back.

She nodded tightly. Finally they were in the garage and she wanted to run to their car, her high heels clicking and echoing in the concrete structure.

Traffic got in their way, even though it wasn't rush hour yet. "Dammit, move!" Kassidy shouted futilely at a car driving slowly in front of them. Chris reached out and took her hand again.

"Sssh. It's okay, Kass. We're just a few minutes away."

She squeezed his fingers, closed her eyes and tried to focus on breathing. What if her mom died? She wouldn't. She wouldn't die. But she could be paralyzed or brain damaged or...

"I'll let you out here," Chris said, pulling up in front of the emergency entrance. "I'll find somewhere to park and come right in."

"O-okay." She wanted him with her, but she stepped out of the car and hurried into the building. The unmistakable odor of hospital antiseptic stung her nostrils and turned her stomach as she ran up to the desk.

"I'm looking for Hope Langdon."

The woman clicked through some screens on a computer. "Are you family?" She looked at Kassidy over her black-framed glasses.

"Yes," she said in a rush. "She's my mother."

The woman glanced over her shoulder. "Tess, can you take this woman back to exam room three? It's the daughter."

The daughter. The daughter. Kassidy followed the nurse. There were two daughters. Where was Hailey? Her dad probably hadn't even called her. *But what if Mom...*

Stop. It was going to be okay.

The nurse held the door open and Kassidy walked in, her heart fluttering, afraid of what she was going to see. Her dad stood there beside the hospital bed while a nurse checked some monitors or something.

"Dad. I'm here." She rushed over to her father.

"Kassidy." He turned to her, his face pale and anxious.

"Is she okay? What happened, Dad?"

"I'm okay." Her mother spoke, her words a whisper, and relief poured through Kassidy, weakening her knees. She leaned on the bed, trying to stay upright.

"Mom. Oh, thank god."

Her mom looked worse than her dad, her face so pale the blue veins in her temples looked like bruises. And she did have

121

bruises...and cuts, a gash across her nose, scrapes on her cheekbones, and Kassidy could see an angry red mark on her left collarbone. She reached for her Mom's hand lying on the bed.

"She's got a broken pelvis," Dad said. "They did an x-ray and they're still going to do a CT scan. She might have internal injuries. And she might need surgery. Depending on what type of fracture." His mouth trembled. Kassidy hated seeing her dad, always big and strong and dependable, so shaken like this.

The nurse spoke up. "If it's a type A, she won't need surgery," she said. "She'll just need bed rest. Type B or C are more serious."

Kassidy nodded and swallowed through a dry throat. "Okay. When will she have the CT scan?"

"Should only be a few minutes and we'll take her in."

"Okay." Kassidy looked back at her mom and smiled. "Does it hurt, Mom?"

"Like hell," her mom said with an attempt at a smile. "They've given me some drugs, though."

"That's good." She squeezed her hand then looked up as Chris came charging in, eyes flashing. He seemed to take up a lot of space in the exam room, his presence solid and reassuring. Kassidy held out her other hand to him. He strode over, laying one hand on Dad's shoulder and taking Kassidy's with his other.

"Dave," Chris said. "How's Hope?"

Kassidy's parents loved Chris and he liked them too, which made life much easier than for friends Kassidy knew who hated their in-laws.

"She's okay, we think," Dad said, straightening his shoulders in the presence of another man. He repeated what

Kassidy had just learned.

"Well, apart from a few bruises and scrapes, you look as gorgeous as ever," Chris told Hope, earning another wisp of a smile from Mom.

Kassidy went warm inside and squeezed Chris's fingers. Thank god he was there. Now she felt like everything really might be okay.

The CT scan confirmed no internal injuries, and as the fracture was a type A, there wasn't much they could do about it, so they sent Mom home with crutches, instructions to rest and a couple of different medications including blood thinners to prevent clots from forming in her legs, which was somewhat alarming.

"We'll follow you home," Kassidy told her parents, shooting a look at Chris, who nodded.

At her parents' home, Kassidy buzzed around, making Mom comfortable. Thankfully they had a den on the main floor with a sofa bed in it where Mom could sleep because stairs were out of the question. Also luckily they had a main-floor bathroom.

She made up the bed, with a quick heated memory flash of doing that with her own sofa bed with Dag just a week ago, got her mom settled in the sofa bed, brought water, magazines, the remote control for the television.

"Are you hungry?" she asked. "I'll make some dinner."

"No." Mom sank into the pillows, eyes closed, still white as the sheets she rested on. "I'm not hungry."

"Okay." Kassidy bit her lip. "You rest. Sleep if you need to. I'll go see if Dad wants something to eat."

She hurried out into the living room with one last look at her mom. Pain had tightened her face, despite the narcotics she'd had. Kassidy hurt just to see her like that.

Chris was checking messages or emails on his BlackBerry. "Gotta call Dag," he said. "We were going to meet for dinner."

"Oh. Damn. That's right."

"Go," Dad said. "You don't have to hang around here all evening. I can look after your mother."

Yeah, but who was going to look after him? "Are you hungry, Dad?" Her father had never really been much of a cook. Give him a steak to grill and he'd be happy, but he wouldn't have a clue how to prepare the steak or anything to go with it besides a beer.

"Well..."

Kassidy smiled. "I'll make some dinner."

"But you have plans," he said. "Don't—"

"It's okay, Dad." She patted his shoulder before going into the kitchen. "It's no big deal. We see Dag all the time."

"Isn't that your friend from San Francisco?" Dad asked Chris as she moved away. She heard them talking as she opened the door of the refrigerator. What could she make?

She studied the contents. Well, it didn't have to be gourmet. She found some ham and eggs. Surely Mom had an onion. She slid open the crisper drawer. Yup. Denver sandwiches. Perfect.

She kicked off her high-heeled pumps and busied herself chopping onions, whisking eggs, toasting bread, keeping her hands busy so the adrenaline rush of energy had somewhere to go. Otherwise she might have just collapsed into a heap of overwrought emotions on the kitchen floor.

Her mother's kitchen was as familiar to her as her own— no, probably more familiar, given she'd only moved into the condo two weeks ago. She easily found utensils, a skillet, plates to serve the sandwiches on. As she was assembling bread and omelets, Chris appeared.

"You okay, sweetheart?" He curved his hand around the nape of her neck and kissed her.

"I think so." Then tears puddled in her eyes and she set down the knife and turned into Chris's arms. "I was so scared."

He wrapped her up in his arms and she let the tears soak the shoulder of his dress shirt. He was still dressed in work clothes, as was she. "Did you talk to Dag?" she asked with a sniffle.

"Yeah. I told him what happened. He asked if there's anything he can do, and said to give you a hug from him."

"Aw. Thanks. I feel bad deserting him."

"I told him to hang out at our place if he wants and we'll be home later."

She lifted her head and peered up at him. "Chris...this is weird. Isn't it?"

"What? You mean Dag and...us?"

"Yes."

Chris pressed his lips together and lifted his hands to frame her face. "Some might think so. Does it feel wrong to you?"

She shook her head. "No."

"Me either." He pressed her face to his chest again. "I don't know why. I don't really want to analyze it. Let's just enjoy it. While he's here."

"He's not going to stay. Is he?"

"I don't know."

She wanted to talk about it, but clearly Chris didn't, and anyway, this was not the time. Stepping out of his arms, she turned back to the counter, and in a moment had sandwiches on plates, which they carried into the living room. They ate, sitting on the couch, her dad looking a little more like himself.

"I just checked on your mom," he said. "She's sleeping."

"That's good." She took a bite of her sandwich, chewed and swallowed, not really tasting it. "It's good that it's the weekend and you'll be here to help her."

"Yeah." He sighed. "This is a good sandwich, Kassie."

She smiled at his old nickname for her. "Thanks."

"I don't know what I'll do Monday." He frowned. "I have an out-of-town trip next week."

"Can you cancel it?"

Her dad was corporate counsel for Palladium Bank.

"I don't think so."

"Well, then, I'll come stay with Mom."

"You need to work."

"We have family sick days we can use. I've never used any." Except they had this big new project they were working on, and already she felt guilty at running out today and leaving everyone in the lurch. If she had to take a few days off, that would screw things up for the whole team.

"That would be great, honey."

She smiled reassuringly at her dad. Of course she'd be there to help them. "And I'll call Hailey. Maybe she can take a turn."

As if. She'd have to tell Hailey what had happened. Hailey wasn't exactly the nurturing type, but maybe she'd come through in a pinch. Maybe she'd look after Mom during the day, since her bartending job was at night, and Kassidy could come in the evenings. That would be fair.

"I'll text her," she said. "She needs to know what

happened." She didn't question her dad about why he hadn't called Hailey, but instead had called Chris. She quickly thumbed in a message then tossed her phone back in her purse.

She did the dishes, tidied up the kitchen and spent a few minutes with her mom, a bit groggy from all the meds. "Sure you're okay, Dad?" she asked before she and Chris left. "Call if you need anything, okay?"

"We'll be fine," he said. He hugged her and she breathed in his familiar aftershave, the same kind she and Hailey used to buy him for Father's Day years ago.

"I'll come by tomorrow," she promised.

He shook his head, smiling. "You don't need to, but I know I can't stop you."

She smiled too. "Nope."

Chapter Eleven

"Some idiot apparently went through a red light."

Dag sat on the brown leather couch in Kassidy and Chris's living room. They'd just gotten back from Kassidy's parents' home after getting her mom home from the hospital.

"She's okay, though?" Dag asked. Kassidy flopped down into a chair across from him, dressed in a narrow white skirt and silky pink-and-mauve-flowered blouse.

"She's in a lot of pain," she said, rubbing her forehead. "But it could be worse." With sigh, she pulled her telephone out of her purse, flipped it open to check it, snapped it shut. "I thought Hailey might have texted back. I guess she's working."

"She doesn't know?"

Kassidy shook her head. "My dad just called Chris, and he came and got me." She gave him a tight little smile. "Hailey and my parents don't get along that well, so I guess she wasn't the first person he thought of."

Huh. He knew Kassidy and Hailey were different, but this was pretty serious. Ah well. Families. He knew only too well how screwed up they could be.

"You look exhausted," Dag said, studying her.

"Thanks." Her wry smile tugged at something inside him.

Chris appeared in the living room, having headed straight

to the bedroom to change out of his suit and tie. Now he wore a pair of loose knee-length gym shorts and a baggy T-shirt.

"Hey, sweetie," he said. "How're you doing?" He sat on the padded arm of the chair she sat in and stroked a hand over her hair.

"I'm okay." She sent him a tired smile then pushed herself up out of the chair. "I should go change too." As she walked out, she asked over her shoulder, "Did you eat, Dag?"

"Yeah. I picked up a sandwich."

Chris took Kassidy's place in the chair. "Holy shit. That was scary."

"Yeah. Sorry, man. I don't know Kassidy's mom, but that's really shitty."

"She's a nice lady," Chris said. "Seeing her like that..." He shook his head. "I need a beer. You?"

"Sure."

They sat and drank beer together, Chris filling him on more details of the accident until Kassidy returned dressed in a pair of sweatpants rolled up to her knees and a gray T-shirt. Her breasts jiggled softly without a bra beneath the thin cotton, momentarily distracting Dag from the fatigue evident on her face.

Dag found himself strangely disturbed by seeing her so distracted and upset. He wanted to do something about that, something to help, but he felt...helpless.

She was Chris's girlfriend, so he hesitated to butt in. But they were friends too. She stood there, staring into space, rubbing the back of her neck.

"C'mere," he said softly, holding a hand out to her. She looked at him and blinked but moved toward him. He took her hand and pulled her down, then pressed her shoulders so she

129

sat on the floor at his feet. He started massaging her shoulders, the muscles tight over her fine bones.

"Oh," she said on a whoosh of breath. "That feels good."

"I'm told I'm pretty good at this," Dag said, a smile lifting the corners of his mouth as he worked at her shoulders.

Her head nodded forward and he pressed with fingers and thumbs, finding all the taut bands and knots, eliciting soft moans of pleasure from her. Warmth spread through his chest.

He glanced up at Chris, who watched, and their eyes met. Chris gave a crooked smile, eyes warm, and Dag returned it and continued massaging, working his way down between her shoulder blades then back up. She was so little.

When his hands started to tire, he slid them through her hair, dragging it back into a low tail, letting it slide out and then gathering it again, over and over.

"So nice," she slurred. Much more relaxed now.

"Good," he said. He bent his head and kissed her shoulder just where the loose neckline of her T-shirt bared it. He didn't intend for it to be any more than that—a shoulder rub and a quick friendly kiss—but she tipped her head back between his knees to look at him with gratitude shining in her eyes, and her mouth was so close he couldn't resist the invitation, and he leaned over a little farther and kissed her mouth.

She responded, opening to him, kissing him back, a soft lingering kiss that had his cock stirring in his jeans. Damn. Here they went again.

They didn't make it to the bedroom, hell, they didn't even bother trying. Chris sat down on the floor beside Kassidy and started removing her clothes, kissing her. Dag helped get the T-shirt over her head and then tossed a fleecy throw blanket to the floor. The two of them laid Kassidy out on it, stripped out of their own clothes then worshiped her pretty body on their hands and knees, sucking her tight little nipples, licking her between her legs, taking turns moving up and down her body until she came in hard, panting shudders.

Then, with the two men standing on either side of her, Kassidy rose to her knees, holding a cock in each hand, sucking first one, then the other. Her tugging fingers pulled them closer, closer to her eager mouth, closer to each other, so close their cocks almost touched. Dag watched with heated, heavy eyes as his cock and Chris's met at Kassidy's mouth. Heat boiled in his balls, his body tightened with anticipation, every nerve ending tingling.

She looked up at them, her mouth wet, eyes wide. "I want to suck you both," she whispered, and Dag felt her breath on the sensitive head of his cock. "At the same time."

Jesus. He wanted to shout, *yes!* But he swallowed the words through a tight throat, glanced at Chris. Chris's jaw was locked, a pulse ticcing there, his eyes narrowed, one hand resting on Kassidy's head. When Dag's eyes met Chris's, the torment there almost knocked him back. Did Chris want that? Did he not want that? Confusion swirled inside Dag as he waited for Chris's response, his cock and balls aching.

"Please," Kassidy whispered, focusing her attention on Chris. "I want to so bad."

Chris's eyes fell closed and he gave a jerky nod. "You can try, baby. You won't be able to get both of us in very far."

Heat flooded Dag's body, weakening his knees, and he took one step closer, planted his feet firmly on the floor as his dick slid along the length of Chris's.

Fuck! His eyes were heavy, but he wanted to watch, wanted to see as Kassidy pumped them together and opened even wider. She could barely take them both in, just the heads, her tongue scalding hot as she licked over his flesh, Chris's cock just as hot and hard against him.

Unable to stop himself, he reached out a hand, for support, for balance, for...pleasure...and rested it on Chris's chest. They both held Kassidy's head with one hand. Chris's other hand hung at his side, fingers clenched. Dag didn't look at Chris, couldn't look at him, stared at Chris's hand. Until finally Chris lifted it and slowly, slowly touched Dag's chest.

Fire streaked through Dag's body, his cock jerked against Kassidy's mouth. Chris slid his hand higher, flattened his palm, his heat scorching Dag's skin. Dag moved his hand too, up to Chris's shoulder, to the back of his neck. Their faces were only about a foot apart, close enough to hear each other breathing in harsh, ragged breaths.

Slick, wet sounds filled the air as Kassidy licked and sucked and played with the thick shafts and murmured her enjoyment. Dag let out a long groan when she rubbed their cocks together. She looked up at them almost apprehensively, her long lashes like starbursts around her eyes. And, making another noise of helpless pleasure, Dag leaned his head against Chris's and tightened his fingers around Chris's nape as he exploded in long, hard spurts.

Chris was quiet, for one who usually talked during sex— Dag knew this—and then he came too, with a muffled groan, and Kassidy took their come into her mouth, on her mouth, on her face, splattered into her dark hair.

"Thank you," she said long moments later as the three of them collapsed together on the couch. "For letting me..."

Dag didn't say a word, and neither did Chris.

Kassidy finally heard back from Hailey Saturday afternoon, when she was on her way over to her parents' house. "Are you going to come see Mom?" she asked into her cell phone, turning onto the street where her parents lived.

"I can't today," Hailey said. "She's okay, isn't she?"

"She's got a fractured pelvis. She's pretty much bedridden for a while."

"Well, that's good," Hailey said, and Kassidy drew the phone away from her ear to stare at it in disbelief.

"That's good?" she repeated, voice rising. "That is not good!"

"She's alive," Hailey said. "I had a late night last night, I'm beat, and I have to work tonight."

"But...well, okay. But next week Dad has to go out of town." Kassidy pulled into the wide driveway in front of the double-car garage. "I thought maybe you could check on Mom during the day when I'm at work, and I'll come by in the evenings."

"I can't," Hailey said. Kassidy gritted her teeth. "I'm really busy all next week."

"Doing what?" Kassidy sat in her parked car, staring at the doors of the garage painted the same taupe color as the house.

"I'm just busy," Hailey said, an edge in her voice.

Kassidy felt like flinging the phone against the garage. "Fine," she said tightly, getting out of the car and slamming the door shut. "Whatever." She snapped her phone shut and stalked into the house.

Inside the foyer, she took a deep breath before facing her mom and dad. Her hands trembled and she tried to control them as she dropped her phone into her purse then moved into the house.

"Hello!" she called. "It's me, Kassidy."

She walked into the den and found her dad sitting in a chair beside the bed, both of them watching television. Her mom looked a little better but still bashed up and pale.

"Kassidy," Mom said with a faint smile. "Hi."

"Hi, Mom." Kassidy approached the bed with a smile and smoothed her mom's hair back. "How are you doing?"

She visited with her mom for a while then threw in a load of laundry for her dad. He could do laundry, but he didn't like to, and he needed clothes for his business trip. Kassidy took inventory in the kitchen for easy meals her dad could make, but didn't find much, so she made a list and then went to the grocery store. She unloaded groceries, made two big pans of lasagna and slid them into the oven to bake. She'd take home one of them for Dag and Chris and her.

"You're such a good girl," her mom said later, her voice blurry from pain meds. "Thank you, Kassie."

She was the good girl. Always the good girl. Except for the naughty threesome she had going on in her bedroom with two men. Her stomach clenched at the thought. What would her mom think if she knew about that? About how bad Kassidy was really being. Kassidy sucked her bottom lip in briefly.

What she was doing with Dag and Chris wasn't hurting anyone. It wasn't as if she were doing something deliberately bad to someone else—breaking a law or harming anyone.

Although a glimmer of concern did hover in the back of her mind about where this was all going and the fact that, hell yeah, someone could definitely get hurt by what they were doing. She just wasn't sure who it was going to be.

She pasted on another smile for her mom. "Dad says you'll be okay tomorrow, so I'll come back Monday when he's gone."

"Don't you have to work?"

"We have some family days we can use for things like this."

The small knot in her stomach tightened at the thought of

the project at work she needed to work on, but she had a plan—she'd stop by in the morning, make sure Mom had everything she needed, get to work, do a few things and gather up some work she could do at home, then come back and stay with her mom for the rest of the day. It would only be a few days and then Dad would be back, and Mom would be able to get up and around on her crutches a bit more, hopefully.

So that's what she did, but Tuesday night she'd done all she could do on the project away from the office and she was stressing about how she was going to get her tasks done by deadline and still look after her mom.

"God, I wish I could help," Chris said, shoving a hand through his hair. "But I'm swamped myself."

"It's those layoffs, isn't it?"

The company was moving forward with outsourcing. Working in Human Resources she knew all about it, but she didn't like it—cutting staff was never a good thing—and she knew Chris didn't either, but didn't have much choice.

"Yeah." He sighed. "Fuck. I'm in meetings all day and I might even have to fly to Seattle this week."

"Oh no." She stared at him in dismay. "Not now."

"I hope not. I'll try to avoid it."

"I'll go check on your mom," Dag spoke up, and both Kassidy and Chris turned to him in surprise. One corner of his mouth tilted up. "What? So she doesn't know me. I feel like a useless piece of shit sitting here while you two run yourselves ragged."

"I'm okay," Kassidy said automatically. "You don't have to do that."

"I know I don't have to, I want to," he replied evenly. "Come with me in the morning to introduce me and I'll stay with her for a while and you can go to work."

"Don't you have meetings tomorrow?" Dag had been busy all week too, with seemingly back-to-back meetings and constant phone calls and emails on his BlackBerry. He'd worked most evenings, too, and Kassidy had come to realize that contrary to her impression about him having everything dropped into his lap with no effort, Dag was as much as a workaholic as Chris was. Maybe more. He seemed driven to turn this idea he had into reality.

"Not until four o'clock. You can come after work and that should cover things pretty well."

"Yeah. She can be alone for a couple of hours." She nibbled her bottom lip and regarded him. "Thank you, Dag."

"Thanks, man." Chris laid a hand on Dag's shoulder. Dag looked up at Chris, and Kassidy saw a flash of something in Dag's eyes, something...disturbing. Dag looked at Chris as if he wanted to eat him.

She swallowed and blinked, but the hunger was gone and Dag just smiled easily. "No sweat, man," he said. "Anytime."

So the next morning Kassidy led Dag into her parents' home and introduced him to her mom. Predictably, her mom protested that she didn't need someone with her all day and she certainly couldn't impose on someone she didn't even know.

"It's no trouble, Mrs. Langdon," Dag said, with his devilish charming smile, and Kassidy watched her mom soften at his irresistible appeal.

"Call me Hope," she said. "I feel terrible about this. I'm sure you're a busy young man..."

"I may have to take a few calls," Dag said, smiling. "And I've got my computer to keep me busy with some work, but otherwise I'm yours for the rest of the day. I'm looking forward to knowing all about Kassidy's childhood. I want to hear all the stories about what kind of bratty kid she was."

Hope laughed. "Sorry, there aren't any stories like that. Kassidy was a perfect angel."

"There must be something." His dimples deepened and Kassidy shook her head.

"Don't tell him, Mom," she said, smiling. "He'll hold it against me."

Her eyes and Dag's met above the bed and heat sizzled for a few seconds.

"I wouldn't hold that against you," he said softly, and she knew exactly where his mind was and what he would hold against her. And her insides softened and warmed.

"I better go," she said hastily, picking up her purse. "Thank you again, Dag, and just call my cell phone if you need anything."

What would her mother tell him? God. Once again, she didn't want Dag to think she was a boring goody-two-shoes, although at this point he had to have a fairly good idea that she was definitely no angel.

Chapter Twelve

"You should just stay with us," Chris said, then clenched his jaw. Fuck. Where the hell had that come from?

Dag laughed as if it were a joke. They were in the kitchen making dinner. Kassidy had gone over to her mom's place after work, just for a quick check in, and Dag had had the idea to make dinner for her. A damn good idea, Chris had to admit, ashamed he hadn't thought of it himself. Kassidy was running herself to pieces between her mom and her work since the accident two weeks ago.

"Seriously," he said, stirring the pot of pasta. "I mean, you've been in Chicago for nearly a month. You're spending a fucking fortune for a hotel room and you're hardly ever there." He didn't look at Dag. His stomach tightened into hard knots.

Since that night when Kassidy had—Christ, what had she done? Sucked them both? Pulled them close and rubbed their cocks together? Yeah, that and a whole lot more. Since then, Chris had found his head swimming with sizzling images, his body responding with heat and hardness. He tried to get those pictures out of his mind, the vision of his cock and Dag's together seared into his senses. The feel of Dag's cock against his, so goddamn wrong. So goddamn hot.

Dag nodded slowly. "Yeah. I guess that's true. But what does Kassidy think about that?"

"She'll be fine with it." Chris was sure of that. He hadn't talked to her about it, but he knew she'd be okay with it. What he didn't know was why the hell he was even suggesting it. Was he sick? Was he asking for something? Was he daring himself to see what he'd do with Dag around all the time?

"Well...okay. I do seem to end up here most of the time. Not sure how much longer I'll be in town."

Chris didn't know whether to laugh or curse. He struggled for composure. "I thought maybe you were thinking of moving back to Chicago. Permanently."

Dag's face, too, stayed neutral. His wrist twisted as he opened a can of tomatoes. "I haven't decided that."

"Yeah. Okay." Chris rubbed the back of his neck. "Well, tomorrow you can get your stuff and bring it back here."

The sound of the door opening had him lifting his head.

"I'm home!" Kassidy called. She appeared in the kitchen doorway, sniffing. "God, that smells good! Garlic! What are you doing?"

"Making you dinner. Hey, sweetheart." Chris moved over to kiss her forehead, almost feeling relieved she was home.

"How's your mom?" Dag asked.

"Doing okay. Still in a lot of pain." Kassidy rubbed between her eyebrows and sighed.

"You look tired," Chris said. "Go change and I'll pour you a glass of wine. Dinner's almost ready."

"That is so nice." She surveyed the kitchen. "Thanks." And she disappeared again, returning moments later dressed in a pair of beige shorts and a white T-shirt. She accepted the glass of Chardonnay from him with a smile.

"I can't believe you guys are cooking."

"Gotta give Dag the credit." Chris circled his hand around

the nape of her neck and stroked. She felt tight beneath her soft skin, the downy hair at the nape of her neck tickling his palm. This had been a rough couple of weeks. "But I helped." He grinned and took a swallow of his beer. "You've been running your ass off trying to look after your mom and stay on top of things at work. Thank god I didn't have to go to Seattle. And thank god Dag was here to help out too. Thanks again, man." He turned to his friend. Yeah, he was glad Dag was back. Then he remembered.

"Hey, guess what? Dag's going to stay with us," he told Kassidy. "He's paying a fortune for that hotel room and he's never there, so I suggested he just come stay with us while he's here."

She blinked at him. Said nothing. Her silence unnerved him.

"What?" he asked. Her lips tightened. "What's wrong with that?"

"Nothing's wrong with that." But her clipped words told a different story. Shit. He'd been sure she wouldn't mind. He shot a glance at Dag to see if he'd picked up the tension. His frown told him, hell yeah, he had. Again, shit.

Chris debated with himself whether to push her right then and there, get it out in the open, or wait and have the fight in private. He sighed. Drank his beer. He was screwed.

Dag, the perceptive son of a bitch, chose that moment to go to the bathroom. "Dinner should be ready when I'm back," he said as he walked down the hall.

Chris turned to Kassidy. "Hey, sweetie. I didn't think you'd mind if I invited him to stay with us. He practically is, anyway." He regarded her hopefully. His gut clenched.

"It's not that," she hissed, moving closer. "It's just...you should have asked me first. This is my place too."

"Yeah, I know. But like I said..."

"That's not the point! The point is, you need to talk to me before you do stuff like that. We live together now, we make decisions like that together."

"Um...yeah. Okay. I get it." *Sort of. Not. Women.* Again, he blew out a long breath, but when her eyes narrowed, he realized he'd probably come across as pissed off and long-suffering. Okay. He was digging himself into a hole here tonight, despite the cooking of dinner. "I'm sorry, sweetheart. I wasn't thinking. Really. I won't do it again."

Except he probably would, because his logic didn't match with her logic on this. Okay, yeah, he got that he needed to talk to her first about things, but what difference did it make if in the end she agreed? Hell, this was going nowhere fast.

Dag returned and they ate dinner, the atmosphere at the table just slightly less chilly than the wine they drank.

"Okay, what's wrong?" Dag finally asked, sitting back in his chair and crossing his arms across his chest.

Chris and Kassidy exchanged a glance.

"Nothing," Chris said.

"Nothing," Kassidy said.

"Bullshit. Kassidy, are you pissed off that I'm going to stay here?"

"No."

Chris watched now as the two of them shared a look. Maybe she wouldn't be so pissy with Dag.

"I'm mad because nobody asked me," she finally said, and her bottom lip jutted out just a little in a very cute pout. "That's all."

"I said I'm sorry," Chris began.

"Yeah," Dag said. "I was afraid of that. Sorry, Kass. I should

141

have made him ask you first. Before I agreed."

"It's not your fault," she said.

Chris pursed his lips. Apparently it was all his fault.

"You deserve the respect of being asked, at least," Dag said. "Are sure you're okay with it? Because I haven't checked out of the hotel or anything yet. We can just keep going the way we have been."

Her eyes got kind of hazy looking as she thought about something, and Chris wished he knew what the hell it was.

"No," she said with a sigh. "Really. It does make sense." She looked at Chris.

"See?" he said. "That's what I said—"

"Chris!" She stared at him. "You are so damn stubborn! Would you just admit you screwed up?"

He pressed his lips together and took a deep breath. "I apologized—"

"But you didn't even get why!"

She was killing him, and in front of Dag no less, but hey, if Dag was moving in, he was going to see it all, including him making a fool of himself over a woman. So be it. "Fine," he said shortly. "I screwed up. I should have asked you. The fact that you agreed is beside the point."

"Exactly. Thank you." She beamed at him then at Dag. Chris shook his head, but something inside him relaxed and softened. Christ. He loved her. He didn't want her pissed off at him. Much as he hated to admit to making a mistake, goddammit, it was better than living in a deep freeze.

"Double penetration."

Kassidy peered at Chris, her hair a tangled mess in front of her eyes, having just spent the last half hour rolling around in bed with two naked men. Her lips throbbed from all the kissing and sucking and biting. Her pussy ached. She blinked at him.

Dag's hand stroked down her back and over her bottom, lingering there.

Oh dear god.

"Double penetration," Chris said again, voice low and husky. He touched her bottom lip with his fingertips. "Dag and I fucking you at the same time."

Her eyes widened, her pussy clenched. Dag's fingers teased the crease between her cheeks. She looked at him over her shoulder, stretched out naked on the bed. His eyes met hers. His fingers played—up, down, lower into her wetness, trailing a line of her own moisture back up. He tickled the base of her spine and she shivered.

"We've never...uh...done that," she whispered. Her buttocks clenched at Dag's caressing fingertips. Anal sex was beyond her experience...but she supposed not theirs. She licked her lips.

"We'll make it good for you, sweetheart," Chris said, kissing her shoulder. "I'll do your ass. Dag's too big for your first time."

Her womb spasmed. She swallowed hard.

"We'll get you nice and ready," Dag said, still playing there. "You're already so wet..." Again, he trailed moisture up between her cheeks, this time his finger pushing deeper between her flesh, stroking over her anus with a firmer touch. She quivered.

Chris slipped a hand down between her legs and played there too, him from the front, Dag from the back. Chris leaned forward to suck on a nipple, Dag dragged his tongue up her back between her shoulder blades.

Dag reached for a bottle of lube sitting on the table beside the bed. He opened it and squeezed some out onto his fingers then handed it to Chris. Dag's slick fingers probed, brushing over her hole again and again until she felt herself softening there, just a little, and his fingertip pushed inside her. A small cry fell from her lips at the unfamiliar sensation.

"It's okay," Dag whispered, his mouth against the back of her shoulder. He licked her there, kissed her, withdrew his finger then pushed back in. Slowly. Her body adjusted to the intrusion, heat blooming there, spreading through her body.

Chris's fingers pushed inside her too, into her vagina, and she felt his and Dag's hands collide as they worked her. Dag lifted her thigh, opening her more to them. They owned her body, the two of them, knew it, worshiped it, owned it. And she loved it.

"I think she's ready," Dag murmured. "How do you want to do this?"

"You lie down," Chris said, ever the director. "Kassidy, you get on top of him."

After rolling on a condom, Dag stretched out and lifted Kassidy over him, hands on her hips. In a heated daze, she found his thick cock and held it as she lowered herself onto it. His size still amazed her, stretched her, filled her. When she'd worked herself down onto him, all the way, breathless and hot, Chris's hand on her back urged her forward and she lay down on Dag's chest.

He found her mouth and kissed her, long, wet kisses, while Chris now played with her ass from behind, kissing her, parting her cheeks, drizzling lube. "Relax," he said. "Relax, sweetheart."

"Don't clench," Dag whispered against her mouth.

"I can't relax," she whispered, her whole body tight and shivering. "I'm afraid..." She wanted to do it, but she was afraid it was going to hurt and she'd disappoint them if she couldn't.

144

Dag stroked his hands up and down her back, fisted her hair, kissed her again. She felt the nudge of Chris's cock at her anus, just pressing there and holding, not entering her yet. He rubbed a bit, sending a cascade of sensations over her body. Who knew all those nerve endings could be a source of such intense pleasure?

And then, one hand on her hip, he did push into her. She gave a sharp cry at the fiery sting. Her whole body tightened. Chris didn't move, Dag pulsed inside her. "Okay?" Chris asked.

"It hurts," she whispered, tears gathering in her eyes. "I want to, but..."

"Take it slow," Dag said, stroking her hair.

None of them moved for long moments, hearts pounding, breath catching. She knew it must be hard for both of them to do that, and she willed her body to relax. She took a deep breath and buried her face against the side of Dag's neck. "Okay," she said moments later.

Chris pushed in a little farther and she jolted again, flames licking around her ass.

"Bear down," Dag whispered in her ear. "Don't try to tighten on him."

She did what he said, and amazingly Chris slid in farther. Sensation exploded through her body, heat and light, wild and fiery. She cried out again. "I'm okay, I'm okay," she babbled. She bit her lip, kept her face hidden, felt perspiration run down the side of Dag's neck. She licked him there, warm and salty. He shuddered.

The wicked sensation of being filled by two men had fire streaking through her body, lighting up every nerve ending. She let out a long, deep groan of pleasure.

They began to move in her, finding a rhythm together, their cocks stroking not only her but each other, reminding her of the night she'd done that to them, that shockingly forbidden act that had brought them to orgasm so fast she knew they'd liked it, whether they'd wanted to admit it or not. She remembered how they'd leaned their heads together, how they'd clasped each other's shoulders, their cocks joined in her hands, and her tummy did that flip of excitement. That had been a moment of togetherness she hadn't felt in all their threesome encounters, where the two men had displayed some affection for each other as well as her. Could they feel each other inside her? They had to.

Her body burned, sensations sizzling over her flesh, a swirling pleasure inside her coiling up and building. It scared her, the intensity of it—she was afraid her body was literally going to explode with it, it was so huge and ferocious, so all-encompassing, taking over her and lifting her out of herself. She floated and flew, her body surrounded by an edgy shimmer of heat.

Four hands moved on her, two mouths, as Chris bent over to kiss her back, both of them thrusting into her in hard strokes, taking her body, taking her heart, taking her soul. When she did explode, she came apart, crying out over and over again, the sensations so sharply exquisite it was almost beyond bearing.

"Fuck," Chris muttered, fingers digging into her hips. "Dag? You close?"

"Yeah." The word was dragged out of him. His hands tightened in her hair, his hips moving beneath her. "Yeah...fuck...now...aw, Christ."

With matching tortured groans, they came inside her, Chris flooding her ass with his hot come, and she couldn't stop herself from crying out again. "God, oh god, oh god."

They collapsed into a sweaty heap of bodies, gasping for

breath, hearts thundering. All Kassidy knew was sensation, an erotic haze of dazzling pleasure.

They slept for a while, dozing lazily, then Chris disappeared into the bathroom to wash up, and came back with a warm wet cloth that he used to clean her. He'd never done that before, clean her up after sex, and the tenderness of the gesture made her insides go all soft, especially as Dag held her and gave her soft little kisses on her mouth, her cheek, her eyelids while Chris washed her. She felt so incredibly cherished and loved.

When she floated up from sleep a while later, the lamp still on, she studied both men—Chris's light brown hair streaked with gold, his lightly tanned skin, faint shadow of beard and his big, muscled shoulders revealed by the sheets halfway down his back; and Dag's sweep of silky dark hair across his forehead, his complexion swarthier, his beard heavier and darker in that bad-boy way. Her chest constricted—and then fear grabbed hold of her in a tight grip.

What was she afraid of?

She closed her eyes, fighting a wave of panic, wrestling with the urge to scramble out from under the covers and get the hell out of the bed. What had she done? What had they done?

She tried to breathe, slowly, filling her lungs, letting it out little by little. This had all been sexy and fun, but what they'd done had been so erotically intimate, she couldn't help but be affected by it. Emotions rose inside her, a fierce, almost angry rush of intense affection—for both of them—including Dag.

She couldn't feel that way about another man. She was in love with Chris. Since the day they'd met, attraction had deepened into lust and like and then into love. He was everything she wanted. So how could she be feeling this for Dag? Feeling...what felt like...love. A different love, because he was a different man, but no less powerful.

147

Tears burned her eyes and she covered her face with her hands.

"Hey." Chris pulled her hands away from her face and rose above her, concern etching his forehead into furrows. "What's wrong, sweetie? Did we hurt you?"

"No." She rolled her head on the pillow and realized Dag was awake too as his hand came to settle on her tummy. "I'm fine. Just feeling...god, I don't know what I'm feeling. Overwhelmed."

The touch of their hands on her spoke only of tenderness and respect and affection—and made her chest expand and swell with the same feelings for them, and a longing to show them how she felt even if she didn't understand it herself. She wanted Chris to know she loved him—he had to know she loved him, despite the confusion she was experiencing. But she also wanted Dag to know she cared too, because even though he was a tough bad boy who apparently didn't need anyone, she couldn't bear the thought of him feeling excluded, extraneous, unwanted.

Once again, she faced the dilemma of how to please two men at the same time. Last night they'd taken care of her, worshipped her, both of them at the same time, and today she wanted to do that for them. Faced with too many choices, she rolled over and climbed over Dag, kissing his chest, rubbing her cheek against the hair there, nibbling at his nipples. He jerked when she did that, encouraging her to do more.

"Oh sweetheart," he groaned. So she licked and sucked there, and Chris got the hint and moved behind her. He stroked her butt with gentle hands.

"You sore, babe?" he asked, voice husky.

"A little." She lifted her head to look at him over her shoulder, letting the invitation show in her eyes. "But I'm okay."

She gave one last nip to Dag's flat brown nipple then scooted down his body to take him in her mouth. She pushed his thighs wide with an urge to explore him, all of him, and her fingers found his tight balls, stroked over the soft flesh, lightly furred, tugged experimentally. She got another low groan, so her fingers continued playing as her mouth tasted him.

"Fuck me, Chris," she said, long moments later. "While I suck on Dag."

"Oh yeah."

She let her fingers wander lower, behind Dag's balls, and to her surprise, Dag lifted his hips to let her. She stroked around the puckered hole of his anus, remembering the sensations that had evoked in her last night. Was it as pleasurable for him? She hesitated, because once she'd tried this with Chris and he'd immediately stopped her from touching him there. She guessed some men didn't like it, but Dag seemed to...love it. In fact, he pulled his legs back even farther.

"Yeah, baby, oh yeah..." His next words shocked her. "Lick me there. Lick my balls..." And when she did... "Fuck! Oh yeah!"

She dragged her tongue over the loose skin, felt the solid roundness inside, sucked one into her mouth and let it pop out. God, oh god, she loved doing this! She sucked his other testicle, then held his cock up, pushed his balls up too, and licked the taut skin below, inhaling the musky male scent of him there in that most intimate of places. Daringly she kissed his ass cheeks with nibbling kisses and then firmer sucks.

His moans of pleasure, his muttered words of encouragement drove her on and she buried her face there, licking and sucking while Chris entered her from behind. She was so wet he slid inside easily even though her flesh was still swollen and tender. She wished Chris would let her do this,

149

because it felt so good, tasted so good, felt so absolutely giving and caring.

She licked her way back up and took Dag in her mouth, as far as she could anyway, he was so broad and heavy, but she continued to play with his ass with her fingers, daringly even inserting the tip of one finger into his hole. He gasped then groaned with pleasure, and her fingers moved in and out in small thrusts as she sucked him.

Chris filled her from behind, in the position she loved because of the deeper angle, the spot that he hit with every pounding stroke that lit her up inside and started the shimmering glow, the faint buzz of an orgasm beginning. Everything inside her tightened and then she lost her rhythm, her focus, too much to keep fucking Dag's ass with her finger while she sucked him, she just couldn't do it. Her orgasm exploded in her womb, sensation bursting through her body over every nerve ending, leaving her limp and breathless. Then Chris came too, holding her hips against him as he erupted inside her. "Kassidy, god, Kass, you feel good."

When she could, she took Dag in her mouth again, holding her hand tight at the base of his cock, resuming her fingering of his ass, and sucked on him with greedy recklessness.

"Deeper..." Dag grunted, hips lifting. "Just a little...with your finger...deeper...yeah, oh yeah, right there. Jesus!" Then he too spurted, into her mouth, hot and tangy on the back of her tongue.

Chris held his weight off her until she released Dag. Did he know what she was doing to Dag with her fingers? The naughty act thrilled her to her core, and she wished Chris had seen it. Then Chris collapsed over her, rolling her to Dag's side, once again the three of them a sweaty satisfied pile of bodies.

Chapter Thirteen

For the first time, Dag felt like he belonged there in Chris and Kassidy's bed. He'd moved his stuff from the hotel to their place the day before, and when they'd all drifted off into exhausted, sated sleep, it felt good to know he had nowhere else to be. Just there. With them.

In the morning, he recognized how dangerous those thoughts were. What the fuck was he doing? Why had he agreed to stay with them? This was getting so much deeper than he'd even contemplated, but ultimately where could it go?

No fucking where. That's where. His gut cramped as he lay there, gradually rising to wakefulness from the depths of sleep. Chris and Kassidy continued to sleep, Kassidy between them as usual.

Yet it felt like somewhere. It felt like home.

Confusion twisted inside him. He had to start being honest with himself about what he wanted. Coming back to Chicago had been all about Chris—seeing him again, finding out if things had changed. Instead, he'd found Chris in a serious relationship with a woman, which had told him—no, things hadn't changed.

And yet, Dag found himself changing. Yeah, his feelings for Chris were still there. Dammit. Still big and powerful and completely beyond reach. But Kassidy was within reach. And, as in the past, if he could be with Chris as long as he was with someone else too, he'd take it. Except he hadn't counted on the feelings for Kassidy he'd developed.

Her sweetness and compassion pulled at him. Her acceptance of him and even, mind bogglingly, her willingness to let him into their bed.

It wasn't what he'd planned. He hadn't even imagined this happening.

Kassidy stirred beside him, and once again, she and Dag were awake in the bed before Chris. When she saw he was awake, she turned into his arms and snuggled into him. He wrapped her up, held on to her, last night having been a pinnacle of both joy and self-deception for him. Because he hadn't just been fucking Kassidy—he'd been fucking Chris too.

Feeling Chris move inside Kassidy, their bodies moving together like they were fucking each other with her between them, had almost made Dag's heart explode. The joy he'd experienced had been amplified at seeing the pleasure on Chris's face, but it had been ramped up times ten seeing Kassidy's ecstasy too.

Kassidy's hand curled around his shoulder, their legs entwined, and Dag's heart turned over in his chest as he realized just how much he'd come to care for this woman.

Now not only did he have to leave Chris behind when he eventually left, but her too. How the hell was he going to survive that?

He wasn't one for commitment. He liked moving on—to the next new adventure, the next thrill, the next challenge. There was no way in hell he could be thinking about something long term, with anybody, never mind with both Chris *and* Kassidy. He felt like fingers had wrapped around his throat and were squeezing, and he forced his muscles to relax. Kassidy lifted her head and looked up at him as if sensing his discomfort.

"You might be sore today," he said in a low voice.

She smiled. "I might be. That's okay." Then she buried her face against his chest, and mumbled, "I can't believe we did that."

For a good girl, she'd been doing a lot of dirty things lately. Including what she'd done to him. He got the feeling she wasn't entirely at ease with all of this, despite the willingness with which she participated in their three-way sex. He stroked a hand up and down her smooth back.

"I...I..."

"Shh." He pushed her head back down, kept moving his hands over her. "It's okay, Kass."

They lay like that for a while, his hand moving down over the curve of her smooth little ass, back up and into her hair, and down again until her hips started moving against his thigh and he knew she was getting hot again. He lifted her chin and found her mouth, kissed her in long, lush kisses. She tried to press her pussy against him and he knew what she wanted. What she needed.

He reached out and gave Chris a smack on the shoulder. Because it had to be all three of them. "Wha...?" Chris mumbled, opening eyes blurry with sleep.

"Kassidy needs you," Dag said. "Wake up."

Chris lay there blinking, his mouth soft. "Jesus, man, I was sound asleep."

But they started playing, soft and slow, slumberous and lazy, with long, wet kisses, gentle touches and low sounds of pleasure. Dag drifted on a hum of arousal, in no hurry, just taking time to find all the places that made Kassidy sigh and quiver. He wanted to know them all, wanted to be able to please her, absorbing the scent of her, the sound of her pleasure and the feel of her skin soft and silky beneath his fingertips.

Until the doorbell rang.

His body went still.

"Jesus, who the hell is that?" Chris muttered against Kassidy's tummy. She groaned.

"Ignore it," Dag said, his tongue in her ear.

"Mmm."

But it rang again, and then Kassidy's cell phone buzzed on the dresser across the room.

"Oh, for..." She threw herself back onto the pillows and blew out a breath. "What if it's Dad? If something's wrong..."

"I'll go," Chris said, tossing back the covers. He swung his long legs out of bed, grabbed for a pair of boxers and pulled them on, half-hopping across the room, his hard-on making it difficult to pull them up. He cursed and disappeared out of the bedroom.

Kassidy bit her lip and looked at Dag. He smiled. "It's okay, baby." He stroked her hair off her face. "Don't worry, I'm sure it's nothing."

She cast a worried glance at the alarm clock. "It's almost noon," she said. "I didn't realize how late it is." The blinds on the window kept the room nice and dark for lazy late mornings. If they wanted to keep Chris, the morning man, in bed, they had to keep the room dark.

Voices carried from the door down the hall, Chris's and a feminine voice.

"Shit!" Kassidy sat bolt upright. "It's Hailey!"

Dag's brows shot up.

"What the hell's she doing here?" She started to scramble out of the sheets, but he grabbed her wrist.

154

"Chris'll get rid of her." He fucking better get rid of her.

"But, what if... I don't know why she's here." She turned her pretty face to him, squinting, mouth turned down.

He sighed. "Yeah. Go see."

She was just getting out of bed when he heard steps in the hall. He turned his head, expecting to see Chris telling her Hailey was there, but his heart slammed to a stop when he saw Kassidy's sister appear in the open door.

Just as Kassidy climbed naked from the bed in which he was lying, also naked.

Chapter Fourteen

Kassidy froze. Well, first she froze, icy and motionless. Then fiery heat swept over her naked body as she stared into her sister's eyes.

Hailey looked as shocked as she did. Chris appeared behind her, dressed in his plaid boxers, his hand in his hair, mouth open.

Hailey's eyes shifted to Dag, and Kassidy didn't even need to turn around to know exactly what she saw—his long, lean and very naked body only half covered by the sheets, his hair rumpled, his jaw morning sexy with a dark growth of beard.

Her heart crashed into a rapid beat. She opened her mouth but nothing came out. Chris pushed past Hailey and grabbed Kassidy's robe, strode toward her and shielded her from her sister, handing her the robe. She took it automatically, her face burning, breath coming in shallow little spurts.

"What the hell is going on here?" Hailey finally asked. She turned dark eyes to Chris with a long, appraising look, then back to Kassidy, and the corners of her mouth kicked up. "Kassidy. Well, well, well. I cannot believe this."

What could she say? Helplessly she tied the belt of the robe and looked at Chris, then back at Hailey. The words "it's not what it looks like" came to mind, but that was such a lame cliché and so patently untrue. It was totally what it looked like.

"Why are you here, Hailey?" Kassidy finally managed to get some words over her tight lips. "It's not like you to be out so early on a Sunday."

"Yeah. I know." She shrugged. "I came to see if you were going over to Mom and Dad's today. I'll go with you."

"Jesus. You could've called first."

"And missed this?" One eyebrow arched. "Are you kidding me?" She folded her arms across her chest and leaned against the doorframe, eyes moving over both male bodies.

"Hailey. This is..." She swallowed. "This is private."

"Oh yeah."

"I mean...don't tell anyone..." Oh god. "Especially Mom and Dad." She tried to keep the panic out of her voice because it never failed, if Hailey knew something was important to her, she didn't want her to have it, and if Hailey knew Kassidy didn't want her to do something, she'd do it for sure.

Please, Hailey, she begged inside her head.

She shrugged and straightened. "Are you going over there or not?"

"I actually wasn't planning to today."

"What? The good little daughter isn't going over to check on her injured mother?"

"I've been there almost every day for the last two weeks. Dad's there with her today; I think they can manage one day." Then she frowned. "What do you need me there for? Go over by yourself. You haven't even been once."

"Yeah." Hailey's eyes fell away from Kassidy's and her mocking smile disappeared. "I've been busy. I guess I'll do that."

Kassidy led Hailey out of the bedroom, with a roll of her eyes at Chris and Dag over her shoulder as she did so. She took her straight to the door.

"Not offering me coffee, even?" Hailey asked, amusement shading her voice. "I guess you're anxious to get back to...whatever the three of you were doing. In bed."

"Hailey." Kassidy's insides churned. "I..." Once again she didn't know what to say. She'd been caught. In the act. *Flagrante delicto*—was that the term? In a scandalous liaison with Chris and his best friend. She wanted to believe she didn't care what Hailey thought of her, and she'd wanted to be the bad girl for once, but the sad truth was, she was so invested in being the good girl that this threat to her pristine reputation threw her way off balance. "Please don't tell Mom and Dad."

Damn. She didn't want to say that again. She had a feeling that telling Hailey not to do that would send her straight to their house with shocking tales of their older daughter's sexual escapades.

Hailey just laughed. "See ya later, Kass."

And she was gone.

Kassidy stayed there in the foyer for a few long moments, head leaning on the wall. Visions of Hailey driving straight to Mom and Dad's, the shock and horror on their faces when she told them what she'd discovered, had her stomach heaving, her mind reeling, and oh hell, her body still pulsing with unsatisfied lust. But her hunger wasn't about to be slaked as she heard Dag and Chris behind her, and when she turned, they'd emerged from the bedroom fully dressed, both of them wearing identical sheepish expressions.

That mood had been killed.

She sighed. "Well, shit," she said.

Chris walked over to her and pulled her into his arms. "It's okay, Kass," he murmured.

"Who cares what she thinks?" Dag asked, although his eyes were shadowed. "It doesn't matter."

It didn't matter to Dag what people thought. He just did what he wanted, the rebel bad boy. But it mattered to her.

Although the idea that she'd shocked Hailey gave her just a tiny little triumphant thrill. "I just...even if I don't care what Hailey thinks about me, what about all the people she's going to tell? Mom and Dad will die." And she did care what they thought about her.

"She won't tell them," Dag said with confidence.

She looked at him. "Why do you say that? You don't know her. That's exactly the kind of thing she would do."

"It would hurt your parents more than it would hurt you," Dag replied, taking a step nearer to rub her shoulder.

"Except Hailey doesn't care about our parents," she said. "In fact, one of her goals in life is to make them miserable. And I doubt she cares that much about me, either."

"She can't be that bad."

He didn't know her. Kassidy took a deep breath. She wasn't sure she'd tell her parents, either, but the thought of it was enough to have her insides churning furiously.

"Well, there's nothing you can do," Chris said, always practical. "If she tells them, we'll deal with it. I'm with you, sweetheart, you know. If I have to face your parents and try to explain what's happening here, I will."

She regarded him with warm gratitude, knowing this had to be huge for him too. The one who always followed the rules and did what was right...if he had to face her parents and try to explain this all, he'd be dying. She tried to smile as she said, "Maybe you could explain it to me, first."

"Mom's accident changes what I wanted to do for their

anniversary," Kassidy told Chris later that night. "I wanted to have a party, but Mom's not up to it."

"When's the anniversary?"

"Next weekend." She sighed and pouted. Her sexy bottom lip made him want to suck on it. Jesus. All he thought about lately was sex. Living in a *ménage à trois* would do that to you, he guessed.

"You could just wait. Do something when she's better."

"I suppose." The bottom lip came out farther.

"How long have they been married?" Dag asked.

"Thirty years."

"Wow."

"I know. Amazing, huh? We did a big party for their twenty-fifth. Hailey doesn't even want to be involved, so…I don't know." She paused, clearly thinking about what had happened that morning. Her pout turned into a thin-lipped grimace. Chris's chest tightened, remembering how upset she'd been. He'd been pissed off at himself that he hadn't grabbed Hailey and physically stopped her from walking right in. He'd never thought she would go all the way to their bedroom door when he'd told her Kassidy was still in bed. The fact that she'd upset Kassidy made him want to kick Hailey's ass. And not for the first time.

Kassidy sighed again. "Maybe we could just go over there and do a nice dinner for them."

"Seafood on the barbecue," Chris suggested.

"Yeah. That sounds good. I should call Dad and see what he thinks."

Her hand hovered over the phone and he knew what she was thinking—had Hailey said anything to her parents? How would this phone conversation go? Then she picked up the phone and Chris listened to her side of the conversation along with the baseball game on the television, his muscles tightening. Dag sprawled in a chair across from him, looking relaxed and all at home, his stuff in the spare room, but Chris noticed Dag's fingers tapping against the arm of the chair, the slight tightness of his mouth.

"He says that's fine." Kassidy set the phone on the table beside the couch. She swallowed and sank back into the couch, closing her eyes briefly. "He says not to invite lots of people though, Mom's still really tired all the time. Still in quite a bit of pain."

"Just us then," Chris said, muscles relaxing.

"I guess I'll invite Hailey too."

Chris reached for her hand and squeezed it. "I'm sorry, Kass," he said. "I should have tried harder to stop her from walking in like that."

"It's okay."

But it wasn't. She was obviously disturbed by it and had been distracted all day. Was she going to have second thoughts about what they were doing? Chris cast a glance at Dag. He too watched Kassidy with a faint frown.

She blinked and met Chris's eyes. He smiled at her. "I love you, Kass."

She huffed out a breath, almost a laugh. "I love you too." Chris tugged her into his arms, and then remembered Dag sitting across from them. When he lifted his eyes to his friend, the look on Dag's face had Chris's gut clenching. Hell. Yeah, he and Kassidy were a couple. Dag was their third. The intense longing in Dag's eyes caught at Chris and made him wonder. Maybe they were headed for trouble doing this. Maybe it was a huge fucking mistake. It might be short-term gain for long-term pain. It might be instant gratification...but delayed suffering.

But as usual, he had no problem pushing away troubling thoughts to the backside of his brain, and all three of them slept together that night, and every night that week.

Thursday was Chris's turn for stress at work. He'd had to personally tell five people they were losing their jobs.

On the drive home, he was stubbornly silent, not wanting to talk about it, Kassidy's sideways glances swiping over him, her frustration at his bad mood palpable.

He disappeared into the bedroom to change without a word, shedding his clothes. When he went to walk into their closet, he nearly tripped over a pair of high-heeled pumps. Jesus, she had too many fucking shoes. He kicked the shoes out of his way, sending them flying into the back of the closet.

He changed into a pair of baggy shorts and a ratty old T-shirt, emerged from the bedroom to see Kassidy and Dag watching him cautiously.

"What?" he snapped, crossing the living room to the kitchen to search out a beer.

He saw them exchange serious eye contact.

"You okay, man?" Dag asked.

"Yeah, I'm okay. I like firing people."

He yanked open the fridge door and stared inside, searching with his eyes. "Don't we have any goddamn beer?" He lifted a head to glare at Dag.

"I...uh...mighta drank the last one."

"Shit." He slammed the door shut.

"Chris." Kassidy's soft voice held a note of censure that pissed him off even more.

He ran a hand through his hair. Blew out a breath.

"What do you want to do?" Dag asked.

One corner of Chris's mouth pushed in. "What do you mean?"

Dag hitched a shoulder, leaned against the kitchen counter. "I mean, d'you wanna go out and get a beer? Something to eat? Shoot some pool? Punch a bag?"

Chris stared back at him. "Yeah. Hell yeah," he said slowly. "Punching a bag sounds good." He hadn't been to the gym in a couple of weeks. He eyed Dag. How'd Dag remember he used to do that all the time? More importantly, how'd he know that was exactly what Chris needed right then?

Dag grinned. "Better than using us as a punching bag." He straightened. "Come on. Let's go. I assume you have a gym membership somewhere."

"Yeah. Double Tiger Kickboxing."

Dag lifted a brow. "Martial arts?"

"Yeah, but they have equipment there too."

Chris looked at Kassidy. Her head tipped to one side and she gave him a wry smile. "Go on," she said. "If that's what you want to do."

Taking out his frustrations with some intense physical activity was exactly what he needed. And maybe some sex. They could do that later. He grinned, already feeling better, and slung an arm around Dag's neck.

"Okay, buddy, let's go see what you got."

"You can buy me a beer after."

"Ha! You're the one who's loaded. You'll buy the beer."

While they punched and kicked the crap out of a couple of bags, Chris told Dag in between panting breaths about his shitty day, about the guy who'd told him to fuck off and die

163

when he'd told him he was being turned loose, and the other one who'd cried. Dag didn't say much, just listened, and Chris liked that. They picked up fried chicken and beer on the way home, which Kassidy shared with them, and then the three of them had hot, intensely physical sex.

It was good.

Kassidy worked up her nerve and called Hailey about the party she was planning for Saturday. Hailey said nothing about what she'd interrupted the weekend before and sounded like she actually might come to the anniversary celebration.

Friday night Kassidy went shopping for the food. The only good thing about Hailey catching them like that was that she'd completely distracted Kassidy from the troubling feelings she'd been struggling with. Focusing on the shopping she had to do was another welcome distraction, but as she pushed the cart up and down the aisle in the grocery shop she felt a weird out-of-body sensation, as if she were a different person, living a different life, a life that had changed stunningly. When people looked at her, they had no idea what kind of kinky sex life she was leading. That old lady with the thinning white hair and bright red lipstick smiling at her—no idea. The girl with the ring piercing the middle of her nose—*eew*—and thick black eyeliner looked at her and saw an ordinary mid-twenties woman dressed in boring shorts and T-shirt shopping for boring groceries—and had no idea.

She walked in the door of the condo, home sooner than she'd expected to be, and heard sounds from the television in the living room. The guys were no doubt watching sports— again.

She smiled as she dropped the bags to the floor and walked

in. The guys. Her guys. Weird.

The living room was nearly dark and apparently they hadn't heard her come in because the image on the big screen television had her stopping short. A naked woman was centered between two men, holding two erect cocks. They were watching porn!

Kassidy's mouth dropped open and she stared at the TV. She blinked. "Uh...what are you guys doing?" she finally asked. They both jumped, seated side by side on the couch. The guilty look on their faces almost made her laugh, but she could also see they both had hard-ons and flushed cheeks.

What had she interrupted?

She swallowed.

"Kassidy." Chris jumped to his feet and Dag reached for the remote. "You're home already."

She walked in farther, the groceries forgotten, her gaze riveted to the screen. "What are you watching?"

"Uh..." Dag fumbled to stop the movie.

"No, no, don't stop it," she said. "I want to see this."

"Kassidy..." Chris followed her to the couch where she lowered herself beside Dag. She sent him an amused glance. "Geez, you guys. You aren't getting enough kinky sex, you need to watch porn movies?"

"No, uh..."

They both seemed at a loss for words. Kassidy leaned back to watch, intrigued—maybe a little aroused—by the explicit images. Did they think she'd be pissed off? She wasn't that much of a prude. Surely they knew that.

Chris lowered himself to the couch beside her. She wanted to reach over and feel the erections inside their jeans, but just as she was about to do that, the scene changed and another woman joined the threesome on-screen. Another woman who looked familiar...

Holy shit!

It was Hailey.

Chapter Fifteen

Kassidy sat forward, eyes huge, and watched as her sister began removing clothing. "Oh my god!" She slapped her hands over her eyes and bent forward. "Turn it off, turn it off!"

"Jesus fucking Christ."

The movie kept rolling amid a thick silence in the living room. Kassidy peeked at Dag between her fingers and saw him staring open mouthed at the television. She grabbed for the remote and he let her take it. She prodded around for the power button and the television went dark.

The only sound was their breathing, all three of them dragging air into lungs stiffened with shock.

"That couldn't be my sister," she finally managed to choke out.

"Uh..." Again Chris had no words. "It sort of looked like her."

She had to see it again. To convince herself. Because it was just too mind-blowing. But she did not want to watch her sister naked and having sex.

"You look." She handed the remote to Chris then snatched it back. "No, you look." She passed it to Dag. They exchanged a look.

"Kassidy..."

"Please. Just make sure it's her. So when I go kick her ass I'm not doing it for nothing."

Dag clicked on the television, and the pay-per-view movie resumed. She stared at her feet on the carpet, her chest tight, stomach clenched as she heard Hailey's voice moaning and saying, "Oh yeah, fuck me harder."

She wanted to cry. Hailey was having sex with strangers for money. It was the lowest low she could have fallen to, and even though she disapproved of many things about Hailey's life, she would never have imagined that she would do something like this.

"It's her, isn't it?" She still focused on her pink toenails.

"Yup." Chris and Dag both said it at the same time, and Dag stopped the movie again.

"Oh my god. How could she do that?"

"It's not the end of the world," Dag said, voice rough.

She made a strangled sound in her throat and covered her face again.

"You don't think she's wondering that same thing about you, right now?" Dag asked quietly.

Her head shot up and she glared at him.

"I'm just saying..."

"That is entirely different than what we're doing!" she snapped at him.

"Kassidy." Chris rubbed her arm. "It's okay."

"It's not okay! That's my sister! My sister the porn star! God! No wonder she has money all the time. I could never figure out..." Her voice trailed off. "Oh, this is awful. My parents..."

"You're not going to tell them." Chris's voice held a note of authority. She turned to look at him. He shook his head. "No. You're not."

"But..."

"You don't want her to tell them about us."

She stared at him. Then she started laughing. "Well. This is funny."

"Har," Dag said. She shot him a frosty glance.

Why was she angry at both of them? This wasn't their fault. They'd just been watching a dirty movie and had no idea it was going to turn out like this. She sighed and pressed shaky fingers to her eyes. "I can't believe this."

Was Hailey wondering that about her? Was there a difference between what Hailey was doing and what she was doing? Her mind spun all over the place, her stomach tight and hurting.

That night when the three of them went to bed, Kassidy didn't want to have sex.

Kassidy and Chris were about to leave for her parents' place, their car loaded up with food and drink, when Kassidy turned to Dag where he slouched on the sofa and said, "Are you ready?"

"Ready for what?"

"To leave. For the party." She grimaced. "Such as it is."

"Uh...I didn't plan to go."

Her eyes widened. "Why not?"

"It's your family, Kassidy. And I'm not family."

She stared at him, lips parted. "But...yes, you are."

Whatever their relationship was, it wasn't family. It was weird, unconventional, even kinky—but not family.

"You have to come," she said, her eyebrows meeting over

her small nose.

Dag looked to Chris for guidance. Chris nodded, his face completely open, looking almost confused by the fact that Dag wasn't going to join them. And once again, even though Chris had once rejected him in the worst way possible without even knowing it, Dag only felt acceptance and inclusion from him.

Warmth spread inside him, but he shrugged carelessly. "Well, okay, if you're sure. I don't really know your parents, but..."

"You stayed with Mom that day, and you've met my Dad. You're staying with us; of course they'd expect you to come."

He was tempted to make a comment about a boring family barbecue but somehow knew it wasn't going to come out sounding the way he wanted it to—it would only sound hurtful, and even though he only wanted to cover up how much it meant to him to be included with his usual cynicism and jokes, he couldn't do it.

"I'll just go change. Sorry to hold you up."

In the spare room where he kept his things, he changed from baggy athletic shorts and T-shirt into a pair of beige cargo shorts and a white shirt that he wore loose over them, the sleeves rolled up. He didn't know why he wanted to go with them—it was going to be a boring family barbecue, with just Kassidy's parents and them, possibly Hailey. That at least would likely add a little spice to the evening, but then again, he hated the thought of Kassidy being upset by her sister. She'd been pretty freaked out by the whole porn movie thing, had been distracted and brooding ever since.

But he did want to go, strangely felt himself looking forward to it as he quickly changed.

"Okay, let's go," he said as he emerged from the bedroom.

Kassidy smiled at him. She looked pretty in a flowered

orange and yellow sundress, the bodice two tiny triangles over her breasts, held up with equally tiny straps, showing a lot of smooth, golden skin including some nice cleavage. Chris looked good too, as usual, in a pair of plaid shorts and a pink—pink!— polo shirt that only he, with his wide shoulders and muscled arms, could pull off.

"Nice shirt, man," he said, raising a brow. "You borrow that from Kassidy?"

Chris laughed. "Fuck off. Grab that case of beer and let's go."

They got Mrs. Langdon settled on the deck in a comfortably cushioned chair in the shade. The backyard swimming pool shimmered turquoise and aqua in the late-afternoon sun and colorful flowers and greenery spilled out of pots arranged around the deck. It was so far from how Dag had grown up, it made his skin itch. Chris and Kassidy had both had completely different lives than he had. And yet, from the moment he'd met Chris he had never felt inferior or any less. And Kassidy had been the same. Dag's chest tightened at those thoughts, which he pushed away as he directed his best smile at Kassidy's mom.

"How're you doing, Mrs. L.?" he asked.

"I told you, Dag, call me Hope."

"Oh yeah." He winked at her. "Hope. How's the pelvis?"

She made a face. "I suppose it's getting better. It's driving me crazy, though, to sit around and do nothing all this time."

"Good thing it's summer holidays and you're not missing work." He'd learned she was an elementary school principal the day he'd spent with her, a day that once again had been surprisingly enjoyable.

171

She sighed. "Yes, if there was anything good about this whole thing, it's that. I should be more mobile by the end of the summer."

"Do you need a drink?"

"I'd love some iced tea."

"I'll get it for you then." He flashed another smile and returned to the kitchen where Kassidy was unloading the bags of food they'd brought. Chris and Mr. Langdon were already opening beers and talking about the Cubs.

"Dag, good to see you again," Mr. Langdon said, reaching to shake his hand.

"Thanks for having me."

He found iced tea for Hope and a beer for himself, and the men wandered back out onto the deck. It wasn't a wild party, that's for sure, but Dag found himself feeling remarkably relaxed and comfortable, sitting there in the warm sun, drinking beer and talking to Chris and Kassidy's parents. They clearly loved Chris, and a pang of envy twinged in Dag's chest at that. Not that he was jealous of Chris, but Dag had never experienced that easy acceptance by the parents of any of his dates—they were more likely to look at him, sense the badass inside him and try to discourage their daughters from having anything to do with him.

Mr. Langdon was interested in Dag's work and had a lot of questions, smart and knowledgeable, absorbing him in conversation, and then Dag also felt a stab of guilt at the fact that Mr. and Mrs. Langdon were just as accepting of him as Chris and Kassidy, even though he was totally corrupting their sweet daughter.

After a while, Kassidy emerged with a tray loaded with food—bowls of chips and salsa, a layered dip and some stuffed jalapeno peppers she'd made earlier. She laid things out on the table.

"Looks good, Kassie," her dad said to her.

"Thank you for doing this," Hope added. "It wasn't necessary."

"You know we'll take you out for a special dinner when you're feeling up to it," Kassidy said to her mom. "This isn't much, really. But thirty years is something to celebrate. I even brought a bottle of champagne for later."

"You're such a sweetheart," Hope said. Kassidy's cheeks got a little pinker.

The business conversation continued, turning to talk of government bailouts for struggling companies.

"You're opposed to that?" Dave Langdon asked Dag, picking up a chip.

"Absolutely."

"Dag's a *laissez-faire* capitalist," Chris put in with a smile. "Dog-eat-dog Darwinist capitalist."

"Well, I wouldn't go that far," Dag responded. "But a capitalist, yeah. If those businesses can't survive on their own, why should the taxpayers be bailing them out? A business has to make it or break on its own merits. If it can't be financially viable, then what's the reason for its existence?"

"How about to provide jobs to thousands of people," Kassidy spoke up. Dag looked at her. "That's important," she continued. "Some of those businesses are so big they're the backbone of the entire economy. If that many people lose their jobs, think how many other business will suffer because of it— because nobody has money to spend."

"A simplified point, but true," Dag acknowledged. He loved talking about stuff like this—it revved his motor. "I just hate to think of people getting handouts, when some of us..." Yeah it was personal, he fully admitted it. "Had to work our asses off for everything we have. That's the way things should work. You work for what you want."

"You sure taught me that," Chris said. Dag's head whipped around and he stared at Chris.

"Taught you what?"

"That I had to work." Chris gave a rueful smile. "I cruised through high school. My parents had the dough to send me to a good university. You were there on a scholarship that you busted your... I mean..." He shot a glance at Hope. "I mean you had to work hard to get there while I just walked in. And I probably would have just kept walking right out if it hadn't been for you."

Dag clenched his jaw to keep his mouth from falling open in astonishment, reined in his emotions to keep his face neutral.

"Yeah, you were a slacker, all right," he said, forcing a laugh. He couldn't believe Chris actually realized how much he'd changed while they'd gone to school. The fact, that he, Dag, had actually had some kind of positive influence on someone gave him a weird aching feeling inside.

"And the truth is, I wouldn't be where I am now at RBM if it wasn't for that."

Dag's chest constricted. Jesus, the guy was killing him here. He lifted his beer and caught Kassidy's warm gaze on him. She'd thought he was the slacker, but now admiration gleamed in her eyes. For him. Jesus. "See. I knew I'd suck you into my philosophy—living by your own effort. Getting what you deserve rather than getting something you didn't work for. Achievement. Happiness."

"Sounds like you're a follower of Ayn Rand," Dave said.

Dag looked at him with surprise. "Yeah. To a certain extent.

"You're an Objectivist?"

"Again, to a certain extent. *Laissez-faire* capitalism, limited government protecting individual rights to life, liberty and property."

"Entrepreneurs who create by building businesses."

"Yeah." Dag grinned. "That's me. But so is Chris. He invents new technologies."

Chris grinned. "I'll admit I share your views on some things."

"Well, I don't," Kassidy said. She lifted her chin, but her smile told Dag she was prepared to hold a different view but not hold a grudge. He respected that. "Don't Objectivists believe the purpose of life is the pursuit of one's own happiness?"

"Yeah." Now it was her turn to get a surprised glance from him.

"Well, I can't agree. Instead of Darwinist capitalism, how about conscious capitalism?"

Dag's lips quirked. "Wow, Kassidy. Idealistic much?"

She shrugged. "Call me idealistic if you want. I've heard it before. But I believe in it."

"Of course you do—" He bit his tongue. He'd almost called her "baby" in front of her parents. "Tell me more about that."

"Every business should have a deeper purpose than just maximizing profits. People want business to do more than just make money. And conscious leaders work toward that deeper purpose. It's not just about delivering value to stakeholders, and it's not just about personal gain."

"Well, pursuit of one's personal gain, or one's own happiness, doesn't mean at the expense of others," Dag replied. "You have to have respect for facts, for reality, and you have to live by objective principles, which includes respecting the rights of others. So it's not necessarily selfish. And..." His grin spread and he watched Kassidy's face. "If you can't be happy yourself, how can you make someone else happy?"

She met his gaze head on and smiled too. "Okay, I get that. Kind of like, if you can't love yourself, how do you expect anyone else to love you." She lifted a brow and their gazes locked. And held.

Christ, she was smart.

"Hey, everyone."

They all turned at the sound of the voice from the sliding doors. Hailey stood there, dressed in a skintight, short black dress. Dag thought he saw a flicker of uncertainty in her eyes as she surveyed the group talking and laughing, all at ease with each other there in the sunshine. And at that moment he realized that Hailey's cocked hip and slightly mocking smile covered up something—something like what he often felt inside when he used that bad-boy attitude. Interesting.

"Hailey! You came." Hope sounded genuinely pleased about that.

"Sure. I have to work tonight, but not until eight, so I can stay for a while."

"That's great!"

"Would you like a drink?" Kassidy offered, and Dag noted the coolness in her demeanor as she spoke to her sister, the stiffness in her spine. "I'm having wine, but we have beer and iced tea."

"A beer would be great."

"I'll bring it out." Kassidy disappeared back into the kitchen like the hostess of the party, which she was.

Dag felt Hailey's knowing gaze on him and he lifted his chin, arched an eyebrow and held her gaze challengingly. *Go ahead, make my day and spill it,* he messaged her. *Just try it.* She might think she was tough, but he was tougher, especially when it came to protecting Chris and Kassidy. Hailey's glance slid away as she talked to her parents.

Kassidy returned moments later carrying a wineglass and a tall glass of sparkling amber beer. Dag watched her. Her pretty mouth was tense, her eyes blinked rapidly even though she smiled and appeared to chat normally with Hailey. He could feel how the entire atmosphere had changed though, although Dave and Hope didn't seem to notice. Dag could see the worry shading Chris's eyes, knew how he felt because he felt exactly the same—protective of Kassidy.

He didn't give a shit if Hailey wanted to spill her guts and rat him out—if Hope and Dave hated him, so what, he'd be gone and never see them again. It was Kassidy he worried about, worried too because he knew how disturbed she was by what her sister was doing.

And he didn't even want to let his mind drift toward the thought that he'd seen Hailey naked with another man's cock in her mouth—Jesus H. Christ.

After a while of drinking and munching on snacks, and conversation that had turned brittle and superficial, Kassidy stood. "We should start cooking," she said brightly. "Dad, can you start up the grill?"

"You bet, Kassie."

Dave went over to the deluxe stainless steel barbecue on the side of the deck. Dag followed Kassidy into the kitchen.

"You okay?"

She paused, hands resting on the island countertop. He wanted to put his arms around her and hug her but resisted the urge, given...everything.

"Yeah." She blew out a breath then met his eyes. "I have to

talk to her."

He nodded. He would have been perfectly fine just forgetting the whole thing, never letting Hailey know they knew. He could be good at pretending. He'd been pretending most of his life. But he understood that Kassidy was concerned about Hailey.

He grabbed another beer. "I'll send her in."

"Dag. Wait."

He turned and looked over his shoulder.

"I was wrong about you. When we first met."

He smiled crookedly at her. "Yeah. You were."

They exchanged a long, weighty look and then he turned and went back outside.

Chris watched Hailey disappear through the sliding doors into the kitchen where Kassidy was. He looked at Dag, who met his gaze and lifted a brow. Dag's mouth was firm and straight, and Chris's gut clenched. He went to stand, and Dag gave a brief shake of his head. Chris subsided back into the cushioned wicker chair and lifted his beer to his mouth.

Damn. He didn't know what Kassidy was going to say, but he really wanted to be in there. And he could tell, so did Dag. Dag didn't sit back down in his chair but perched on the deck railing beside Chris, listening to Hope and Dave talk. Then he felt Dag's hand on his shoulder, a brief squeeze. He didn't look at Dag, wanted to reach up and cover Dag's hand with his own, but the touch was fleeting. He nodded, smiled at Kassidy's parents, not even hearing what they were saying. Only good thing about this whole mess was that the three of them shared it, which was weird but somehow comforting. Together he and

Kassidy were a couple and he'd always felt they made a good team—her, soft and sweet and sensitive, him, tough, aggressive, maybe a little stubborn. Okay, a lot stubborn. But having Dag with them, on their side, just made him feel even stronger.

How did life get so fucking complicated?

"Dag said you wanted to talk to me."

"Yes." Kassidy set her trembling hands on the counter and faced her sister.

Hailey met her gaze with raised eyebrows.

"Hailey. We saw you...in a movie the other night."

Hailey blinked.

"A porn movie."

Several beats of silence passed. "You were watching porn?" Hailey gave a tight laugh. "This gets better and better. Little angel Kassidy is turning into such a naughty girl!"

Kassidy wasn't going to get caught up in that. She recognized exactly what Hailey was doing. "Never mind me," she said firmly. "I'm worried about you, Hailey. Why are you doing that?"

"Why do you think?" Hailey reached for a pretzel in a bowl on the counter and popped it into her mouth.

"Well, I'm guessing it's for the money, but god! Hailey, how can you demean yourself like that? You're so smart and you have so much going for you! If you need more money, go back to college, finish your degree, get a better job than bartending!"

"Why do you think it's demeaning?" Hailey asked coolly.

"Hailey! The things you do...with men you don't even know...how can you do that?"

"You're not exactly in a position to be judging me, big sister." Hailey crossed her arms and leaned against the counter. "With what I saw the other day..."

"This isn't about me!" Kassidy's fingers tightened on the cool granite counter. She took a breath. "And you're right. I'm not judging you. I'm just...worried about you. Truly."

"Well, don't. I'm fine. I enjoy what I do. I'm having fun. I'm professional, respected, well paid...it's not big deal. And I don't see what's so different about it than what you're doing."

"There's a huge difference. What I'm doing....isn't..." She stopped, at a loss to try to explain the difference. She could feel it inside her, the powerful difference, but putting it into words was hard. "What I'm doing is about love," she finally said.

Hailey gave a shout of laughter. "You're telling me you're in love with two men?"

Kassidy bit her lower lip. Her stomach churned and she pressed a hand there. She'd been trying to avoid thinking about that, but when Hailey said the words, she knew it was true. She'd come to care for Dag. A lot. She wasn't sure if she'd say she was in love with him—but she definitely cared for him. "We're not hurting anyone," she choked out. "We're all mature, consenting adults."

"Well, I'm not hurting anyone either," Hailey said, straightening. She smiled. "And we're all mature consenting adults making adult movies. And I don't feel demeaned by it. So what's the problem?"

"Mom and Dad would die if they knew."

Hailey's eyes narrowed and her gaze zoomed in on Kassidy. But she gave a negligent shrug. "You won't tell them."

Kassidy stared back at her and lifted her chin. "What makes you think that?"

Hailey laughed. "I don't actually give a shit if they find out. But I know you won't tell them because you're such a soft-hearted little angel. You wouldn't want to hurt them."

Kassidy gritted her teeth. "Fine. I won't tell them about you if you won't tell them about me."

Hailey rolled her eyes. "God, are we five years old again?" And she turned and walked out of the kitchen, back onto the deck.

She couldn't go back out there. Her whole body was shaking, her stomach hurting, her chest squeezing. She closed her eyes and set her elbows on the counter, rested her head in her hands.

Maybe she was making too big a deal of this. It just seemed so...awful, what Hailey was doing. Whereas she...what she was doing was...not. It wasn't.

Who was she to judge her? She couldn't judge anyone for choices they made. Much as she tried to defend what she and Chris and Dag were doing, most people would think it was wrong. Sinful. Depraved.

But she didn't care and she supposed she could understand that Hailey felt the same way.

"Hey." She felt a gentle hand on her back. Dag's voice stroked over her. "You okay?"

"Yes." She straightened, pushed her hair back and smiled at him, although her lips felt tight. "I'm fine."

"Hailey's gone. She decided she couldn't stay for dinner after all."

"Shit." Hailey'd finally shown up at a family event and Kassidy had ruined it. Tears stung her eyes and she blinked rapidly. "That probably hurt Mom and Dad's feelings."

"Yeah, a little, I think."

He studied her, and the concern she saw there told her one important thing—Dag cared for her too.

Chapter Sixteen

"You can't use that objectivist crap to justify porn."

They walked into the condo, continuing the heated discussion that had started on the way home in the car.

Dag laughed. "What? You can't see that porn is a form of art?"

"Art! Well, okay, some of it might be. But really, it has to have some kind of artistic value."

"The debate of art versus porn wages on," Chris said, dropping car keys to the small console table inside the door. "We could argue this for hours. I have a better idea."

Dag looked at Chris and caught the evil glint in his eye just as Kassidy did too and she burst out laughing. "We're not making our own porn movie."

He caught her around the waist and nuzzled her neck. "Aw, why not?"

"I know you're worried about your sister, Kassidy, but she's a big girl," Dag said.

"I know." Kassidy sighed. "I just wish... Oh never mind."

"What, sweetheart?" Chris followed her into the living room.

"Yeah, what?" Dag reached out and ran a hand down her hair. He'd longed to touch her all evening, wanting to make her feel better about what had happened, but his role in that family setting was extremely ambiguous.

"I just wish I had a different relationship with my sister. I've always wished Hailey and I could be friends."

"You aren't necessarily friends with someone just because you're related," Dag murmured.

She turned her eyes up to him. "Is that part of the objectivist philosophy too?"

"Yeah. Sort of. We develop relationships with people we share values with—common interests in things like sports, art, music, philosophical outlooks, political beliefs. That includes our families."

"I always believed you may not like your family, but you have to love them. Because they're family."

"Do you feel guilty because you don't love Hailey?"

A long heavy silence filled the room, and Dag saw that Chris was listening intently too, waiting. "I do love her," she said finally. "She's my sister. But I do feel guilty for not liking her." She put a hand to her mouth. "I do."

"Don't." Dag slid his arms around her and pulled her against him in a warm hug that felt so damn good. "Don't feel guilty. Think about it rationally. Just because you're related to her doesn't mean you have anything in common besides the fact that you're sisters."

"That's kind of sad, though," she said, peering up at him. "Is that how you feel about your family?"

"That's how I had to feel about my family," he said grimly, his mouth tightening. "For me to survive, I had to believe that. Because I hate my family."

"Oh Dag. That can't be true."

"It's true." He glanced at Chris. He'd talked to Chris about his family, only once, years ago, when they were getting to know each other, and Chris had known that topic was off limits ever since. But Kassidy didn't know. "My dad disappeared when I was a baby. My mom was an alcoholic who cared more about getting her next drink and getting another man than she did about me."

Her eyes filled with pain and sorrow. He closed his own against the sight. He hated pity. "Don't feel sorry for me," he said, voice gritty. He opened his eyes and smiled down at her. "I'm fine. I made it. I'm only telling you this so you'll understand and not feel guilty about your feelings for Hailey. If you're going to love someone, it's gonna be the people you choose to be family. Like...like...Chris." His voice faltered on the last words, and tension in the room thickened as all three became painfully aware once again of the unique nature of their relationship. That it was her and Chris who had the relationship, not him. "You choose your partner, your spouse. That's who you love," he finished, still smiling, his chest still aching.

"I understand that." She laid a hand on his cheek and smiled at him. Her bottom lip trembled and she looked as if she wanted to say something but hesitated. "Dag..." He didn't want to go where her mind might be heading, so he bent and gave her lips a quick kiss.

A kiss that quickly turned heated. Chris joined them, close up against Kassidy's backside, pulling her hair aside and laying his mouth on the bare skin of her shoulder, moving the tiny strap aside and kissing her there.

"Even though I don't understand this," Kassidy whispered. "Even though I suspect it's very, very wrong...can I tell you guys how lucky I feel to have both of you in my life?"

Dag's gut clenched. Amazing—that was exactly how he felt about Chris and Kassidy, the feelings that had swamped him earlier at her parents' home.

"It's not wrong," he replied, sliding his mouth over her soft cheek. "Sex promotes happiness. That's our goal—to be happy, right?"

Kassidy gave a delicate little snort even as her head fell back to allow both men access to her throat and shoulders. "More objectivism?"

He smiled against her jaw. "Yeah. Sex isn't just physical pleasure. It's a celebration of existence." *And an expression of love*, but he stopped himself from saying those words aloud. "Celebrating life is essential to happiness. So, it's moral to make choices that allow that celebration and immoral to deny it. We're celebrating life."

"I think you can use philosophy to justify anything," Chris muttered from behind Kassidy, and Dag laughed.

"I probably could," he agreed. "But are either of you arguing with me right now?"

"No," Chris said.

"No," Kassidy said on a sigh. "No."

They moved to the bedroom in what was becoming a familiar rhythm of three.

"Wanna make you feel good, baby doll," Dag murmured against the thin skin of her neck. "So good."

"Yes," she whispered, eyes closed, head to one side. "Make me feel good."

"You're so sweet," Chris said, pushing the bodice of her dress down. As Dag had suspected all day, she wore no bra beneath and her perfect round breasts gleamed in the lamplight.

"Oh yeah."

While Chris helped her out of the dress, Dag bent to take her nipple in his mouth, a delicious hard little nub and she moaned when he sucked on it. Soon she stood naked between them.

"I hate it when you feel bad, sweetheart," Chris added, nuzzling her hair.

"You guys..." Her voice choked up.

"C'mere." Chris took her hand and led her to the bed. "Lie down." He reached behind his neck and pulled the goofy pink polo shirt off over his head, muscles rippling in the dim light.

Dag followed his lead, unbuttoning his shirt and shrugging out of it, his eyes moving between Kassidy's soft femininity and Chris's male strength. When he and Chris were both naked, Chris turned his head and met his gaze, his eyes gleaming. "Let's make her feel good."

"Yeah."

As usual, Chris was the one who chose the position—this time he lay on the bed and moved Kassidy into reverse cowgirl. Nice. She faced Dag, her eyes dark and heavy-lidded, her mouth pouty. Dag filled his hands with her breasts as he moved over Chris's legs, his cock jutting in front of him. Christ, he was hard enough to hit a baseball with it. Kassidy's stiff little nipples poked his palms.

Then Chris tugged her down, so she lay on top of him, exposing her pussy to Dag.

"Lick her," Chris instructed Dag in a hoarse voice. "Get her good and ready and then I'll fuck her ass and you can fuck her pussy."

Dag smiled. Sounded like a plan. He leaned over Kassidy, supporting his weight on his arms and kissed her, long and lush, as Chris's hands slid over her breasts and belly stretched out above him. When Dag lifted away, Chris used one hand to grip her jaw and turn her face to him so he could kiss her too. Fuck, that was hot. Dag's cock surged and he stroked himself,

187

moving back down between both their legs.

Oh yeah, hell yeah, she was so wet and pretty. He inhaled the delicate warm scent of her he'd gotten to know so well, closed his eyes as a wave of emotion rolled over him. When he opened his eyes, the image of Chris's big masculine hands on her small body, holding her in position, nearly undid him. Christ.

He kissed her inner thighs, so soft, quivering, gave a tiny nip at the tendon there, bringing a gasp from Kassidy. He smiled against her flesh, licked his way up the crease between thigh and pussy, kissing and sucking gently. He loved doing this. He could do it forever. The taste of her melting on his tongue, the hot feel of her against his lips—loved it. Fucking loved it. And Chris's cock was right there too, thick and shiny, roped with prominent veins, his balls tight and high beneath.

Dag dragged in a breath. He stared at Chris's cock and his balls, right there in front of his face, all smooth and tempting. Chris's hand appeared and fisted his cock, and Dag helped Kassidy lift up a little as Chris moved his shaft, searching for her back entrance. Kassidy gave a soft cry as he found it.

"No," Dag murmured. "First her pussy. She's so wet."

Chris grunted and took a few moments to work his cock inside her pussy. Then Dag watched with utter fascination as Chris thrust up into her. Daringly, he set his hands on Chris's inner thighs, to brace himself as he leaned in to kiss Kassidy's swollen clit. Chris's big thigh muscles tightened beneath his palms, but he kept his rhythm, and the room filled with his groans, Kassidy's breathless panting and Dag's suckling noises as he drew Kassidy's clit into his mouth. She gave a soft cry.

Dag's fingers tightened on Chris's hair-covered legs, and he licked Kassidy, suckled slowly, licked her soft folds, down, lower, right down to...Chris's cock. Unable to resist, he drew his tongue over that distended shaft, over the hard ridge of vein, tasting of Kassidy's sweet cream.

"Ungh! Jesus Christ!"

Chris's whole body jerked as something stroked his cock. He couldn't see what it was but it sure as hell wasn't Kassidy touching him like that, her hands clasped over her own breasts. A harsh tremor shook his body and to his dismay, he slid out of her hot pussy.

"Shit," he muttered.

"Got it," Dag said from down below, and goddammit if Dag didn't take hold of Chris's cock. Jesus. Surely to god he was just going to quickly direct it back inside Kassidy...

Please...oh god...no. No.

Dag was holding him, stroking his length, shafting him with a practiced hand that knew exactly how hard and how fast. Chris groaned. "Dag..." A shudder raced over him, sensation tore through him, wrenching, fiery sensation. "What the..."

"It's okay," Dag murmured.

Then Kassidy tipped her head, looked into his face. "I was so close..."

Oh Christ. They couldn't stop now. They had to stop this, though, this was wrong, this was bad... It took all his self-control not to toss Kassidy aside and leap off the bed. He gritted his teeth, as pleasure, dark, forbidden pleasure, exploded inside him.

And when Dag's mouth took him in, he thought his heart might burst out of his chest. "Fuck!" he cried out, but his voice emerged as a feeble croak. Heated suction surrounded him, flames licked over his body. Kassidy whimpered, tensed, squirmed a bit. "It's okay, sweetheart," he gritted out. "Oh fuck…"

"What?"

She lifted her head and looked down their bodies and saw…well, Christ only knew what she saw. Chris's head was glued to the pillow, his body a sparking mass of sensation as Dag's hard mouth dragged up and down his cock, sucking and licking him with reckless enthusiasm. What the fuck was he doing? Had the guy lost his fucking mind? Jesus!

And Jesus, that felt good.

"Oh god." Kassidy's moan sank into his consciousness. "Oh god that's hot."

Words failed him; the only words that kept running through his mind were curses, the worst curse words he knew as his blood stirred in a rush of heat and a cascade of sparks.

They could not be doing this. Could. Not.

They were doing it and, holy hell, it felt good.

No. Bad. It felt bad. It had to feel bad. More curses clamored in his head, and he squeezed his eyes shut against the flames raging beneath his skin. He should make Dag stop. He should…but he couldn't. Instead, he wanted to beg him *not* to stop.

Then things got worse, much worse, as Dag held up Chris's cock, rubbed it against Kassidy's pussy, and licked his balls. Wicked throbbing sensations built inside him, and when Dag's fingers started teasing his asshole, his hips jerked. "Dag…" The word dragged out of him on a long groan.

"Chris." Kassidy lifted an arm, touched his face, kissed his jaw. "Chris. It's okay."

No, it's not. He could barely form words, as every nerve ending jumped, sensations sharp and hot exploded in his balls and raced up his spine. "Aw fuck. Dag, Jesus..." He'd never even let Kassidy touch him like that, it was so forbidden, so bad, so very bad. And then Dag's finger breached him. His eyes stung at the sensations, the sharp slice of pain, the unfamiliar, almost unpleasant feeling...until Dag's finger touched something else, something inside him, something amazing, and a burst of pleasure shot through him, so extreme it made him blind and deaf and feel as if his body was lifting off the bed. "Jesus fucking Christ."

And he came. Not even inside Kassidy. He came in Dag's mouth, Dag's lips and tongue and cheeks sucking greedily. "No," Chris almost sobbed. "No, no..."

"Chris." Kassidy touched his face again, pressed her mouth to his. "Oh Chris..."

Dag sucked him dry, licked him clean, let his shaft slide from his mouth and then Kassidy gasped as Dag no doubt returned to her pussy.

"Oh yes," she moaned again, plucking her own nipples. Shit. He should be doing that. Too bad he couldn't lift his arms. Dag would take care of her. His head muzzy, thoughts spinning out of control, Chris drifted, hot and undone. Kassidy made little girl pleasure noises, her body tensed and tightened, and she gave a soft cry as she came.

Feverish, almost delirious, Chris babbled something, knew in the far back of his mind it didn't even sound like human language that Dag or Kassidy could understand. Dag sprawled on the bed next to them, breathing heavily, one big hand still resting on Chris's thigh.

And then Kassidy, sweet generous Kassidy, slid off Chris's limp body and moved over Dag. "Dag," she whispered, reaching for his cock. "Now you."

"Aw, Kass, baby." Dag's fingers slid into her hair as she

knelt beside him. Chris's chest ached, his throat felt tight, his eyes hurt. Normally he loved to watch Kassidy give Dag head, but at that moment, he could hardly bear to open his eyes in case he looked at Dag. He could never look at him again.

Chapter Seventeen

"What do you mean, he's gone?"

Kassidy rounded on Chris, the pot of coffee held above her mug.

"Jesus, Kass, watch what you're doing." Chris grabbed for her hand as coffee poured all over the counter and dribbled down the front of one maple cabinet.

"Oh shit." She reached for a towel and swiped at the mess.

"For Chrissake, be careful," Chris snapped. "You could burn someone like that."

She mopped up the coffee, his words like a slap. "I'm sorry," she muttered. "You don't need to bite my head off."

Chris rubbed the back of his neck, took the towel and wiped up the coffee that had dripped to the hardwood floor. "Sorry."

"Where is he?"

"He left."

She stared at him, questions clogging up her brain. "But, I don't get it. Where did he go? Why?"

"Oh for— I don't know. I think he's going back to San Francisco. Probably going back to the hotel for now."

"But..." The kitchen shifted around her and she set a hand on the counter to steady herself. "But, I don't get it." She narrowed her eyes at Chris. He looked like shit, she had to say. His eyes were red and a pulse ticced in his tight jaw. "Is this because of last night?"

"No."

He continued mopping without looking at her, then stood, turned and hung the damp towel on the rack.

She snatched it away from him. "That needs to go in the laundry," she snapped. "Chris. What's going on?"

"I told you, I don't know."

She balled up the damp towel in her fists. "Yes, you do." Then she smacked his chest. "What did you say to him?"

He continued to avoid her eyes. "What happened last night shouldn't have. We just...both agreed to that. And that it was best if he go."

Kassidy's face felt tight and hot, her stomach cramped. "I'm trying to understand," she said slowly, her throat aching. "Help me understand."

Finally he looked her in the eye. Briefly. "Kassidy. You know what...fuck." He rubbed his face. "I can't even talk about this. You know what he did last night. He can't do that. We can't do that."

"You loved it!" She stared at him. "You came like a volcano! If you hated it that much, why didn't you stop him?"

"I tried! I was..."

"Bullshit!" She sucked in air in quick, shallow breaths. "Bullshit, Chris. What's so wrong if it felt good?"

He stared at her, his mouth pressed into a grim line. "I can't believe you just said that."

She shook her head. "I can't believe you just said that. It's okay for me to sleep with two guys? For me to have two cocks inside me? For me to do all the wild and wicked things we've done? It's okay for you to share your girlfriend with your best friend, which you've done many times I might add, but it's not okay for two men to touch each other?"

He closed his eyes and turned away. "That about sums it up, yeah."

"Oh, for... Chris." She stretched a hand out to touch his shoulder. "Tell me. Is it that repulsive to you that Dag touched you like that?"

"Jesus Christ!" He shrugged her hand off and she took a step back, feeling a knife twisting inside her. "I just...can't do that."

She just gazed at his back, the old, well-washed gray T-shirt hanging from his wide shoulders, tensed up almost level with his ears. "I don't know what to say. I just don't."

"Look. Yes, Dag and I have had threesomes in the past. But it was never for him and me—it was about the girls. Both of us sharing and enjoying her and giving her two times the pleasure."

"Because you're both such studs," she added with a touch of bitterness.

"No. That's not what I meant."

"You know what?" She fixed her gaze on him. "I don't totally buy that. That it's not for you and him. You two get something out of doing that—I know you like to watch, but it's more than that." She paused. "You and Dag have feelings for each other."

Chris's narrowed to slits. "We're friends."

"Yeah. Friends." She shook her head. She eyed him. How far should she push him? He was on the edge as it was, body tense, jaw locked. Her heart felt full and heavy. "I've never been totally able to get my head around this whole thing. It confuses me. I don't know what's right or wrong anymore. But I do know one thing. Yesterday I felt lucky to have both of you, but it wasn't because of the sex. It was because you guys both looked out for me yesterday. No, not just yesterday—every day. You both care about me. Both of you. You wanted to make me feel better, to look after me. That meant—" She had to stop and swallow, her throat thick with tears. "That meant so much to me."

"Jesus Christ." Chris whirled around. "Are you in love with Dag?"

Her chest ached so much she could hardly breath, almost couldn't speak. "I-I don't know."

"Fuck me! You have got to be kidding me! This wasn't supposed to turn out like this!"

"Chris, wait. It doesn't mean I don't love you. But I care about Dag. I can't deny that. I couldn't sleep with him and do the things we've done with him if I didn't care about him. You should know that. You should be happy about that."

He gazed back at her, confusing swirling in his eyes.

"I love you, Chris. You know I do."

"Yeah." His voice was low and tight. "I know it. And I love you too, sweetheart." He put out his arms and she moved into them, against his big, warm body, got folded up in his embrace. "God, Kassidy, you scared the crap out of me." They stood there holding each other for a long moment, and then he said, "So we're good?"

Slowly she drew her head back. "No. No, Chris. We're not good." She met his eyes. "I need to know what happened with Dag."

She walked through the lobby of the hotel where she and Dag and Chris had had dinner weeks ago. Dag hadn't answered his cell phone, but when she'd called the hotel they'd put her through to his room, and without caller ID, he'd picked up. He sounded different—fractured, distant—but he gave her his room number even though he tried to tell her not to come.

She didn't listen to him. Chris wouldn't talk to her, wouldn't tell her what had happened and once again, even though Chris said Dag would be fine, Dag was always fine, even though Dag was a tough bad boy who apparently didn't need anyone, she couldn't bear the thought of him being hurt.

Her heart strained in her chest with hard, painful beats as she rode the elevator to the tenth floor. Room 1010. Easy to remember. She rubbed her lips together and pressed her hand to her stomach.

She stepped off the elevator, and as she stood in front of the door of room 1010, she knew her life was about to change. If she knocked on that door, she had to deal with whatever happened, and a feeling grew inside her, intuition, premonition, she didn't know, but she did know this was going to rock her world forever. Since Dag had come back, their lives had taken a sharp turn into craziness, although as time went on, what they were doing felt more and more natural and comfortable and right. But the fear had been there all along, simmering underneath everything and now she knew why. Because their lives were going to blow up. It was happening now, right now, right this minute, and she didn't know if they were all going to live through it, or if they did, if they'd ever be the same.

She knocked on the door, bowed her head as she waited for Dag to answer. He took so long, she was afraid he'd left after her call, and she sank her teeth into her bottom lip and lifted her head just as the door opened.

Oh hell. She thought Chris had looked bad. Dag's hair was all over the place, he hadn't shaved for a couple of days, which yesterday had looked sexy and stubbly, today looked...rough. Dangerous. But his eyes were the most dangerous of all, because for once he couldn't hide the pain and vulnerability beneath that badass attitude.

"Kassidy. I was hoping you'd change your mind and not come."

"Sorry." She slipped past him and into the room, inhaling his scent as she brushed against his body.

It was only noon, but Dag had opened the mini bar and several small bottles of Scotch sat on the dark wood dresser. The room was bare otherwise, his bags tossed in the closet, nothing unpacked, an impersonal, anonymous hotel room. He wore the beige cargo shorts he'd worn yesterday with a white T-shirt, and he crossed the carpet on his big bare feet toward her where she stood by the window.

"Chris won't tell me what happened," she said without any preamble. "So I came to find out from you."

"What makes you think I'll tell you?"

"You will."

His mouth tightened. "If Chris doesn't want you to know, then I'm not going to tell you."

"Yes, you are."

He gave a bark of laughter and rubbed his hand over his forehead. "Kassidy. Go back to your boyfriend. This was all a fucking big mistake. Let's just let it go before things get worse."

"How can things get any worse?" Her heart ached and she took a step toward him. "You and Chris are both dying. And...so am I. I care about you, Dag. About both of you."

It was daring, saying that. She hadn't told him she loved

him, but he had to know she cared, that's why she was there. Something flickered in his eyes.

"I just want to understand," she whispered. She clasped her hands in front of her. "Please. Maybe it was a mistake. Maybe we can never go back...but I want to understand. I need to."

"Shit."

She sank into a chair because her legs went wobbly as if all the strength had drained out of them through her feet.

"I know Chris doesn't always want to talk about things," she continued. "But you've always talked to me."

He shook his head and sat on the edge of the king-size bed. "Kassidy." His somber eyes regarded her steadily. "I can talk to you about my own shit. But I can't tell you what's going on in Chris's head." He rubbed the back of his skull. "Hell, *I* don't know what's going on in Chris's head."

"I don't think Chris knows what's going on in Chris's head," she muttered.

Dag snorted. "Yeah." He sighed. "I fucked up. Big time. You know it."

She pressed her trembling lips together. "If you knew that, why did you do it?" She held up a hand. "Sorry. That sounded accusing. I didn't mean it to. I just want to know."

He gave a short nod, dropped his head and looked at the floor, his hands between his knees. She wanted to rush over and sit beside him, throw her arms around him. She tightened her leg muscles to keep her in the chair, gripped her fingers together.

Then he raised his head, and agony and longing blazed in his dark eyes. "I love Chris," he said simply. "I've loved him forever."

She stared back at him, breathing in tiny shallow breaths. "You mean..."

He nodded again but held her gaze. "Does that disgust you?"

"No. Of course not." Disgust was nowhere on her emotional radar at that moment. "I just... Are you gay?"

He shrugged. "I guess you'd say I'm bi. I've always been attracted to both men and women. Chris is the only guy I've ever had feelings like that for, though."

"He told me you were a man whore. That you slept your way through college. With girls."

Dag choked on a laugh. "Yeah. That'd be true. I like sex, lots of sex, what can I say? And I wasn't going to get any from Chris. He made that pretty damn clear."

Her face scrunched up. "You told him...?"

"No. Christ, no. I just knew from conversations we had he was in no way open to that. And I mean, *in no way.*"

She nodded.

"It hurt," Dag added, voice low and taut. "Hurt like hell. But I valued his friendship. Hell, he accepted me for who I was, busted-up family and poor-as-dirt, complete misfit. Not many people have ever done that."

Her head was whirling with this information that shouldn't have stunned her like it did. She'd just had no idea. But thinking back to the last few weeks, she felt as though she had known. With some kind of deep-down instinctive knowledge, it made sense to her.

But she was still confused. "Did you tell him—last night? Or this morning?" He'd been gone when she woke up so she didn't know when the big showdown had occurred. "Is that why he made you leave?"

Dag's mouth curled. "Why do you think he made me leave?"

Her mouth fell open. "Well... Oh shit. I don't know. I assumed..."

"Chris doesn't make me do anything. But no. I didn't tell him that. He freaked out about what happened and told me to get out. I knew I had to leave."

Her eyes prickled. Her heart cracked and ached. "Oh Dag." The words came out in a rough whisper. "I'm so sorry."

"I'm going back to San Francisco, Kassidy."

Her bottom lip trembled and her heart stuttered. "When?"

"I booked a flight for Tuesday morning. I have a few business things to deal with tomorrow, the rest I'll have to handle from there."

"Oh." She sucked on her bottom lip and looked down at her hands, a little blurry through her tears. How could he leave? What would they do without him? She felt as if someone were wrenching her heart out of her chest.

"I know I fucked up," Dag said. "I shouldn't have done what I did. It was just so hard...not to. Ya know? We'd all gotten really close and it...just happened." He scrubbed a hand over his face and his eyes looked kind of red too.

She met his eyes. "But...the weird thing is—he liked it. I know he did."

Dag was silent.

"He wouldn't admit it to me," she added. She laid her hands on her knees, bare beneath the hem of her skirt, and curled her fingers around them, her heart slowly splintering into painful shards. "He's so damn stubborn. I-I accused him of having feelings for you. And that was before I even knew..."

His eyes shot wide open. "What the hell? You said what? Why?"

One corner of her mouth lifted and she hitched a shoulder. "Call it woman's intuition. Little things. I should have figured things out a long time ago."

"No. Whatever." He closed his eyes briefly. "Jesus." His eyes opened. "That's not right, Kass. I know he doesn't feel that way. He never has and he never will. In my screwed-up way, I wanted to be close to him, but as usual, I made a mess of things. Don't tell Chris this. Please? I'm just going to get the hell out of town again, and leave you two to live your lives."

"Why did you come back?" she asked. "Why?"

He hitched one shoulder. "I just wanted to see him again. I guess I had some kind of crazy hope that maybe..." His voice trailed off. "It was stupid."

He'd wanted to see Chris again. He'd hoped they could be together.

And then a question hit her, like a smack in the face. Had he been using her to get closer to Chris?

Oh god. She'd thought he cared about her. She cared about him. Stupid, stupid, stupid. The pain clamped down on her, crushing her, a knife turning slowly inside her. She felt like she might throw up. She stood. Her legs wobbled as she walked across the hotel room, not looking at Dag. She couldn't look at him. In fact she could barely see, other than a small round window in front of her, everything else faded to black. She fumbled at the hotel door.

"Kassidy." Dag spoke behind her, his voice ragged. She paused, bent her head, looked at the door knob. A harsh sob swelled inside her and she tightened her stomach muscles to keep it from bursting out, breathed in through her nose. She yanked the door open and walked out, down the hall and out of Dag's life.

Chapter Eighteen

She couldn't go home. Chris was there. She couldn't go to her parents. There was only one place she could go.

Hailey opened the door of her small apartment and the surprise on her face quickly morphed into concern. "Hey," she said, eyebrows pulled together. "Are you okay?"

Kassidy shook her head. She walked in, collapsed onto a chair and buried her face in her hands.

"Kassidy."

She felt the warmth of Hailey's hand as she touched her back. They weren't the kind of sisters who hugged and touched each other. Hell, they barely talked to each other sometimes. But the gesture comforted her in some small, weird way.

"I'm okay," she finally said, lifting her head. She dragged her palms over wet cheeks, pushed her hair off her face. "I think."

"What the hell happened?" Hailey took a seat on her couch, her knees almost touching Kassidy's at a right angle. Hailey's legs were bare beneath the frayed edge of a pair of jean cut-offs. "It's not Mom, is it?"

"No." She squeezed the word out of a tight throat. "Not Mom."

She leaned back and rested her head against the back of

the chair, closed her eyes. Pain throbbed inside her, along with a swirl of confusion. "It's a long story."

"I'm sure it is." But Hailey's voice held none of her usual mocking tone. "Did you come here to tell me? Or just to...come here?"

"I don't know. I just know I can't go home."

Hailey frowned. "You and Chris? Did you have a fight?"

"Sort of. My life is so messed up, Hailey." She pressed the heels of her hands to her aching eyes. "I don't know what's going on and I don't know what to do."

Silence blanketed the room, but that was okay. Hailey probably didn't know what to say and wisely didn't say anything.

Finally Hailey did speak. "I know you probably don't want advice from me, and that's okay. I'm not exactly the best person to give advice anyway. But if you just want to talk...sometimes that helps."

"Yeah." Kassidy moved her head, eyes still closed. "Yeah. Okay."

She told Hailey about her and Chris and Dag. Hailey listened and didn't say much, and Kassidy appreciated that. She did not want someone judging her or telling her what a stupid idiot she'd been—because she already knew that.

"So Dag's in love with Chris," Hailey repeated slowly. "And Chris has no idea?"

"Nope. Never has. And Dag doesn't want him to know."

"Well. That sucks for Dag." She eyed Kassidy curiously. "So why are you so upset?"

That was the big question, wasn't it? Kassidy drew her shredded dignity around her as best she could, tried to gather up her running-wild thoughts. "I think I...sort of fell in love with

Dag."

Hailey's mouth opened. Closed. She blinked.

"Not like you think," Kassidy added. "I still love Chris. I think...oh god, this is crazy. I think I love both of them."

Hailey blinked again. "Oh."

Kassidy licked her lips, looked at her hands, her fingers twisting together. "But it hurts. I thought Dag cared about me too, and it hurts to think he was just using to me to get to Chris."

"Ah."

Kassidy lifted her head. Once again, Hailey had a holy-fucking-shit look on her face, though she said only that one word.

"And I'm terrified. Because I think Chris might have feelings for Dag. He won't admit it. He's such a stubborn ass."

"What makes you think that?" Hailey's words were a bare whisper, her eyes wide.

Kassidy couldn't tell her what had happened last night. It was too personal. Too secret. Chris would kill her if Hailey knew about that. "I just...have a feeling. Some things...that happened." She shrugged.

"I can't believe that, Kassidy. Really. Chris loves you. He's crazy about you. It's so obvious, always has been." Hailey gave a short laugh. "It's enough to make me jealous."

Jealous? Kassidy peered at her sister through gritty, swollen eyes. Hailey jealous of her? Yeah right.

"That's not to say he doesn't care about Dag. But..."

"Would a guy let another guy suck his dick if he wasn't into that?"

Hailey didn't even flinch. She met Kassidy's gaze steadily. "I've met people who are...just...attracted to other people. It doesn't matter if they're male or female. It's just some kind of chemistry or attraction."

Kassidy nodded. Was that Dag? Mind-bogglingly, she was grateful for Hailey's experience and her acceptance of the question for what it was. Jesus, her world had turned upside down and inside out.

Then, her body trembling, her stomach in knots, she spoke aloud the words that scared her the most, the ones she had to drag from way down deep inside, hoping that saying them aloud would take the fear out of them. "If Chris cares about Dag...and Dag cares about him...where does that leave me?"

"Oh Kassie." Hailey swallowed. "You're fine. I told you Chris loves you. Go home to him. Talk to him. Dag's leaving and you two will be fine."

"Can I just let Dag leave? Can I just let that happen, knowing they might...never see each other again? That they might..."

Hailey's face flickered with emotions. "Are you asking for my advice?"

"No. I don't know. I don't know what to do! How can I live with myself if I never tell Chris the truth...about how Dag feels for him? What if that makes a difference? I'm so afraid! What if he really wants to be with Dag? Can I spend the rest of my life wondering that, keeping that secret inside me?"

Hailey bit her lip.

"But if I tell him, what if he decides he'd rather be with Dag than with me?"

"He wouldn't do that." Hailey leaned forward. "Chris loves you, Kass. You know that."

Kassidy nodded, twisting her fingers together so tightly they hurt. Her eyes stung with more tears. "I just don't want to lose him! But...maybe I already have." The agony inside her burst out then in harsh, painful sobs and she bent over the arm of the chair, crying in breath-stealing, gut-wrenching gusts.

Why had they done this crazy ménage thing? How could they have blindly thought they could just all have sex together without any of this happening? They must have been out of their minds. The enormity of it rose up inside her, terrible, unbearable, painful.

They'd messed up their lives so thoroughly Kassidy couldn't see at that point how this was ever going to be okay. And maybe that's what she deserved.

"I'm sorry," she gasped long moments later. Hailey handed her tissues. "Thanks."

"It's okay. I'm sorry too. I wish I could do more to help."

She shook her head, mopping up. Her face felt hot and tight, eyes burning. "I got myself into this. But thanks."

Stunningly, Hailey reached out and took her hand. "Kassidy. I..." She looked at Kassidy and nibbled her bottom lip again, her eyes dark with anxiety. "I...know we haven't been close. It's hard to be your sister."

Kassidy's eyes flew wide. What?

"You're so goddamn perfect," Hailey continued in a low voice. "I couldn't ever be as good as you. So I didn't even try. I just tried to be bad. But I want you to know I never would wish this on you. Truly. Your perfect life, your perfect job, your perfect boyfriend. I envied you. Even when I discovered you having a hot threesome with two gorgeous guys, I was envious. But I never... I hate seeing you like this. I really do."

"Oh Hailey." Kassidy stared at her, mouth open. Hailey was jealous of her? That was just freaky. Because she'd been jealous of Hailey.

Life was so strange. When you could be jealous of the things someone else had at the same time they were jealous of what you had. Why couldn't everyone just be grateful for who they were and what they had without comparing it to others? Why was she like that with Hailey? Just because they were sisters? Was it because Kassidy really did deep down inside love her and that's why she had the power to make her so angry, so frustrated, the power to make her feel so insecure and inferior? But then Hailey must care about Kassidy too, if she made her feel the same way. They made each other feel bad even though they never intended to, even though you were supposed to make the people you cared about feel good. There was something wrong with that, but she couldn't figure it all out at that moment; it was beyond her.

Hailey reached for Kassidy's hands and they sat there for a moment, all four of their hands clasped together.

Kassidy sighed. "Oh Hailey. How can you be jealous of me, for being so good? When all I wanted was to be bad for once. That's what got me into this mess. I was tired of being the good girl. You made me feel like some kind of boring prude, and I wanted some adventure, I wanted to do something naughty."

"That's why you did that?" Hailey's eyebrows flew up into her hairline.

"Well. That was part of it." Kassidy paused. "Thank you," she finally said. "For being here for me. I still don't know what to do, but thank you."

Hailey nodded, her mouth soft and trembly, her throat working. "And just for the record, I think Dag cares about you too." Hailey met her eyes. "That night at Mom and Dad's, he was acting very protective of you. And I'm telling you Chris loves you too. I don't think you have to worry about your relationship with him."

Kassidy blinked wetly at her. She swallowed. And at that moment, even though Hailey didn't say it, Kassidy thought that maybe Hailey loved her too.

Dag had said you didn't have to love family. He'd said you loved the people you chose to love. But Kassidy wasn't so sure it was a choice—her feelings for Hailey were there.

Was it a choice to love Chris? She'd always thought falling in love was something that happened to you, not something you chose. Did she choose to love Dag? Maybe you could love more than one person, if you chose to. Could you?

Could Dag? Could Chris?

Chris sprawled on the couch, bare feet propped on the coffee table, a baseball game on the television. He had no fucking clue what the score was, in fact, he didn't even know who the hell was playing. He just stared at it while his mind churned.

He'd called Kassidy's cell phone but she wasn't answering. Where the hell had she gone? What was she so pissed off about? It gave him a headache thinking about all this emotional crap and he didn't like it, not one bit. His gut felt like a stone had lodged inside it and his chest ached. He glared at the television. Wanted to punch it.

Fuck.

He blamed fucking Dag. Why had he had to go and do something so lame-assed stupid? But that memory had the disturbing effect of making his dick twitch.

Jesus Christ. He could not be turned on by that. It was fucking insane. No wonder Kassidy was pissed off at him.

No, that wasn't right. He heaved a sigh. That's not what she was mad about. She was pissed off at him, but he wasn't getting why.

Because he'd sent Dag away?

Yeah, that might be it. She'd been all riled up when he'd invited Dag to stay without consulting her. This time she probably wanted him to talk to her before he'd asked Dag to leave. Except he hadn't exactly asked Dag to leave, hadn't admitted to her that he'd kicked Dag's ass out of there.

That had been a fucking clusterfuck of a scene, confronting Dag that morning. He'd dragged Dag's ass out of bed before Kassidy woke up, then told him to pack his stuff and get the hell out.

His gut cramped. He rubbed the sharp pain in the middle of his chest. What a fucking mess.

The sound of the door opening had him jumping to his feet.

Kassidy.

"Hey," he said, relief pouring through him like Niagara Falls. She walked in, looking like she'd come from a fucking funeral.

"I went to see Dag."

He took a step back, feeling like he'd been punched in the stomach. "Dag." She'd been gone a long time. Hours. Shit.

"Yeah."

Christ, she looked like hell. He'd never seen her so distraught—her eyes all red and swollen, her nose red, lips puffy, face blotchy. She was such a beautiful mess.

"Are you okay? C'mere, sweetheart, you've been crying..."

"Oh Chris."

She melted into his arms and he held her tightly, pressed his face against her hair, inhaled the familiar scent of it. They stood there, swaying a little, hearts beating in tandem. "I love you, sweetheart. I do. So much."

"Really?"

She looked up at him with big, wet eyes.

"Of course." He frowned. "I know I pissed you off. I should have talked to you before I asked Dag to leave, but...I was mad too, and..."

She choked on a laugh. "You think that's why I'm mad at you?"

"Hell, I don't have a hot fucking clue why you're mad at me," he said helplessly. "You know I'm not good at shit like this. Are you mad because of the whole threesome thing? That we made you do that?"

"I did it of my own free will," she said. "I can't blame you or Dag for that. I had the chance to stop it and I didn't. And I loved it." Her voice snagged on the last words and she swiped some tears. "I'm sure as hell mad at myself for doing it though, considering how things have turned out."

"It's okay, sweetheart. It's okay. Dag's gone, and we're going to be fine."

"That's what Hailey said."

He frowned. "You went to see Hailey?"

"I didn't know where else to go. You know what? It was good." She waved a hand. "I'll tell you about that later. But we need to talk."

Shit. Sure they did, and he'd rather eat a pair of Kassidy's high-heeled shoes than have this conversation, but it was going to happen, sure as shit, he knew that. He sighed.

"Let's sit."

They sat side by side on the couch, Kassidy turned to face him. His heart constricted at the sight of her poor little face all swollen and red, the misery in her eyes, the quivering of her soft

211

mouth. He touched his fingertips to her bottom lip.

"I went to see Dag. We talked. He says he's leaving Tuesday morning to go back to San Francisco."

Chris nodded. His body tightened, heart ached.

Kassidy drew in a long breath and let it out on a shaky exhale. "He told me something. Something in confidence. He doesn't want you to know this, but I..." She stopped and breathed again. Chris's gut clenched even more. "I've thought about it and I decided I have to tell you. I can't live the rest of our lives keeping this from you." Her eyes met his, hers liquid and dark, full of emotion.

"What is it?" His voice came out scratchy. He cleared his throat. "Oh fuck, Kass. Don't tell me."

He turned away and closed his eyes, blades slicing his insides open. He'd been afraid Kassidy had fallen in love with Dag. She'd gone to him. Had Dag fallen in love with her too?

Chapter Nineteen

Fuck. Fuck everything in the world. If he lost Kassidy... Pain seized Chris in a crushing grip.

He'd already lost Dag. That was bad enough. But to lose both of them...to each other? He wanted to puke up the coffee he'd downed earlier.

"I have to tell you," she said softly. "You're not going to like it."

No. No. No. His head spun.

"Chris. Dag's in love with you."

The words pierced the fog swirling in his brain. He knew it. He fucking— *What?* His brain screeched to a halt like a record on a turntable. What had she said? His head snapped around.

"He's... What did you say?" His eyes squinted at her.

"He's in love with you. He always has been."

He blinked at her. Wheels turning, processing information, but the hard drive in his brain was short circuiting and it wasn't computing. "You're telling me he's gay?"

Dag had sucked his cock. Licked his balls. Put his finger... Chris shook his head. "He can't be gay."

"He says he likes men and women. But he's in love with you." Her voice cracked. She sucked in another quivering breath. "I had to tell you. So I know...whatever happens...we're not living a lie."

He stared at her, his forehead tight, body rigid. "Living a lie."

She nodded, holding his gaze.

"What are you saying?" he asked carefully.

"I'm just saying...if you have any feelings for Dag...any...you need to tell him. To talk to him about it. To figure out what you want to do about it."

"He's my friend."

His brain went empty. Total vacuum.

"I know," she whispered, touching his cheek. "I know you love him as a friend. I know that, Chris. You missed him so much. You were so happy he was back. I've seen you together, how much fun you have, how much you guys care about each other. I should have realized sooner what it all meant..." She closed her eyes. "But maybe I was in denial too, thinking that I could be part of it."

Still blank. Nothing. Wheels turning.

"Uh...no, Kass."

"You should go talk to him." Her fingers caressed his jaw, rubbing over the stubble he hadn't bothered to shave off that morning. "Whatever. Only you really know how you feel. But you can't let him leave like this."

Oh, hell yeah, he could.

Hell no, he couldn't.

Gut twisting, chest throbbing, head spinning, he could only stare at her. How could she be telling him to do that? How could she send him away? Who did she love? Him? Or Dag? It made no sense. "I love you, Kassidy."

"I know." Her mouth quivered into a small smile. "I know."

"What if I don't? I mean, what if I don't go talk to him."

She gazed at him. "I don't know, Chris. I don't know if we can be together unless you sort this out."

"I don't get it. If you're thinking that I've been in the closet and hiding it from you all this time, that's the—"

She shook her head. "I don't think that. But if you don't talk to him, if you don't figure out yourself what your feelings are for him, I'll spend the rest of our lives wondering about it. Hurting for Dag. Hurting for us. If you go see Dag and you guys talk and you come back to me, and Dag goes back to San Francisco and that's the way our lives are going to be—fine." A flicker of what looked like pain passed over her face. "If you go see Dag and you..." A small sob hiccupped her words. "If things turn out differently, well, then..."

Chris shook his head.

"I just don't want to spend the rest of our lives not knowing the truth."

"Kassidy. I'll go see him if it will make you happy. But you gotta believe me—I don't want to lose you."

"Go see him."

"I'll...think about it."

"He's leaving Tuesday morning."

Pressure built inside him. "I'll...maybe tomorrow."

How was she supposed to concentrate on work?

Kassidy almost considered going home sick Monday morning, but she'd missed so much time lately because of her mother she just couldn't do it. The project was already behind schedule and she had a million things to do, not to mention check on her mother. Mom had another doctor appointment this week and she needed to make sure her dad was able to take her, and she had training proposals to review and...she couldn't focus on any of that because she kept going over and over in her head her conversations with Dag and Chris.

And Chris, the big stubborn jerk, was sitting in his office pretending their life hadn't just fallen apart, procrastinating on going to see Dag, and Dag was leaving...*leaving!* Tomorrow!

"Kassidy, did you sign off on those invoices?" Her boss, Paul, appeared in her office door.

"Um. Yeah. I gave them to...no, they're right here. But I signed them..." She handed them over.

"No. You didn't." He frowned at them.

"Oh. Sorry! Here, I'll just..." She reached for them.

"Did you review them?"

"Yes, of course. I mean, I think I did..."

"Kassidy, are you okay?" He squinted at her.

"Of course! I'm fine." She flashed a smile.

"How's your mom doing?"

"She's doing okay. It will be a while before she's...before..." To her horror and embarrassment her throat tightened on a huge sob and tears started running down her face.

"Oh Jeez." Paul backed up a step. "Uh, Kass...you want...you should...why don't you go home."

"No." She snatched up some tissues from the box on her desk. "No, I can't go home. I mean, I'm fine."

"But..."

"I'm sorry." God, how unprofessional, breaking down in tears in the office. "I'm just a little stressed right now. I just need a minute."

"I'll send uh...Laura to check on you." He disappeared.

She laid her head down on the desk. God, all she needed was to fall apart at work and get canned right now. She had to get a grip. It took all she had to get the tears under control, repair her makeup, and then head to the elevator to go see Chris.

He was in a meeting.

"Tell him to call me when he's out," she said to his admin assistant with a smile. Jessica was looking at her oddly, no doubt observing her swollen eyes and red nose, which she'd tried to camouflage with powder. In a couple of hours, rumors would be winding their way through the office grapevine that she and Chris were having "problems". She knew how it worked.

Ha. If people only knew! The thought of the grapevine getting hold of the real juicy scuttlebutt almost made her laugh as she took the elevator back to her own office.

Chris didn't call her.

She refused to go back to his office and add more juice to the rumor mill, so she called him and left one voice mail message, sent him one text message. Goddammit, he was ignoring her.

He was going to ignore this problem until Dag was gone and it was too late to do anything about it. Stubborn, stubborn, stubborn!

But why was she pushing him? She knew the risk she was taking. Maybe whatever happened, happened, and it would all be for the best. Impotent anger rose inside her, though, and in a stellar display of passive-aggressiveness, she left the office half an hour early and took the train home. Without Chris.

Dag had polished off the better part of a bottle of Scotch provided by room service—not one of those useless little bottles out of the mini bar—and was thinking about going down to the hotel restaurant for something to eat when he heard the knock on his door.

Who the hell was that? He hadn't ordered any more booze, although that wasn't a bad idea. He climbed to his feet from where he slouched in the chair, lurched across the room. Without bothering to check through the peephole, he yanked the door open.

Chris.

His heart stopped.

He stared.

Then his heart slammed in his chest like a sledgehammer. "What are you doing here?"

Chris stood there in a damn suit and tie and stared back at Dag through baleful, shadowed eyes.

"Oh fuck," Dag groaned, shoving a hand in his hair. "She told you."

"Yeah. Let me in, asshole."

Dag stepped aside. Chris walked by him, filling the hotel room with his presence.

"Look," Dag began. "I told her not to tell you. I don't want you feeling sorry for me. I'm fine. I'm always fine. I—"

"Shut the fuck up."

Dag snapped his mouth closed. Chris stood there, body tense, hands clenched. He didn't exactly look happy about all this, but that definitely wasn't pity shining in his eyes.

Dag narrowed his eyes at his friend. "Don't tell me what to do," he snapped. "You kicked me out, now it's my turn. Get out."

"You're drunk."

"I am not."

"Yes, you are. Jeez."

"So what? I felt like getting shitfaced. What's it to you?"

Chris rolled his eyes.

"And why're you here anyway?" Dag planted his feet apart and folded his arms across his chest, frowning at Chris.

"Kassidy made me come."

Great.

"She has this fucking weird idea that—" He stopped.

"Yeah. I know. She told me. I know she's wrong. Don't worry, Chris. I dealt with this a long time ago."

"I hate this shit."

"I know."

Chris sighed. "I've been thinking about it all day. All last night too. Thinking about how I'd feel if I lost Kassidy. I love her, Dag."

"I know."

"It would kill me."

"Yeah. Oh, goddammit, you do feel sorry for me. Jesus Christ, Chris..."

Chris took three steps across the carpet and was in his face, his fist grabbing hold of Dag's T-shirt. "I don't fucking feel sorry for you, all right? Would you get off the damn pity train?"

Dag thrust his arm up between his body and Chris's, dislodging his grip of his shirt. He shoved Chris away from him.

"Hey!" Chris stumbled but came back at him, shoved him back. Dag grabbed hold of him, fury and frustration boiling up inside him, boiling over, out of control, and he swung at Chris's face, connecting with his jaw. It wasn't the hardest punch,

Chris holding on to him too, but Chris grunted and swore.

They wrestled, shoving, trying to land punches, a haze of red in front of Dag's eyes, until Chris hooked one foot around his leg and took him to the floor. Hard. Stars sparkled in front of his eyes, his breath whooshed out of him. "Fuck you!" He drew back to pummel Chris, and then realized Chris had him pinned beneath him on the floor. Chris outweighed him, not by much, though their strength was probably evenly matched, but Chris was looking down at him, his face only inches from his, breathing heavily. His pupils exploded, his lips parted.

They stared at each other.

The world shrank away, Dag's awareness narrowing to the face in front of him, the hard body pressed to his, the heat of Chris's skin scorching him, Chris's eyes burning him.

"Fuck you," Dag whispered. He reached a hand up, grabbed Chris's tie and yanked his head toward him until Chris's mouth smashed into his. Chris made some kind of sound, something deep down and agonized, and then Dag's heart nearly exploded as Chris kissed him back.

Their mouths moved against each other, hard, grinding, teeth knocking, opening wider. Dag's tongue plunged into Chris's mouth, bringing another tortured sound from Chris's throat.

This couldn't be happening. Dag's head spun, his hands tightened on the other man. Chris. Chris. Oh god, it was Chris, kissing him, and fuck, it was heaven.

Their tongues slid, Dag nipped Chris's bottom lip then licked it, sucked his tongue into his mouth until Chris gasped. "Jesus."

This was probably another fucking huge mistake he was going to regret, but he couldn't stop now, couldn't stop breathing, couldn't stop his heart from beating, couldn't stop kissing Chris.

He'd dreamed of this. He'd beaten off thinking about this, he'd fucked other men pretending they were Chris. He'd wanted this, always, this man, with everything he had—his body, his heart, his soul. With a long, deep groan, he rolled, pushing Chris's heavy body off him, moving over him. His cock surged to life, and he pressed against Chris's pelvis as he kissed him again and again, brutal, ferocious kisses of pent-up need and repressed longing.

"Fuck you," he whispered again against Chris's mouth. "I don't know whether to love you or hate you."

"I'm leaning toward hating you right now," Chris gasped.

"Don't try to tell me you didn't want that. Jesus, you are so fucking stubborn."

Chris said nothing.

Dag looked down at him, their chests heaving against each other.

"Christ, Chris. Don't do this to me."

"I don't know what the fuck I want! All right?"

They stared back at each other, silence expanding around them, only the sound of their rasping breaths filling the room, Chris's green eyes wide, his lips wet and shiny.

Fuck he was gorgeous. Dag closed his eyes briefly against the sight, and against the mix of emotions swirling in Chris's eyes—denial, confusion, arousal.

Chris finally said, "Get the hell off me."

"No." And Dag kissed him again. Long, sliding kisses, savoring the feel of Chris's mouth under his, Chris's tongue in his mouth, in case this was the last time, the only time he ever got to do this. He cupped Chris's jaw, slid his other hand into his hair, the strands short and silky, his skull large and firm beneath.

Dag's cock throbbed insistently, sensation sizzling over his flesh, need stabbing into his balls in sharp, hot spears. Fiery heat built inside him and he rocked his hips urgently against Chris, shifting so he could feel...oh yeah, Chris was hard too. He might be confused or in denial or who the hell knew what he was feeling, but his body wanted this even if he didn't.

Dag shoved Chris's suit jacket out of the way so there was less fabric between their hot skin, slid a hand down and rubbed Chris's erection, straining beneath the fly of his trousers.

"Jesus," he breathed into Chris's mouth. "You're so fucking hard."

Chris groaned, turned his head away from Dag's mouth. "Dag..."

"You want this."

Dag moved his weight until his aching hard-on pressed against Chris, and he rubbed and shifted against him, sensation building inside him, tighter and hotter. He could come like this, just like this, not even inside him, just being with him...and he could make him come too.

But he couldn't do it. Not like this.

He groaned and rolled off Chris onto his back on the floor, his cock throbbing, his lungs straining. He stared at the ceiling, at the stippled texture of the white plaster.

"We have to talk," he finally said. He should sit up, but he didn't move.

Finally Chris rolled over and got to his knees. "Yeah. Get up." He rubbed flushed cheeks, swiped a hand over his brow. "Tell me. Tell me about it."

Dag stared back at him, heart pounding. Could he do it? Ever since they'd met years ago, he'd wanted this, but had so feared losing Chris's friendship that he'd locked it away inside him. Locked it away and thrown away the key.

He pushed himself to sitting and they sat there on the floor, clothes rumpled, hair messed, breathing rapidly. "Aw, fuck, Chris." He sucked in a long breath of courage. "I fell in love with you right from the start," he confessed in a low voice. "It just happened."

"Shit."

"Yeah."

"I never knew, man."

"I know. It's okay. I wouldn't have told you because...I valued our friendship. I didn't want to lose that. You were such a lazy-ass slacker, I don't know why I cared about you."

"Musta been my good looks."

Dag's heart stuttered and he choked on a laugh at Chris's unexpected joke. "Yeah, right." His smile faded. "I never wanted you to know."

"Had you been with...guys before?"

"Yeah. Some."

"I never knew that."

"I know. You made it pretty clear that disgusted you."

Chris bent his head. "Uh. That's not exactly true."

Dag stared at the top of Chris's head. "What do you mean?"

Chapter Twenty

Kassidy sat in the condo, alone. She should make some dinner. Chris was late, really late, but he still might show up, and she should eat anyway, even if he didn't, but the thought of food just made her stomach heave.

He hadn't returned her calls or responded to her text message. She had no idea what was going on. Was he pissed off at her for bugging him? Or for going home without him? Had he gone to see Dag?

She gazed at the three creamy pillar candles on the coffee table, sitting on the pretty carved dark wood holders Dag had picked out. The rule of three. Heat flashed in her chest.

She rose to her feet, wandered into their bedroom and flopped down on the bed, facedown, breathing in the sheets that still smelled like Chris and Dag, their masculine scents mingled with fabric softener and her own scent. Tears prickled her eyes and she stubbornly fought them back. She'd cried enough goddamn tears over this.

She rolled to her back.

Had she had some crazy idea that she could love both of them, and they'd love her back and they'd live happily ever after? Who did such a thing?

It probably happened more often than people knew. Nobody would talk about it though.

But it was crazy.

And she'd been crazy stupid to fall in love with Dag, because he'd likely only used her so he could be with Chris. Another knife sliced through her at that thought. She'd really thought he'd cared about her—once again, crazy stupid.

She remembered the tenderness of his touch, the warmth in his eyes as he looked at her, the affection and passion in his voice. She'd thought that had been for her. But it had all been for Chris. He'd come back for Chris.

She squeezed her eyes shut, though, remembering Dag looking at her like that. God, she was confused. But maybe this pain and misery, maybe losing everything was what she deserved. She was a good girl and she'd done bad things. Now she deserved whatever she got.

After several heavy beats of silence, Chris lifted his head and met Dag's eyes. Anguish tightened his features, the corners of his eyes, his mouth, his square jaw. "When I was fourteen years old, my dad caught me…fooling around with another guy. My friend Cam."

Dag sucked in a breath. "Jesus."

"We were young, horny, hormonal—attracted to each other on some level, I guess, but too young and stupid to know what was going on. Things got hot and heavy and my dad walked in on us—holy fucking shit, did he flip out. I thought he was going to have a heart attack."

Dag had met Chris's parents a couple of times. His dad was a really nice guy but definitely a straight-laced conservative, stern and uncompromising. No doubt where Chris got his stubbornness from.

"He beat the crap out of me," Chris continued in a low voice. "Really worked me over. He and my mom didn't speak for weeks over it. He wouldn't tell her why, and neither would I."

Dag felt his stomach drop. Chris's upbringing had seemed so privileged, so normal. He would never in a million years have thought his old man had ever beat him.

Chris's gaze met Dag's. "I swore I'd never do that again. You can imagine the effect that had on a teenage kid."

"Uh. Yeah." Shit. Dag's heart constricted. Then he gave a crooked grin. "That just shows the difference between us, huh? If that'd happened to me with my old man, I'd've been out screwing every guy in sight. Just to defy him. In fact..." He shrugged. "Maybe that's what I was doing." He met Chris's eyes. "I'm sorry that happened to you."

"I'm not going to lie and say I lusted after you all those years. I turned that part of me off. I wouldn't let myself go there. But you know I care about you, man. And I gotta think..." He rubbed the back of his neck, looked up at the ceiling, blinking. "That having all those threesomes with you was..."

"A way for us to be together."

Chris's eyes closed, his mouth a straight line, and he gave a barely perceptible nod.

Dag reached for Chris's hand, twined his fingers between Chris's and clasped it tightly.

"For me too," he murmured. "Except I always knew it."

"It was so hot," Chris said, voice low. "Seeing you like that, being with you like that." He swallowed. "Why'd you leave, Dag?"

"I had to leave. I knew it was never gonna happen between us, so I had to go. L.A. was okay, but I moved to San Francisco thinking things were more open there and maybe I'd find someone else. I fucked my way through guys, girls, threesomes, foursomes. I never found anyone else."

"Ah hell, Dag."

Chris's eyes looked glossy as he again met Dag's.

"I told you, don't feel sorry for me, asshole."

"And I told you, I don't, dickhead." Chris rubbed his eyes.

Dag shifted his body over the carpet, closer to Chris, cupped his jaw and lifted his face, looked at Chris's mouth. His eyelids dropped. He moved closer. And he kissed Chris. Their mouths connected, opened, Chris's tongue swept over his and Dag felt Chris's hand lift and fist in the back of his T-shirt as the kiss deepened and heated.

Chris pulled away. "Stop."

"No."

"Stop, dammit." Chris grabbed Dag's head with two hands and held him away from him. His eyes blazed at him. "All right, damn you, I want this. I want *you*. Fuck." His eyes dropped closed and he swallowed. "But I can't do this to Kassidy."

Dag's heart plunged. He stared back at Chris.

Chris met his gaze steadily. "I can't do this...without Kassidy."

The sound of the door opening alerted Kassidy and she lifted her head, turned her face to the bedroom door. The outside door of the condo clicked shut. It had to be Chris. She pushed herself off the bed, ready to rush out to see him, but she paused. Her stomach tightened and her mouth went dry. She swallowed, took a long breath, no idea what she was about to face.

She stood and wiped her palms on the knee-length shorts

227

she wore, then lifted her chin and walked out of the bedroom. In the living room she came face-to-face with Chris...and Dag.

She stared at them, eyes moving back and forth between them. They stood side by side, both big and gorgeous, Dag's silky dark hair hanging over those wicked dark eyes, Chris's short golden-brown hair all mussed and his suit wrinkled. She blinked.

"Hi, honey, I'm home," he said, one corner of his mouth lifting.

A smile trembled on her lips. "I see that."

"I went to see Dag."

"I see that too."

She shivered and curled her fingers into her palms.

"Kassidy." Dag's voice stroked over her, his eyes warmed her. She held his gaze. She was still so afraid. Maybe he saw the fear in her eyes, as his eyebrows drew down and his smile faded. "Hey. What's wrong?"

"What's wrong?" She almost choked on the words. "What's wrong?"

"I mean, you look terrified." He took a step toward her, his frown deepening. "Don't be afraid."

Was he crazy? Her life was being ripped apart and he told her not to be afraid? She just shook her head.

"Hey. We better talk. Let's sit down."

She let him take her hand and lead her on shaky legs to the couch where he sat on one side of her and Chris sat on the other, after tossing his suit jacket onto a chair and loosening his tie.

She couldn't get her throat to work, couldn't speak as she waited for them to tell her what was going on. She wanted to appear light and nonchalant about it all, but everything inside her shivered and shook.

"Do you really love us both, Kassidy?" Chris spoke first.

She turned to him with a glare. She glanced at Dag. "Um..."

Chris took her hand in both of his, his big, warm hands playing with her fingers, stroking over the back of her knuckles. "You said you cared about Dag."

She shot Dag another glance. She really didn't want to spill her guts like this right off the hop without knowing what had happened between them. Putting herself out there, making herself more vulnerable than she already was, was not what she wanted to do just then.

Dag took her other hand. "Kassidy. Look at me."

She met his eyes.

"I'm falling in love with you," he said.

Her heart stopped beating, then started again in painful, unsteady beats. She heard it in her ears; that was all she heard. How could that be? Only yesterday, he'd told her he was in love with Chris.

"I told you I love Chris," he continued as if recognizing her confusion, fingers moving over hers. "But I didn't tell you how I felt about you. That these weeks with you...have been special. Your sweetness and caring and generosity—your acceptance of me, just like Chris—you've pulled me in. Just like Chris." A small smile touched his lips. "Both of us. When I told Chris I loved you, I thought he was going to punch me again."

"Again?" She eyed the purplish mark on Chris's chin. "Looks like he's the one who got punched."

"Yeah. We both landed a couple."

"Oh, you guys." She blew out a breath.

"We're fine. Anyway..."

"You have to tell me more," she whispered. "Please. I can't

229

do this."

They told her more. They told her everything. They told her what she never dared hope or dream she'd hear.

"Doesn't it kind of make sense?" Dag asked, his fingers moving over hers. "That if Chris loves you, and I love Chris, that maybe I could love you too? We've always been attracted to the same girls..."

"So you both slept with them," she finished dryly. "Most guys would fight over a girl you both like. You two just share her."

A smile tugged at Chris's lips. "Well yeah. Isn't that better?"

She shook her head, trying not to smile back at him, and failing. At one time that idea would have shocked her to her core. Now she just accepted it.

"We love you, Kass. And we...I..." Dag shot Chris a faint smile. "I love Chris and maybe one day he'll love me too, but for now...we both want the three of us to be together."

Her heart expanded and softened in her chest, her world brightening, surrounding her with brilliant light and vivid colors. "Really?"

Dag nodded.

She turned to Chris, her question in her eyes and as usual he read it. "Yes. Really."

She held his gaze long and steady. "Chris..."

He clutched her hand, raised it to his lips and kissed her knuckles. "I want it, Kass. I want...both of you."

She sat there for a long moment, everything rolling around in her mind, trying to reconcile it all and make it make sense. She was afraid to hope, because she knew she didn't deserve what they were offering her. "I don't know if I can do this," she finally said.

They both looked back at her with carefully controlled expressions.

"Why not, Kassidy?" Dag asked.

"Everything was such a mess. I should never have done this. I'm not...I wanted adventure, I wanted to be wild and crazy and wicked. Like you. Like Hailey. But I'm not meant for that. I just wanted to be a little bit bad, but people got hurt and now I don't want to be bad..." Her voice trailed off as her throat closed up, hurting, and she couldn't talk anymore.

"Kassidy." Dag lifted her chin and made her look at him. He swam in her vision, swimming in tears. "What we did...that doesn't make you a bad person."

She stared back at him, her throat aching painfully.

"You did it out of love. Didn't you?"

Yes. God, yes. She'd even tried to tell Hailey that once. She gave a small nod.

"Some people might consider what we did bad. But you never intended to hurt anyone, and you're not a bad person. You're the most compassionate, giving, sweetest person I know. You care about your sister even when she's not all that loveable. You look after your parents. You look after us. That's why I care about you."

The tears spilled over, scalding hot. She nodded again, a small sob escaping her, her throat relaxing. "Th-thank you."

"I know this is...unconventional," he continued. "But I don't think more love can ever be a bad thing. Lord knows, I haven't had a lot of love in my life."

Oh geez. Now he was squeezing her heart in both fists. She struggled to get her voice under control. "But what does this mean? What are we going to do?"

Dag used his thumbs to wipe her tears away, took her

hand again, and then, in a gesture she watched with swelling emotion, he reached and took Chris's other hand too, two big, masculine hands joined, all of them joined together. In a circle. Her throat ached again, ferociously.

"I don't know, Kassidy," he said honestly, their eyes meeting. "This is new to all of us."

"Are you going to stay here?" She looked at Dag.

His lips quirked. "Here, in Chicago? Or here, in your condo?"

Her gaze moved to Chris's face. "Did you guys talk about this?"

"Not much," Chris admitted. "We...wanted you to be part of it."

"Oh." Her heart expanded even more. "Please stay," she whispered to Dag, tightening her fingers on his. "Here. With us."

Dag held her gaze for a few seconds then dropped his eyes. "We need to talk about that. What that would be like."

She glanced at Chris. "It would be like it *has* been. The three of us together."

Dag looked up at her again. "You two are a couple," he said, his voice low. He looked at Chris then back at her. "I'm not part of that."

Kassidy's heart clenched as she understood in a flash how he was feeling and some of her own doubts and fears faded away with her desire to reassure him. "Oh Dag. Apparently we're not just a couple anymore. We're a...threesome. All of us."

He nodded, still looking unsure. She lifted a hand and laid it on his cheek. "Chris told you," she said softly. "I care about you too, Dag. I don't understand it myself. I love Chris so much and I don't want to lose him, but I feel like I'm..." She hesitated. No. No more dancing around it. "I'm in love with you too."

He covered her hand with his and met her eyes again, uncertainty fading into a blaze of emotion in his eyes. He shifted her hand so he could kiss her palm.

"I know how it feels," he said hoarsely. "Because I feel the same. Loving two people—it's kind of crazy."

"I know. But you just said it. More love can never be a bad thing, right?"

"Right. I just think we need to talk about how this will all work."

"Okay." She shifted and sat back on the couch, nestled between them. "Let's talk."

"Okay. So I move in here and live with the two of you. What will you tell people?" Dag asked

She nibbled her bottom lip. Good question.

Chris groaned. "We can't tell people. Jesus."

Dag shot him a look. "You know I don't give a shit what people think."

"Dag, man, think about it," Chris said. "You may think I worry too much about that, about following the rules, about appearances. But it's not just me...it's Kassidy too. We work for a big company, people talk." He paused. "I can't jeopardize my job. My career."

Kassidy could just imagine the grapevine at work going berserk with this kind of story. *Nice little Kassidy Langdon shacked up with two guys...one of the guys is her boyfriend, and the other is her boyfriend's boyfriend.* And what would they say about Chris? She groaned. "Maybe we just don't tell them anything. Maybe it's just our business what happens here in our home."

The three of them exchanged glances. Dag might be a rebel on the outside, but inside—he wanted what everyone wants.

And she and Chris—well, they weren't rebels, despite this crazy thing they were contemplating. Would Dag understand that?

"They'll know Dag's living here," Chris said.

"Yes. I don't intend to hide that. But..." She paused. "We don't have to explain everything."

"Think about this," Dag said quietly. "If one of us was hurt, who would be next of kin? You two have a relationship, even if you're not married. What am I?"

Kassidy licked her lips, a heavy feeling settling over her as she remembered rushing into the ER when her mom had been hurt. They would only let family in to see her. "I don't know, Dag. But if something like that happened, I'd tell the truth, if it meant not being able to see you if you were hurt, or look after you."

He nodded and they both looked at Chris. He grimaced and rubbed his face. She sensed the struggle inside him, how much he wanted this, how much he cared for both her and Dag, and yet how he'd been denying his feelings for Dag for so long, now it was hard to admit them. Chris leveled a look at Dag then tipped his head back.

Kassidy sank her teeth into her bottom lip, slanted a look at Dag who waited too for Chris's response.

"Oh man," Chris groaned. "Yeah. I'd do the same."

Kassidy leaned her head into Chris's shoulder at his words, feeling a little of the tension ease out of Dag's body pressed against her other side.

"And think about this," Dag said. "What about children?"

Her eyes flew open wide. "Well, that's jumping the gun a little."

"You guys haven't talked about that? Marriage? Kids?"

She bit her lip and looked at Chris. Of course she'd thought that moving in together was a prelude to marriage. She loved Chris with all her heart and didn't want to spend her life with anyone else. Well, anyone but Dag. Oh hell, this did complicate things.

"We haven't really," Chris said. "But I know you, Kassidy. I know you want marriage. And kids."

She slid her gaze back and forth between them then nodded. "Yes. I do." She didn't want to be a mother yet. But some day, she definitely wanted that. She wanted to have Chris's baby. And her stomach flipped at the realization that—holy shit—she could see herself having Dag's baby too. She pressed a hand to her stomach and closed her eyes.

"Yeah," she whispered. "You're right, Dag. This is complicated."

Her mind spun for a moment, trying to envision the future for them. Were they really in this for the long term? Were they really talking about a lifetime commitment and children? How could they raise children in a family like that? Maybe she couldn't do this. Maybe they were insane for even thinking about it.

But the alternative made her heart hurt and her skin go cold. She opened her eyes. "I don't know the answers," she said, voice shaky. "Yes, I want children some day. Are we really talking that far ahead though? Do you guys want kids?"

They both got an identical panicked expression on their faces that maybe should have scared her, but instead amused her and reassured her. She smiled. "You don't need to look so terrified."

Dag made a choked noise. "I *am* terrified," he said. "Fuck. Commitment? The idea of committing to one person has always freaked me out, never mind two. Talking about having kids? Jesus Christ."

"You brought it up!"

"I know, I know."

"I don't mean having a baby tomorrow," she said. "Okay, look. Chris and I moved in together. We've never really talked about the specifics of getting married or having kids. I think..." She met Chris's eyes. "I think you want kids some day." He slowly nodded. "But we were willing to make the commitment of living together without knowing that. This isn't really that different. We take things one step at a time, right?" She turned to Dag.

He too nodded. "What about your families?" he asked.

She frowned. "What about them?"

"What will you tell them?"

She'd been so freaked out about her parents knowing what she, Chris and Dag were doing, and now here they were discussing making this a permanent arrangement. "We don't have to tell them. They like you. Maybe after a while, when you're even more a part of my family, we can sort of...break it to them..."

He nodded, his eyes full of emotion. "Yeah. That could work."

"No." Chris spoke up.

She and Dag both swiveled their heads to look at him.

He shook his head. "No," he said again. "We have to tell them."

Her breath stuck in her chest. "Chris..."

"My family's not such an issue," he said. "They live far away. But I'll tell them." His jaw tightened and she could only imagine the guts that would take. Her heart swelled with love for him. "I'll tell them if they're coming to visit, or if we go see them." He met Dag's eyes. "It's not fair to you to sneak around and deny your relationship with us."

Dag's eyes got very shiny. He reached over and grabbed Chris's hand in a tight grip.

"People at work are one thing," Chris continued. "We don't need to announce anything and it's our own business. But family...and friends...need to know the truth." He sucked in a breath. "I know you don't want to disappoint them, Kass. I know you've always been their angel. But they'll still love you. They might have a hard time understanding at first, but they love you."

"Christ, man," Dag said hoarsely. "You're killing me here."

A smile flickered on Chris's lips.

"But Kassidy's right," Dag said. "Maybe we should just wait until I've been around longer, and ease them into it."

Kassidy nodded and leaned into Chris.

Chris lifted his chin. "I'd do it," he said. "I'd tell them right now. But if you think it's better to wait a while...okay."

They all nodded.

"I'll tell Hailey," Kassidy said. She closed her eyes briefly, thinking about her last conversation with her sister. This time, she knew Hailey wouldn't judge her or tell their parents before she was ready. Her heart squeezed.

"And one more thing," Dag said.

Now Kassidy bumped her forehead against his shoulder. "What else?"

"Where am I going to sleep?"

Oh god. That was his question?

"Thank god we bought that king-size bed when we moved in here," Chris said, echoing her own thoughts, and all three of them laughed.

"Okay," Dag said.

"Anything else?" she asked Dag.

"Oh probably," he said, leaning down to brush his lips over her cheek. "Probably a million things. I guess we'll figure some of it out as we go."

"We'll figure it out together," Chris said.

Kassidy let out a long breath. "Thank you." Her lips trembled. She could hardly breathe, excitement and joy bubbled up so fiercely inside her. "I was afraid I was going to lose both of you." Tears blurred her vision.

"I think that's what we were all afraid of," Dag said with a rough chuckle. "I was pretty damn sure that's what had happened to me."

"Yeah." Chris sighed. "Me too, dammit." He rubbed his mouth. Emotion filled his eyes, and even though he hated all this emotional crap, as he would call it, she sensed his relief that things were working out. She also sensed his hesitation, and she knew at that moment, despite his courage at being willing to speak up and tell her parents, he was still afraid, still confused.

She reached up and touched his face. "It'll be okay," she whispered, using his own words. "I promise. I'll be with you."

He closed his eyes, covered her hand with his and pressed it to his face. "Yeah. I need you, Kass."

"I'm here."

She moved into his arms, and he wrapped her up, his body hot and damp with perspiration as if he'd been running miles and miles, and she felt his trembling too. "I love you," she murmured against his lips. "I love you."

"Love you too, sweetheart, so much."

His mouth found hers and clung in a long, heartfelt kiss.

Then she turned to Dag, who sat so close, watching with a soft expression on his face. "I love you too," she whispered. "And thank you."

He lifted an eyebrow, smiling. "For what?"

"For not being jealous. When I kiss Chris. When we make love."

"I was jealous of you. At first."

She drew back a bit. "You were?"

"Hell yeah. When I got here. That night we had dinner. I knew Chris was seeing someone, but I didn't know you'd moved in together. I had this faint stupid hope that maybe things had changed, but when I saw you, and I saw how much in love with you Chris is..." He hitched a big shoulder. "I was jealous, damn jealous."

"Oh." Her chest tightened.

"But..." He reached out and smoothed some strands of her hair back. "It wasn't long before I was attracted to you too. Which wasn't exactly what I'd planned, and god knows I didn't need any more complications in my fucked-up life."

Her eyes searched inside his, seeing the truth of what he was saying. She turned to Chris. "What about you? You've never been jealous of me and Dag."

He moved his head slowly, side to side. "No. I never have been. I don't know if I can explain it..." He paused, searching for words. "I feel happy when you're happy—even if it's with him. And I want to give to Dag. I feel like I'm giving him something when you and he...make love."

"And I felt like you were giving *me* something," she said with a smile. "Like you'd given me a special gift I didn't even know I'd wanted." And she wanted to give him that too. So much.

"There's no room for jealousy in this," Dag said in a firm voice. "For any of us. Ever. If anyone ever feels that way, you gotta say something." And his gaze zeroed in fiercely on Chris.

Chris choked on a laugh, gave him a wry smile. "Yeah, yeah, I know you mean me. Okay, so I'm not good at talking about that. I'll try to be better."

Dag tipped Kassidy's chin up then and kissed her. He tasted of Scotch and the same minty gum Chris tasted of, and she knew then that they'd kissed. A thrill of heat ran through her and her pussy clenched. Dag must have felt it because he deepened the kiss, fingers hard on her jaw, his tongue licking into her mouth, his mouth opening wider on hers.

Her breasts swelled and her nipples tingled. She moved from Dag's mouth to Chris's then back again, her hands sliding around the backs of both their necks. "I love you guys," she whispered, the complete preposterousness of it only a vague brush at the edges of her mind. Time drifted as they kissed and touched, and with her hands on their necks, she brought both their faces closer to hers...closer to each other.

She pulled back, not far, just a bit, all of them breathing the same air, sitting there on the couch. "I want you to kiss again," she whispered.

Chapter Twenty-One

Chris's eyes flickered. "Again?"

"Yes. I know you kissed."

He and Dag shared a look. Everything inside her pulled up tight and hard as she waited. She shifted back just a bit more so they had room. She relaxed her hold on their necks. She wasn't going to push them together.

They looked at each other. The air around them caught on fire, flames licking over her skin. Their eyelids drooped, their faces moved closer together. And they kissed.

Dag slid his hand around the back of Chris's neck too, over hers, and his did tighten and pull Chris toward him. Their mouths connected in an open-mouthed, fierce kiss. With identical low groans, they ground their mouths together and she watched with hot fascination.

It was beautiful. That was all she could think. Beautiful. She saw tongues as their mouths lifted, joined again, the heat flaring higher around them. Chris's hand slid to Dag's shoulder and tightened there, but his other hand was on her leg, and he held on tightly to her too.

"Jesus." Chris drew back, gasping, his mouth wet. He slanted a glance her way, his eyes questioning. She smiled at him and drew his head to hers so she could kiss him again.

"I wanna do more than kiss you," Dag said to Chris, his voice a black velvet brush over her senses.

Chris licked his lips. She'd never seen him look so hesitant and it made her heart swell a little.

Was he sure about this? God, she didn't want him to do things he was going to regret. But...they'd talked. They'd kissed. They'd come home to her, together. He had to want this or they wouldn't be here.

"Like what?" Chris finally asked, tipping his chin up. Dag rubbed a thumb over Chris's bottom lip.

"I wanna suck your cock," Dag said. The air squeezed right out of Kassidy's lungs and Chris's lips parted. "And then I wanna fuck your ass."

Oh dear god. A small moan leaked out of her mouth. Her body was melting, her pussy clenching hard at his words.

"Jesus," Chris muttered.

Her gaze dropped to his fly and, oh yeah, he was as hard as a flagpole beneath his suit trousers. She guessed that took care of her worries that he might be doing something he didn't really want to.

"Here?" Chris asked. "Or in the bedroom?"

He was always the one giving direction, and she had to smile at him letting Dag take the lead. How long would that last?

But this was new to him, all new, scary new, she could still see the flashes in his eyes that told her he was still a little apprehensive.

She grabbed his hand and squeezed, and he turned his gaze to her. "Need you, sweetheart," he said, voice rough and shaky. "You have to be there."

"I know." She held his gaze steadily. "I'm here. Always

here." She glanced at Dag. "We're both here for you, you know that."

"Yeah." His eyes closed briefly.

"In the bedroom," Dag said abruptly. "Now."

He led the way back to the bedroom where Kassidy had shed tears not that long ago. And even though over the last few weeks the three of them had grown so comfortable together and it no longer felt weird to be doing this, tonight felt...different. She, too, felt a little unsure. Her guys had always been focused on her—undressing her, kissing her, making her come over and over again. She loved it.

But tonight wasn't just about her. She stood there, her teeth sinking into her bottom lip. Dag looked up and caught her eye. He smiled.

He moved toward her, all long legs and lean muscle, a wicked promise in his dark eyes. "Kassidy." He bent his head and kissed her and his hands started removing her clothes—the unsexy sweat pants she'd changed into after work, the thin T-shirt, the cotton bra. Chris stepped up behind her and they fell into their rhythm, the cadence of three, one lifting, one pulling, until she stood between the walls of heat that were their bodies, one in front, one behind. Lust sliced through her, her heart pattering in a rapid beat, their hands and mouths sending sparks sizzling over her skin, through her skin, right inside her where they sparkled and shimmered.

"Oh yeah," she whispered, running her fingers through Dag's silky hair, burying her other hand in Chris's shorter hair at the back of his head. "Yes."

"Three of us," Dag murmured against her ear. "All together. At the same time. Chris fucking you. Me fucking Chris."

She shivered, her insides burning with desperate need.

"But first..." Dag turned to Chris. "Take off your clothes."

Chris dragged his tie over his head, and then shed his rumpled shirt and pants. Dag stripped too, the two of them watching each other undress, while she watched both of them with avid eyes. "You too, baby doll."

She pushed the sweatpants down over her hips and pulled her T-shirt off, all the while watching the lamplight slide over Dag's olive skin, highlighting the muscles beneath as he moved closer to Chris, grabbed him and drew him up against him. They kissed again, long, hard kisses, full-body kisses, naked bodies pressed together, all ripped muscle and hair-dusted skin. Dag groaned and thrust both hands into Chris's hair, holding his head, deepening the angle of the kiss.

It should feel weird watching your boyfriend kiss another man. It should feel wrong. It should feel hurtful. But all she felt was a huge surge of emotion so powerful it brought tears to her eyes. Relief. Joy. Love.

She touched her fingertips to her lips as she watched, her body turning to liquid. Chris grabbed hold of Dag's shoulders and held on and they kissed again and again.

Then Dag pulled back and reached for her, pulled her to them. Heat from their bodies surrounded her and he kissed her mouth then slid his hands down Chris's neck, over his shoulders and onto his chest. His fingertips rubbed over Chris's nipples, almost experimentally, and Chris let out a soft groan. And then Dag reached between them and took hold of Chris's cock. Chris stood there, eyes closed, fingers digging into Dag's shoulders.

She moved around behind Chris, slid her arms around him, and rested her chin on his shoulder to watch. She didn't know if Chris pushed Dag to the floor or if Dag just went down of his own volition, but Dag sank to his knees in front of Chris, still holding his cock. He looked up at Chris, up the length of his body. She watched their gazes connect, her heart still hammering away in her chest, and then Dag's gaze moved just a fraction, and his eyes met hers. She smiled at him. His eyes flickered with warmth and then he turned his attention back to Chris.

"I have to taste you," he said to Chris. "I'm gonna suck you. Next time you'll come in my mouth, but not..." He glanced at Kassidy. "Not this time. I just wanna taste you."

Chris gave a short nod, and when Dag took him in his mouth, his head fell back toward her. His fingers tangled in Dag's hair and her mouth opened at the same time Dag's did as he took Chris in.

"Christ," Chris moaned, his face tight. "Jesus Christ."

She rubbed over his chest while Dag sucked on him, licked him with such emotion and tenderness she thought her heart might explode. She loved watching this, the way Dag closed his eyes, rubbed the head of Chris's cock over his lips, swirled his tongue around it, then opened so wide and took him deep.

Chris's body vibrated in her arms. It thrilled her to observe Dag finally getting to demonstrate the feelings he had for Chris with action, and to see Chris finding out how good it could be.

Was there something wrong with her? Was she abnormal in some way, that this excited her, turned her on beyond belief, but also aroused a torrent of tender emotions inside her?

She loved them. She loved them both. She wanted them to be happy.

Dag filled his mouth with Chris, the thick length, the clean taste of him, and inhaled his warm, masculine scent. He rubbed up one thigh, fingertips grazing a lean hipbone then slipped a hand between Chris's legs to find his balls and fondle them. Jesus, they were tight, pulled up against his body, and hot, so hot. Chris groaned again and his fingers tugged sharply at Dag's hair, sending shivers cascading over him.

His fingers played more, sliding even farther back as he had that night everything had gone to hell. Chris had loved it, he'd exploded in his mouth once his finger had found his gland, and he wanted to do it again. But even more, he wanted to be inside Chris.

"Oh," Kassidy breathed from behind Chris. "Let me do that. Please."

Dag let Chris's dick slide from his mouth and looked at Kassidy. Passion glazed her eyes and she reached a hand between Chris's legs from behind. "I've...always wanted to."

"Christ," Chris moaned. Dag smiled and rose to his feet.

"Tonight, buddy, you get to find out what it's like to be the center of attention." He led Chris to the bed, and with a hard shove had him lying on his back. Kassidy moved between his legs, and Dag threw himself down beside Chris and took hold of his cock again.

"Mmm." Kassidy started licking, her little tongue stroking up over Chris's thighs, then between them. Dag lifted Chris's shaft out of her way, bent his head to resume sucking on him while Kassidy licked Chris's balls and slid her fingers beneath him. "Lift your legs," she instructed Chris moments later. Chris bent his legs and dug his heels into the edge of the bed, and Kassidy disappeared farther, the top of her dark head visible as Dag sucked long and lusciously. He rubbed over Chris's chest with his free hand, felt the tremors shaking him, gave one nipple a pinch just to feel the jerk of his body.

Kassidy made soft little pleasure sounds, and Chris tightened and lifted off the bed. "Here," Dag muttered, releasing him again. "Like this..." And he grabbed Chris's knees and shoved them back, exposing his ass to Kassidy.

"Oh yes," she sighed. "Yes." She too trembled as she bent her head again. "Chris, oh Chris, you taste so good, I love doing this."

Dag watched her tongue him, nibble at his ass cheeks then lick lower and lower.

"Fuck!" Chris cried out, his face tight. "Oh fuck, that feels good."

"You wouldn't let me do this," Kassidy murmured, then resumed licking, teasing with her tongue in that sensitive area. Dag's own groin ached in sympathy, in longing too, wanting to be touched that way. He knew how incredible it felt, knew what Chris was experiencing, and it thrilled him.

"Play with his hole," he directed Kassidy, handing her a bottle of lube he'd grabbed from the nightstand. He held Chris's cock up and out of the way so he could see what she was doing, the skin of Chris's balls and perineum stretched taut and beautiful. "We have to get him ready. It's gonna be...tight."

"Mmm." Her finger brushed over Chris's hole, now slick with lube, and Chris groaned and writhed at the touch. She did it again and again, then finally pushed inside. Just the tip of her finger, not far, and Dag almost exploded just watching her slender digit disappear into Chris.

She pumped a little bit, a few times, her eyes wide and hot, her other hand cupping his balls, massaging lightly. "Does that feel good, Chris?" she asked.

"Oh fuck, yeah." Chris's hands fisted into the duvet, his knuckles white.

Seeing the pleasure on both their faces was a rush, so achingly hot and lovely. Dag's whole body burned and throbbed.

Kassidy's intent expression as she focused her attention there in that most intimate of places, Chris's face tight with bliss—it was almost enough to bring tears to a guy's eyes. Not

247

him. He blinked at the stinging feeling in the corners of his eyes. Jesus, he never cried. Never.

He had to be inside Chris, now, but he gathered every particle of restraint he had. "Try two fingers," he told Kassidy. She did so and a long, rough sound came from Chris.

"There," she whispered. "There you go...so good."

Just a little longer. Rushing things would not be good for Chris, not this time, his first time. Dag bent his head and rubbed his cheek over Chris's hip bone, pressed open-mouthed kisses there, across the soft skin between his navel and the brown curls. He took him in his mouth again. So good, so thick and hard against his tongue.

"Okay, Jesus," Chris gasped. "You gotta stop or..."

Dag again let Chris's cock slide out, letting the edge of his teeth drag over the crown, making Chris hiss.

"Okay," he said, and he met Kassidy's eyes. "Gonna do it now."

She bit her lip and nodded, cheeks flushed pretty and pink, eyes sparkling.

"You lie down," he gently directed her. "On your back, baby. That way you can see both of us."

"Yes." She nodded and scrambled over Chris's body to do as Dag asked. Chris rolled and, before he moved over Kassidy, Dag reached for Chris's neck, pulled him close and gave him a fast, hard kiss on the mouth.

Above his girlfriend, Chris paused, weight on his hands. "I love you, Kassidy," he whispered, and then he kissed her, another fast hard kiss.

He was dying. The pleasure was so intense it hurt, and Chris knew they'd barely started. He lifted his mouth from

Kassidy's, the sweet softness so different from Dag's darker, harder mouth. At the far back of his mind, he couldn't believe he was doing this, but yet he knew he wanted it, so damn much it scared him. He wanted Dag, like this.

Dag. All the times they'd been together. He'd never known how Dag felt, never even thought about it, just got lost in pleasure, his own pleasure, the girl's pleasure, even Dag's pleasure. It had all just been mindless, thoughtless bliss. Until now.

He focused on Kassidy's face, though, her mouth, the curve of her cheek, the love shining in her eyes. He couldn't do this without her. He'd told Dag that, almost thinking that might make a difference, but then Dag had blown his mind by telling him he was falling in love with Kassidy too. "Let's go home," he'd said to Chris. "Home to Kassidy."

Gratitude swelled in his chest so huge it almost choked him, gratitude and relief that he'd found this woman who'd pushed him to look inside himself and have the courage to admit how he felt and what he wanted. Who else would ever have understood or accepted something so bizarre?

And gratitude to Dag too, for all he'd given him, for all he'd given Kassidy, for also accepting Chris's need for there to be three of them.

Chris pushed into Kassidy, and her body pulled him in, so hot, scalding him, so wet, bathing him, and he watched her face as he filled her, the haze in her eyes, the curve of her mouth into the sweetest smile. "Love you," he said.

"I love you too."

Dag's hands moved on his hips, his thighs. Heat spiraled. Fire streaked through his veins and every nerve ending jumped as he waited, abs tense, for what was coming. It had been so fucking good, that night Dag had made him come. When he'd nailed his gland like that, he'd thought the top of his head was going to fly off. So the anticipation was both good and nervous, the unfamiliar sensations of being invaded there disturbing yet erotic.

Dag's fingers slid between the cheeks of his ass, so wicked, so dangerous, hot shivers rippled over his skin.

"Want me to wear a condom?" Dag murmured behind him. Chris jerked his head around.

"Uh...no."

"Sure?" Dag dragged his tongue over his shoulder. Warm pleasure poured through him.

"Yeah." Chris choked out the word. "You've been fucking Kassidy without a condom. You said you were tested. You're good."

"Yeah. And Kassidy's the only one I've been with."

Dag reached for the bottle of lube and squirted some into his hand. The cool slickness startled Chris as Dag spread it then he squeezed more into his palm and spread it over his cock.

Jesus. Now wasn't a good time to think about how big Dag was. His butt cheeks clenched hard even as Dag's lubed-up fingers probed.

"Relax." Kassidy's voice whispered over him, her fingers stroking his tight shoulders. "I can feel you tense up. Relax."

"Yeah." Dag echoed her words, again licked his tongue up Chris's back, moved lower and bit one cheek. Chris jumped.

Dag's fingers probed and pushed then parted his cheeks. Chris squeezed his eyes closed, willed his body to relax even as every cell shouted out for more, more, more. Kassidy's soft murmurs and tender caresses, Dag's hands, and then, oh Christ, Dag's cock, the big blunt head probing at his asshole.

"Aw, fuuuuck..."

The pain seared him, heat flamed over his ass, washing up over his whole body. He froze in place, teeth sinking into his bottom lip. Kassidy reach a hand up to his cheek, pulled him to face her. "It's okay," she whispered again. Racing bolts of electricity zapped through his body, straight to his balls, torturously tight. Dag's fingers dug into his hips as he pushed in farther and Chris groaned.

Dampness broke out on his skin, on his forehead, his chest. Every nerve ending was sensitized to the point of pain, especially his ass, burning with a fire that seared him.

"Feel the burn?" Dag asked behind him, stroking a hand up his back.

"Yeah."

"Gonna make you burn more." And with another hard thrust that had Chris crying out, he was in him, filling him, filling his ass.

"Fuck!" he cried again, but now Dag was in, he was hitting that spot, that gland that sent his mind spinning right out of his body. Nothing existed but sensation, he was wrapped up in it, Kassidy's hot wetness rippling around his cock, buried deep in her sweet pussy, her hands drifting over his body as her eyes lost focus, Dag's thick spear of flesh inside him, his body slamming into his ass as he fucked him.

"Feels so good," Kassidy moaned. "So good. I feel you both...every time Dag pushes in, I feel it too."

"Both...fucking...you," Dag said tightly. He bent over Chris, his hands sliding around to his chest, pinching his nipples. More pleasure streaked through his body. Too much, it was almost too much to bear, pleasure so intense he burned from it.

"Yeah," she agreed. "I love it. I love you."

And Chris knew she was saying that both of them. He squeezed his eyes shut against the emotion that exploded inside him, too much, too much...

Kassidy tipped her pelvis up a little more into Chris's thrusts. "Close," she whispered, eyes falling closed. "I'm close..."

"Me...too." Dag pumped into him, the pressure and drag and pull inside him and on his cock as he tried to keep moving inside Kassidy had sensation climbing inside him, his skin burning, his balls tightening, pressure building.

"Come, sweetheart, come now," he panted, 'cause he was done, couldn't control it, and then he burst, totally blasted off inside her, her contractions around him milking him, squeezing him.

"Yeah, oh yeah," Dag groaned, rested his head against him and then he pumped faster, rose to grip Chris's hips as he pounded into him, fast, furious so damn good, flooding his channel with his come. "God, Chris, god. Love this. Love you. So. Damn. Much."

"Dag." Chris couldn't stop the words that spilled out of him. "Love you too, man. Love you too."

Kassidy drifted back to reality slowly, floating on a cloud of bliss, a haze of pleasure.

It was real. What Dag talked about—his crazy philosophical ideas. That reality exists independent of consciousness. That Chris's feelings for Dag had existed, no less real because he hadn't admitted them. That what exists doesn't exist because one thinks it does, it simply exists, regardless of anyone's awareness or knowledge.

Four hands moved over her body, cupping her aching breasts, squeezing gently, rubbing her nipples. One mouth on hers, one on her neck, kissing, licking, sucking. They'd done this before. But this time was different.

This time they were three—the rule of three.

About the Author

Kelly Jamieson lives in Winnipeg, Canada and is the author of over twenty romance novels and novellas. Her writing has been described as "emotionally complex", "sweet and satisfying" and "blisteringly sexy". If she can stop herself from reading or writing, she loves to cook. She has shelves of cookbooks that she reads at length. She also enjoys gardening in the summer, and in the winter she likes to read gardening magazines and seed catalogues (there might be a theme here...). She also loves shopping, especially for clothes and shoes. She loves hearing from readers, so please visit her website at www.kellyjamieson.com or contact her at info@kellyjamieson.com.

SAMHAIN
PUBLISHING

www.samhainpublishing.com

Green for the planet.
Great for your wallet.

SAMHAIN
PUBLISHING

It's all about the story...

Romance

HORROR

Retro ROMANCE

www.samhainpublishing.com

CPSIA information can be obtained at www.ICGtesting.com
Printed in the USA
BVOW011039170113

310902BV00002B/222/P